"I enjoyed *The Manna Enzyme* immensely. This is a work of truly admirable originality. The satire is masterful. . . . There is compassion too, and black humor, and the plot is laid out in all its intricacies by a master storyteller. I was reminded . . . of Aldous Huxley and Raymond Chandler, to whose talents Mr. Hoyt adds his own remarkable gifts. A splendid work then . . . a book to rejoice over."

—Leonard Wibberly, author of
The Mouse That Roared

THE MANNA ENZYME

Look for all these Tor books by Richard Hoyt

THE MANNA ENZYME

RICHARD HOYT

TOR

A TOM DOHERTY ASSOCIATES BOOK

THE MANNA ENZYME

Copyright © 1982 by Richard Hoyt

Excerpts from *The Love Song of J. Alfred Prufrock* by T.S. Eliot are reprinted from his volume *Collected Poems 1909–1962* by permission of Harcourt Brace Jovanovich, Inc. and Faber and Faber, Ltd.

The recipes on pages 17–18 and 61 from *The Spice Cookbook* by Avanelle S. Day and Lillie M. Stuckey are reprinted by permission of David White, Inc., 1 Pleasant Ave., Port Washington, N.Y. 11050. Copyright © 1964 by Avanelle S. Day and Lillie M. Stuckey.

First Tor printing: February 1987

A TOR Book

Published by Tom Doherty Associates, Inc.
49 West 24 Street
New York, N.Y. 11010

ISBN: 0-812-50493-3
CAN. ED.: 0-812-50494-1

Library of Congress Catalog Card Number: 81-16970

Printed in the United States of America

0 9 8 7 6 5 4 3 2 1

For Bill Noble

"I like the Walrus best," said Alice: "because he was a *little* sorry for the poor oysters."

"He ate more than the Carpenter, though," said Tweedledee. "You see he held his handkerchief in front, so that the Carpenter couldn't count how many he took: contrariwise."

"That was mean!" Alice said indignantly. "Then I like the Carpenter best—if he didn't eat so many as the Walrus."

"But he ate as many as he could get," said Tweedledum.

This was a puzzler. After a pause, Alice began, "Well! They were *both* very unpleasant characters—" Here she checked herself in some alarm, at hearing something that sounded to her like the puffing of a large steam-engine in the wood near them, though she feared it was more likely to be a wild beast. "Are there any lions or tigers about here?" she asked timidly.

—LEWIS CARROLL
From *Through the Looking-Glass*

CHAPTER

1

As far as Fidel Castro was concerned the worst part of being Premier was that he was treated as an object of curiosity, like a baboon or an ape in a zoo. He didn't have any privacy. That was a fact of life he shared with entertainers, actors, and athletes. The difference was they could get away. They could put on dark glasses or a wig and blend in. If they were very wealthy, and such celebrities usually were, they could escape to havens for the rich where their problems were understood: Acapulco, Palm Springs, Palm Beach, Monaco. The American President had access to Camp David or he could go to sea on the Presidential yacht. The Soviet Premier could hunt or fish at dachas well isolated from proletarians. There were resorts on the Black Sea reserved for use by the party elite—they had grave responsibilities, after all, and worked hard.

But it was different with Fidel. When he stuck with khaki fatigues as a symbol of the revolution and his origins as a guerrilla in the Sierra Maestra, he didn't realize the conse-

1

quences for the future. In the first weeks, he wore the fatigues as a matter of pride. Later, he decided they were lucky. Castro was superstitious. Like a winning baseball pitcher stays with the same jockstrap or an entertainer has a pair of lucky socks, Castro thought there was a connection between his fatigues and success. He had begun in fatigues and in fatigues he had ridden in victory through the streets of Havana. If he were to put on a tie and jacket he would not only be going the way of Fulgencio Batista, *he would destroy a spell*. The very idea of not wearing fatigues made him nervous; it was unthinkable.

In fatigues lay power. There were ideological reasons to justify them; they were simple, utilitarian, and reasonably comfortable—just the thing for the austere sacrifices required of the revolution. There was little difference between his fatigues and those of his soldiers; in that respect they were equals. While other national leaders *talked* of being equal, Fidel actually was—in appearance if not reality. Of course, there were differences between Fidel and a sugarcane worker; everybody knew that. But still, when Fidel made an appearance in the fields he went in khaki. Fidel Castro wore fatigues. People expected them. Khaki discouraged subversive talk of a privileged elite.

Castro's fear, secret to be sure—he told no one, ever—was that if he should appear one day dressed in slacks and comfortable jacket he would lose everything. There would be a cynical nodding of heads. Those close to him, those who feared his power, would become bold—perhaps think the unthinkable: that Fidel Castro was replaceable. Even blue jeans and simple cotton shirts were denied him.

The thing is, Fidel Castro got tired of wearing fatigues. He was condemned by his fear of bad luck and disaster. He got up every morning and put on the same shorts, the same trousers, the same canvas belt with the same damned brass buckle, the same boots, everything the same. He had done that for more than twenty years! The only way to break the spell, he concluded, was to deliver to the poor people a triumph even more grand than the socialist state of Cuba. It would have to be a strike against exploiters that would enable him to step onto the stage with a new image, in new clothes. No, that wouldn't do it either. It would have to be something that *required* him to change clothes.

What would that be? Fidel had no idea. As it turned out, Fidel Castro's opportunity for liberation from fatigues and the spell of 1959 came in New York, where he went to address the United Nations. As everyone who has been to New York knows very well, anything is possible there. On an earlier trip to New York, Fidel and his comrades had been accused of killing, plucking, and butchering a chicken in their hotel room. The Cubans denied it, of course, but it was too outrageous an accusation not to be true. Nobody would make up something like that, not even the gringos. It was embarrassing. Before the new trip he assembled his traveling party in

Havana and told them this time, dammit, there would be none of that shit!

In preparing for the journey he had a feeling that fate owed him one—he had done his best. His people were prospering despite economic sanctions placed on them by the United States. He had the feeling again on his way to the airport for the flight to New York.

It was on the airplane that his security chief, Diego Rodríguez, first reported the possibility of the manna enzyme. Castro listened, gave Rodríguez instructions on what to do, and ordered him to get rid of a young man named Paco Ortiz, the Premier's valet. Ortiz was a Soviet spy. The Cubans knew that.

The manna enzyme. Castro never dreamed that his patience could be so rewarded, that the gods could be so kind. It was a humbling experience for a man who had forgotten what it was to be humble. Well, that wasn't true entirely; there were always the Soviets around to remind him of his limits.

Confirmation came the next day when Fidel decided to strike out on his own to eat breakfast. He loved American breakfasts. The New York City Police Department, United Nations officials, and his own security people said he couldn't do it, couldn't leave his bulletproof limousine, but he decided they could fuck themselves: he was Fidel Castro. He would do what he damned well pleased. So with people yapping and barking like fox terriers, staring and pointing, Señor Castro, surrounded by cops and hard-faced men in blue suits, took a walk. On the way Rodríguez gave him more details about the manna enzyme and Raúl Vivanco.

Fidel knew immediately he would have a holiday. He would escape. He would get out of his fatigues. He would shake the spell that had held him in khaki.

He chose a café at random and there, discussing the manna enzyme with Rodríguez, had the best breakfast of his life: ham, eggs over easy, hash browns, toast with strawberry jam, and several cups of good American coffee, the kind you couldn't get in Cuba. He drank the coffee with the realization that he would even be able to shave. Castro sweated a lot and his face itched with that damned beard. The hot weather in Cuba is great for growing sugarcane but if you have a full beard, ¡Mierda!

The coffee was so good.

DAY ONE

EDDIE PERINI'S ITALIAN CLAM SOUP*

40 little-neck clams
¼ cup olive oil
1 clove garlic
3 anchovy fillets, chopped
1 tablespoon chopped parsley
½ cup dry red wine
1 tablespoon tomato paste

1½ cups warm water
½ teaspoon salt
½ teaspoon freshly ground black pepper
¼ teaspoon orégano
8 thin slices Italian bread, fried in olive oil

1. Wash the clams and scrub well with a vegetable brush.

2. Place the oil in a large saucepan, add the garlic and brown. Discard the garlic. Add the anchovies, parsley and wine to the oil and cook five minutes.

3. Add the tomato paste, water, salt and pepper and cook three to four minutes.

4. Add the clams, cover the pan and cook until all the shells are open, or a maximum of five minutes. Add the orégano and cook two minutes longer.

5. Place two slices fried bread in each soup dish; pour the soup over them. (SERVES FOUR)

CHAPTER

2

THE REASON EDDIE PERINI WAS THERE IN THE
Masonic Temple in Portland, Oregon, with
Bobby Goldman was because he had taken to
heart George Orwell's dictum never to repeat
any word or phrase he had seen in print
before. That's tough for a sportswriter. Even
tougher is Orwell's advice to break all the
rules of clear writing rather than say anything outright barbarous.

For a sportswriter, avoiding the barbarous
borders on the impossible. Perini was not as
good a writer as Steve Duin, the sports
columnist who had every second fan in town
hating him for his honesty, but he did his
best. Heads turned when Perini screwed a
dart board onto the wall nearest his desk.
His editors shrugged; this was Eddie Perini,
after all, who covered the Trail Blazers but
regarded basketball as a mere game and thus
amused everyone in the building.

Once, when the flu had ravaged the
newsroom and the city editor was down to
interns, he had Perini cover city hall for a
few days. Perini regarded that confusion as a

game also. The mayor did not think it was funny. Neither did the city editor.

What Perini did was throw darts while he wrote his stories in his head—or at least the leads. Then he would sit down at his desk and enter it into the *Oregonian*'s computer. While he wasn't Heywood Hale Broun, he wasn't half bad. Signs soon appeared on his desk saying, "Dart Players Do It from 2.37 Meters," and "Dart God, Where Art Thou?" Perini bought 23-gram tungsten-copper darts so he could play in style.

Which is why Perini found himself waiting with Bobby Goldman, a trainer for Leeds United—on a one-year leave to travel with the Portland Trail Blazers and learn how Americans treat knee and ankle injuries—to face Bill Dennis and Roger Christal, two of the best shots in Portland. Some people called Dennis "Billy Bye-Bye" because you barely got going in a game with him and zing, it was bye-bye. Christal worked with computers and had a smooth, flawless throw that wasted no motion. They were both winners and were confident, so they won even more.

Perini and Goldman, one win from money, waited nervously on folding metal chairs, contemplating plastic cups of draft beer and wondering if their nerve and luck would hold. Perini rolled his darts on his thigh out of restlessness.

Bobby Goldman stared at the hardwood floor. "Zen darts, Eddie. You have to clear the crap. You need a clear head for the outs. Better to think of something else."

Perini was silent. He stared through the triple twenty, picturing it, fixing it in his mind's eye. He had read a magazine article on something called psychocybernetics and was convinced that was the answer to his dart game.

Goldman looked up from the door. "Say, do you want to hear a story? My father found something. We should talk. Do us good."

Perini shrugged: he couldn't keep his mind off the fact that they had to shoot against Christal and Dennis. "We've got twenty minutes before we're up."

"Listen, do you know the Old Testament, Eddie?"

Perini looked at him. "What're you talking about?"

"Give me a minute. Six weeks after they left Egypt, the children of Israel reached the Wilderness of Sin—between Elim and Sinai. It was there that Yahweh caused manna to come from the heavens. He gave them two days' food on the sixth day, for the seventh day was the Sabbath. The sons of Israel ate manna for forty years, up to the time they reached the frontier of the Land of Canaan."

"These Old Testament names are marvelous," Perini said.

Goldman sighed. "Look, my old man discovered something: he wanted to give it a suitable name, which is why he went to the Old Testament. That was the day before yesterday and I helped him, so this stuff is all fresh. It's there, in Numbers, in Deuteronomy, in Nehemia, in Psalms and Hebrews.

In Wisdom, Eddie, it says manna conforms to the taste of whoever eats it—it transforms itself into what each eater wishes."

"Jesus!" said Perini.

"That's New Testament, asshole. Have you ever seen what a horse can do to an acre of grass?"

Perini looked at him. "What? I don't know. Horses shit in parades. I saw horses in the Rose Parade once. They had white nylon bags under their butts to catch the dumplings. But what do horses have to do with the Wilderness of Sin or the Land of Canaan?"

"A horse'll eat an acre of grass to the roots in a week; there'll be nothing left but dirt. Just dirt. Damnedest thing you ever saw. Sheep'll do the same thing."

Bobby Goldman moved his metal chair to face Perini and leaned forward, his hands on his thighs. "Listen, I want to tell you what he found. This is between us now. No one else."

"Go for it," said Perini.

Goldman didn't get the chance. They were interrupted by Roger Christal, who leaned down to them, his belly hanging over his belt. "I believe you're up, gents. You want to give us a cork?"

"You want to let us throw a couple first?" asked Perini.

"Whatever," said Christal.

Perini and Goldman took three turns each for warm-ups. Eddie shot the bull against Dennis while Bobby waited on his metal chair. Dennis wired the bull. Perini was a half an inch off and high. Dennis would

shoot first. "Have a good one," said Perini.
He shook hands with Dennis and Christal,
thumbs up. He turned toward Bobby Goldman's chair. Goldman pitched sideways onto
the floor.

There was a moment when nobody moved,
not Eddie, not anybody. They had assembled
there in the Masonic Temple in Portland to
shoot darts. It was a strange, unreal moment, the memory of which would linger for
those who saw Bobby Goldman.

He had a tungsten-nickel dart with black
flights protruding from his chest in the area
where his heart was.

Eddie Perini was the first to move. "Somebody call the goddamn hospital!" he shouted
and was at Bobby's side. He pulled the dart
with a snap of his wrist. Goldman looked
bewildered. "You're gonna be all right,
Bobby," Perini said.

"This is crazy. Somebody's trying to kill
me. I was just sitting here."

"Nobody's gonna kill you with a goddamn
dart, Bobby. You'll be okay."

Bobby Goldman had an odd look on his
face. Something awful had just occurred to
him. "No, listen, somebody *is* trying to kill
me."

"Who, for God's sake?"

Goldman smiled. His eyelids began to droop.
He coughed weakly. "If something happens
to me you have to help, Eddie. Nobody else
knows."

"Knows what?" Perini looked up at the
dart players, who were staring at them.

"About the manna enzyme." Goldman

coughed weakly once again. "If something happens to me you're the only one who can help. You have to promise."

"Promise what?"

Bobby Goldman yawned, "Promise to go see my father. If they find him they'll get him too."

"They?"

The dart players, still gripped by the trance of what looked like a tragedy, parted for attendants bearing a stretcher. The ambulance had arrived.

Goldman motioned Perini closer. "Ride with me to the hospital, Eddie. We have to talk."

Perini tried to follow the stretcher to the ambulance but was stopped by a medic, a large black man who reminded Perini of Muhammad Ali. "Back off, chum," said the attendant.

Goldman tapped the medic weakly on the arm. "Please, he comes. If I'm dying I want him to be there. It's important to me."

"Listen, man, we have our regs."

"Fuck the regs," Perini said.

The black man understood. "Fuck the regs."

Perini followed Bobby Goldman into the ambulance and waited while the medic attached a monitor to record Goldman's pulse and vital signs. Goldman waited, heavy-lidded, barely able to breathe.

"Well?" Perini asked the black man.

"Not good. He's slowing down." The medic punched Goldman's symptoms onto a computer terminal. "The vital signs go direct," he said, holding on to a stainless steel bar to

steady himself as the ambulance worked its
way through the late-afternoon traffic. "I
can't imagine a dart doing all that damage.
Watch there."

Perini watched. The VDT returned the ver-
dict from the hospital's computer: "Stand
by."

The black man looked surprised. "That
mother's generally right on and right now."

"Eddie, listen. Go see my dad."

The medic wiped Goldman's brow, which
was beginning to sweat. "Go ahead, talk to
him, man. The computer needs more time."

"What kind of help does your father need,
Bobby?"

"Tell him I want him to protect himself
and the enzyme. He shouldn't risk trying to
see me. You can do that, can't you, Eddie?"

The attendant took a deep breath. "Coming up now." He watched the terminal. "Pre-
liminary diagnosis: poisoning, curare deriv-
ative. Recommended treatment: intravenous
injection of one ampule of Prostigmin. Pro-
jected result: symptoms instantly reversed,
ninety-six-percent effective."

The medic jerked open one door of the
elaborate medical cabinet on one side of the
ambulance.

"You have that stuff?" Perini asked.

"You got that right," the medic said. He
drew the Prostigmin into a hypodermic. He
turned to Goldman but it was too late.

Bobby Goldman was dead, killed by a
poisoned dart, twenty-six grams, manufac-
tured by Accudart of London, and lodged in

the fifth anterior intercostal space. In short, he took an out dart square in the heart.

Ten minutes later, Eddie Perini called Bernard Goldman from a pay phone and told him what had happened to his son.

There was a moment of silence over the phone and the elder Goldman began to cry softly into the receiver. "He's dead? Bobby? At a dart tournament?"

"He seemed to think you may be in danger as well, Dr. Goldman."

Goldman was still weeping. "My wife died of cancer just two years ago, did you know that? Now Bobby. It's almost more than a man can take."

"I think you better get out of your house, Dr. Goldman. Bobby seemed to think whoever killed him may be after you as well."

Bernard Goldman tried to stop crying. "Bobby's right about that, Mr. Perini."

"They call me Eddie. Do you have any weapons in the house?"

"I have a shotgun. I was planning on going pheasant hunting in the fall."

"Load it—with fours, sixes, bird shot, whatever you have. Lock your house. Don't answer the door, not for anybody, not even a cop. Only me."

"I have to see my son."

"No you don't. I gave Bobby my word I'd do my best to see whatever happened to him doesn't happen to you. The last thing he wanted was for you to get killed trying to see his corpse. I'll pick you up. I have a mustache and will be wearing a white Panama

with the front and back turned down,
planter-style."

"What if they follow you?"

Eddie Perini laughed. "There are a couple of
things I'm not half bad at: out darts and
losing people."

"I don't understand."

"I used to be a spook for Uncle Sam,
Dr. Goldman."

"You followed people?"

"Well, that too," said Eddie Perini.

DAY TWO

FIDEL CASTRO'S SHRIMP AND AVOCADO SALAD

3 medium-size
  avocados
3 tablespoons fresh
  lemon juice
¼ teaspoon garlic
  powder
¼ teaspoon ground
  tumeric
¼ teaspoon ground
  poultry seasoning
¼ teaspoon ground
  black pepper
¼ teaspoon ground red
  pepper

1 teaspoon salt
1 tablespoon cider
  vinegar
1 tablespoon salad oil
1½ cups cooked,
  deveined shrimp
1½ cups (2 medium)
  diced tomatoes
2 tablespoons
  mayonnaise
Watercress

1. Halve and pit avocados. Scoop out the halves
to make the cavities ½ inch larger, saving the
scooped-out portion for use in the filling. Brush
lemon juice on the insides of the halves and on
the reserved portion to prevent discoloration.
2. Combine remaining lemon juice with the
next 8 ingredients in a bowl large enough to mix

salad. Dice scooped-out avocado and add to sea-
sonings along with shrimp, tomato, and mayonnaise. Mix lightly. Spoon into avocado halves.
Garnish with watercress. (SERVES SIX)

CHAPTER

3

• TOP SECRET •

Federal Bureau of Investigation

SURVEILLANCE: Cuban U.N. Delegation, New York

SUBJECT: Fidel Castro

INTSUM: C123, parabolic

REPORTING: Technicians A. James, R. Hamm. Transcript, J. Rodgers. Translation, W. Pember.

At 0714 hours, 9 June 198-, SUBJECT FIDEL CASTRO, after insisting to the New York Police Department that HE is free to do what HE pleases when HE pleases, decided HE wanted to leave the Plaza Hotel for breakfast. Accompanied by HIS

security chief, Diego Rodríguez, CASTRO
left the hotel. Ignoring anti-CASTRO pick-
ets and crowds of onlookers, HE walked
to Paul's, a sidewalk café on East Fifty-
second Street. SUBJECT and Rodríguez
were under surveillance of team AAH,
commanded by J-16655, assisted by
K-90874, Q-45556, W-46324, and B-23245.
The two men at a window seat (details
in INTSUM: C123-Y4, Surveillance). Technicians Hamm and James were dispatched
to the scene with parabolic listening
gear. They arrived at 0804 hours. J-16655
and K-90874 approached law offices located across the street from Paul's.
K-90874 secured the use of the street-
side office of attorney Anthony Klauss.
Gear was in place at 0818 hours. Less
than fifteen minutes of conversation was
recorded before circumstances made further use of the parabolic impossible.

CASTRO: So you got him. He's dead.

RODRÍGUEZ: Yes. He's dead.

CASTRO: And his father's in the mountains there.

RODRÍGUEZ: In the mountains.

CASTRO: Vivanco, he's sure about this?

RODRÍGUEZ: Yes. I know it sounds incredible but Vivanco says it's true. These
hash browns are good.

CASTRO: The gringos eat good breakfasts, I'll give them that. You ever have
grits? They're great drenched in butter.
So this Vivanco allegedly studied with
Goldman. How come he can't reproduce
it for us?

RODRÍGUEZ: I went over that with him. He said Goldman just stumbled onto it. Just how, Vivanco doesn't know. He said Goldman attributed it to luck. It's all in Goldman's head.

CASTRO: So tell me again, who knows about this thing?

RODRÍGUEZ: Only Goldman, his son, and Vivanco. The wife died a couple of years ago of cancer.

CASTRO: Just the three?

RODRÍGUEZ: Two now.

CASTRO: You'll have to waste Vivanco also. But first interrogate him again. Use drugs if you have to. Do whatever you need to do. When you're absolutely sure he's telling the truth, absolutely sure, then kill him. But not before.

RODRÍGUEZ: Do whatever.

CASTRO: On something like this, yes. If he's damaged in the process we'll have to accept that. The worms won't care. Vivanco will forget all about it when he's dead.

RODRÍGUEZ: Why would he dream up a story like this? That's what I can't imagine.

CASTRO: I can't imagine. But remember, we may be dealing with a gringo scheme here.

RODRÍGUEZ: Laurence?

CASTRO: Yes, Laurence. There's no telling what Laurence will do. He's a liar. The Russians tell me you can never believe him. He's crazy.

RODRÍGUEZ: I still don't understand what

he'd have to gain, floating a story like this. I think Vivanco's telling the truth.

CASTRO: It sounds right but you never know.

RODRÍGUEZ: Laurence.

CASTRO: Laurence. If Vivanco's a double, you find out. If he's not, he'll have given the ultimate sacrifice for the poor people of the world.

RODRÍGUEZ (*coughs*): That's one way of putting it.

CASTRO: I don't like it either but we don't have a choice. We have to think about Laurence, always. Vivanco did come to us with his story.

RODRÍGUEZ: Yes, he did.

CASTRO: Now you tell me this man Goldman is in the mountains. Where in the mountains?

RODRÍGUEZ: In the Cascades that run north-south about a hundred fifty miles from the Oregon Coast. We know exactly where he is. He told Vivanco. He's up there in a maroon Volkswagen bus. Vivanco gave us the license number, everything we need.

CASTRO (*laughs*): *Was* up in the mountains! He won't be there now, friend. His son was murdered.

RODRÍGUEZ: No.

CASTRO: No? He'll be back in Portland. Where would you be?

RODRÍGUEZ: He's not back in Portland. He's still in the mountains. Vivanco says he never listens to the radio. His Volkswagen doesn't have a radio. He doesn't own a portable. He's an intellectual, a thinker. He's up there alone, that's what kind of guy he is. The police are looking for him but they can't find him.

CASTRO: Can't find him? What about the son?

RODRÍGUEZ: The corpse is on ice. I've got a man in Portland watching the situation. It's a big story for the *Oregonian* in Portland. Bobby Goldman is traveling with the Portland Trail Blazers to learn how they keep their players' knees working after all that pounding night after night. He plans to use this information to help British *futbol* players. The student gets killed by poisoned pub dart. (*Silence*) Why do we Cubans have to be so damn flamboyant? (*Silence*) Then his father turns up missing.

CASTRO (*laughs*): Do they think the father did it?

RODRÍGUEZ: No. His friends know he went fishing but they directed the police to the wrong part of the state. Goldman changed his mind at the last minute, Vivanco says.

CASTRO: The wrong part of the state?

RODRÍGUEZ: The police are close to two hundred miles off. They're searching around the Deschutes River.

CASTRO: How long before they conclude he's not there?

RODRÍGUEZ: Days maybe, a week. Who knows? If he's not on the Deschutes, they'll begin searching its tributaries.

CASTRO: So we have time then?

RODRÍGUEZ: Oh, yes. We alone know about the discovery. We alone know where Goldman is. I think we should move quickly but right now we have time.

CASTRO: Time enough to get Dann and Rivera up here?

RODRÍGUEZ: I don't see why not. A day, two days, it shouldn't make that much difference.

CASTRO: Well, where is he exactly?

RODRÍGUEZ: ... (*A uniformed police-man, part of the security perimeter established around the restaurant, blocked the parabolic during* RODRÍGUEZ'S *reply.*)

CASTRO: Is that hard to find?

RODRÍGUEZ (*laughs*): No, not hard at all. All we have to do is buy a road map.

CASTRO: Do you think ... (*A second policeman, joining the first, blocked the remainder of* CASTRO'S *reply.*)

RODRÍGUEZ: I don't know why. Did you get lost in the Maestra? Our man says we can get maps that show everything— logging roads, trails, springs, everything.

CASTRO: There's no immediate worry that you can see?

RODRÍGUEZ: None. We got rid of Ortiz, so the Russians know nothing. Vivanco said only the son knew, and we took care of him.

CASTRO: Good. I want you to get in touch with Dann and Rivera immediately. Don't talk about manna, just get them up here. Then ... (*The remainder of* CASTRO'S *conversation with* RODRÍGUEZ

*was blocked by security people on the
sidewalk outside the restaurant.*)

James Chambliss adjusted his tie and shook
his head. The parabolic report was as curious and suggestive as he'd ever seen. Dann
and Rivera were old comrades of Fidel Castro, friends since the earliest days in the
Sierra Maestra. This manna thing was important enough that Castro wanted them
with him again. Chambliss reread the report
and closed the file. Ever since William Colby
gave the Senate all that it wanted in 1975,
the Company had been forced to play everything by the book. He wished the government would let the Company do its own
domestic CI work. It was outrageous that the
FBI should be working only one parabolic
with Fidel Castro chatting casually with his
chief of security next to a restaurant window. A restaurant window in the City of New
York!

Chambliss was an executive now, deputy
director of plans. But he had served his time
in the field. The first rule was to have a
backup system. That applied to everything
from a rendezvous to a drop-off. Always. A
thick-bodied cop blocks one angle, that's
okay; you're working another.

Fidel Castro was up to something big.
Chambliss wondered who the hell Goldman
and Vivanco were. Whoever Goldman was he
had something Castro wanted dearly and
Goldman's son had somehow gotten in the
way. Goldman was in the mountains of
Oregon. Why would anybody want to go to

the mountains in Oregon? Oregon was one of those clean, dumb places, like Vermont, with trees everywhere. Nothing ever happened in Oregon! A volcano had blown up out there somewhere—what was that, Mount Saint Helens? No, that was in Washington state. The Oregonians were so stupid as to let a Hindu Guru take over a small town and rip everybody off. The city of Portland had even elected a bartender for its mayor. What the hell was going on?

Chambliss dialed the director of the FBI. After the parabolic episode in New York, he didn't trust them to do a simple and obvious follow-up in Portland. Ask a newspaper reporter and the Portland police a few questions and you'd probably have it. But what could Chambliss do? Nothing. He was at the mercy of Murphy's Law.

CHAPTER

4

ANTHONY LAURENCE DIDN'T ARRIVE AT LANGLEY until 2:00 P.M. that day, which was unusual. On impulse he had pulled his Volkswagen Rabbit to the curb by a corner café in Fairfax, Virginia, where he leisurely drank three cups of coffee, ate a Denver omelette, and read *The Washington Post* from cover to cover. He normally wouldn't have gone through Fairfax, preferring to cross the Potomac farther upstream at the Key Bridge. But this morning was different. Laurence told himself that even the director of the Central Intelligence Agency deserves a break once in a while. After the omelette he stopped at a used-book store and spent another hour sitting squat-legged before shelves of thrillers and spy books.

It was all a mistake, of course, a DCI didn't have time for such luxuries. A leisurely meal, a little privacy, and a used-book store are pleasures reserved for other men, men not responsible for the security of the United States. He arrived at Langley feeling anxious, a worrisome knot in the pit of his stomach: considering Fidel Castro's conversation in New York it was no time to drag-ass his way to work. The odds were that some awful, threatening turd would have hit the fan at Langley.

He was right, of course, it was written all over his secretary's face when he got to his office. Her name was Frieda Sondheim, a sloe-eyed, soft woman with a husband and three children; she was in love with Laurence, however, and he knew it. His worries were hers.

"Thank God you're here, Tony. Traffic wants to see you as soon as possible."

"Traffic?" Castro, he thought, it would be about Castro.

"We've been trying to get you all day long. Where have you been?"

Laurence sighed. "Here and there, hanging around with eggs and old books. Why is it we have Chambliss and Driscoll? Do I have to be here every time some Russian passes gas?"

Frieda Sondheim frowned. "Chambliss can be a pain in the butt; you know that. Driscoll gets excited when there's pressure."

"Ahh, well," Laurence said. "What's happened?"

Frieda unlocked a file drawer and removed a single sheet of paper stamped a bright-red TOP SECRET top and bottom. "This," she said.

Laurence skimmed the report. "The Soviets!" He looked surprised.

"Very heavy, strange traffic between Moscow and Berlin."

"Are you working on more there?"

"I'll have it in a minute, Tony."

"Kremlin out mostly or return as well?"

Frieda looked at the paper in her type-writer. "Back and forth, back and forth, back and forth. Charlie says it's crazy." Charlie Davis was in charge of decoding radio communication.

"And we don't know what they're saying?"

Frieda took a package of chewing gum from a desk drawer and began unwrapping it. "No way of knowing, Tony. No hint. They switch patterns before the computer can get a lock on it. The heaviest traffic was between eleven A.M. and noon, when it stopped suddenly. That'd be six P.M. and seven P.M., Moscow time. It's nutty, Charlie says. Says it's like trying to catch a Hoyt Wilhelm knuckler. Who's Hoyt Wilhelm?"

Laurence took a piece of Frieda's gum. "Baseball pitcher, Frieda." It had to be Castro. Whatever he was up to, it had Moscow Center all worked up.

"What's a knuckler?"

Laurence grinned and demonstrated with his right hand. "You hold the baseball like so and push it at the plate. Looks awkward, I know, but the ball doesn't spin so it hops up and down, inside and out. Takes a knack. Batter doesn't have any idea where it's going next. Catcher doesn't either, for that matter. Wilhelm's catchers had to use a special mitt, big sucker."

"Oh?" said Frieda. Baseball bored her. Her husband watched it on television on Monday nights. Other nights he talked about it in bed until he went to sleep, leaving her there staring into the darkness, hand on her pelvis, wondering what it would be like to have a man interested in sex.

Laurence stood up, assumed a stance of a baseball pitcher in deep concentration, looking at an imaginary catcher in the distance. "Easy on the arm, Frieda. Wilhelm lasted until he was almost fifty."

Frieda laughed. "You better leave Mickey Mantle to Hoyt Wilhelm, champ. You've got Russians to worry about."

Russians and Fidel Castro, Laurence thought. "Mickey Mantle retired years ago, love. So did Wilhelm. Punch me up traffic, will you? Thanks, my dear. Hey, Charlie, Frieda tells me you people have a little action going on today."

Charlie Davis groaned. "Where the hell have you been, Tony? We had to put up with Driscoll all morning, running around like he was doing speed or something. Then that turd Chambliss arrived with that bland, efficient face of his. It's nuts, Tony. I haven't seen anything like it in years. Having a bunch of fuzz-cheeked kids down here is bad enough, but Jesus, Tony, Driscoll and Chambliss are too much."

"What do you think is happening?"

"Well, we're running the tapes through again. It'll be a matter of time before we get a fix."

"I have an idea what they're talking about, Charlie. Now don't get offended, but you do not have a need to know, neither does Driscoll nor any of your fuzz-cheeks."

"Oh?" Charlie Davis sounded surprised.

There was an edge to his voice. "What about Chambliss?"

"I want you to pull the tapes and file them with access by my code and my code alone."

"Can't do that, Tony. Regs need a backup. You said Chambliss."

"Sorry. Chambliss too."

"Chambliss it is. I'll pull them, Tony. What about the NSC?"

"Frieda's got your summary here."

"Well, okay. You're DCI, Tony." Charlie Davis didn't like to be excluded from need. He felt he'd been around long enough to prove he could keep his mouth shut.

"Thank you, Charlie. Don't be pissed now. I have my reasons. Someday, maybe, I'll tell you all about it." Castro and the Soviet traffic was too much of a coincidence. Laurence's instincts told him to be very careful.

"No sweat, Tony."

"Thanks, Charlie." Laurence hung up but held on to the receiver. "Punch me the sitters, will you, Frieda? Thank you. William, my man, how're things?"

"Oh, little of this, little of that, Tony."

"Tell me about the Kremlin, William. What do the little birdies tell you about the Kremlin?"

William Shawcroft laughed. "What do you want to know about the Kremlin, Tony?"

"I want to know about the Politburo. What have those little charmers been up to?"

"Funny you should ask that, Tony. Two members are believed to be sunning themselves on the Black Sea. That leaves ten little comrades. Three are out admiring tractors on a tour of communal farms. The seven remaining in Moscow all spent the day at the Kremlin, as near as we can determine. That's unusual."

"Was Karpov there?"

"No. Karpov was in Berlin most of the day. Word we have is the Soviets are worried about a British double. It was a GRU operation with the East Germans involved but they fucked up somehow and crossed it with the KGB, a mistake—the Brits were right on it. Hence Valery Karpov."

Laurence laughed. "Little incest, eh? Bet old Valery was pissed."

"Bet he was." Shawcroft laughed too.

"But Karpov's back at Moscow Center now."

"We think so."

"Well, thank you, William. If anything unusual happens in the next day or so let me know right away."

"Will do, Tony."

Laurence hung up and looked at his watch. "I guess I could phone London and Bonn, see what they make of it. What do you think?"

Frieda Sondheim reached for her pencil and stenographer's pad. "I've never known anybody as cool as you, Tony."

Laurence gave her a self-deprecating grin. "I was a lacrosse goalkeeper in prep school. Taught me not to get excited." The truth was Anthony Laurence's guts were twisted with anxiety. He wondered if the FBI had gotten back to Chambliss on the Portland query.

CHAPTER

5

COMRADE POTEMKIN SHIFTED NERVOUSLY IN his chair while Comrade Karpov read a report on his desk. Karpov closed his eyes in thought, then glanced at Potemkin, took a sip of coffee, and reread the report. Potemkin felt a trickle of sweat slide down his chest. He swallowed. Lenin watched from a painting on the wall.

Karpov took a penknife from his trousers and began making small notches on a pencil. He stared through Potemkin without seeing him. A certain aloofness was expected of the director of the KGB. "So, Alexei Nikolaevich."

Potemkin leaned forward. His collar was a half inch too small. He wanted to loosen it.

Karpov watched his colleague. He threw the notched pencil into a desk drawer and went to work on another. It was a dreadful habit.

Potemkin waited. His stomach gurgled. He was hungry. He hoped Karpov hadn't heard the gurgle. Potemkin cleared his throat.

"Tell me, Alexei Nikolaevich, how many people in your section know about Ural Blue?"

"Besides myself, my deputy Kroslov and two operators. The operators know nothing of the purpose. They only run the patterns. But they must be wondering."

Karpov made a clicking sound with his tongue on the roof of his mouth. "Wondering what, Comrade?"

"Why Blue is handled outside our usual channels and why it made no sense to them."

"They were chosen for their reliability, were they not?"

"Yes, Comrade Karpov."

"Put yourself in the shoes of Charles Davis for a moment, Alexei Nikolaevich. What if Laurence visited London, say, and we monitored a similar pattern from the American Embassy, what would you think?"

"Comrade?" Potemkin looked uncomfortable.

"Go on. Tell me."

"I'd think something big was up with the Americans."

Karpov smiled. He ran the blade of his knife across the pad of his left thumb. "And what would you tell me?"

"I'd tell you, Valery Ivanovich, that our computers report gibberish. No one knows how long it will take to work it out."

"You stopped Blue before I left for the airport at Berlin?"

"I did."

"Is there any way, Comrade Potemkin, that the American computers can give them the answer to Blue in the next few days?"

Potemkin allowed himself a small smile. "We know Charles Davis is a thorough, patient man. He knows his computers, but if the computers got onto Blue he wouldn't believe them. He'd persist. He's a good man, invaluable, and Laurence knows it."

"You and Kroslov are to continue as usual. Your two operators, are they male or female?"

Potemkin brightened. "Female. One of them has the most marvelous set of tits I've ever seen."

Karpov laughed. "No matter. Your two operators are to be given a leave for their hard work and dedication to the State. If they had been men I'd have sent them hunting, maybe, but since they're women they might enjoy the Black Sea. Watched, of course."

"They'll be watched, Valery Ivanovich."

"Married or single, Comrade?"

"Single."

"They'll enjoy the Black Sea."

"Yes, Comrade, they will."

Karpov rose and folded his knife. "That will be all, Comrade Potemkin, you did well."

He followed Potemkin out the door and strolled casually up the hall where his deputy, Alexander Volchak, waited. Volchak, a thin man with rimless spectacles, was picking at a piece of dead skin on the heel of his hand when Karpov entered the conference room. As usual, Volchak looked like he was doing an imitation of a fish. The reason was that he had a pit on his front tooth. He was self-conscious about it and almost constantly ran his tongue around it in tight little circles. That pushed his lips out and made him look like a fish breathing. When he smiled he tried to keep his upper lip from rising too high, thus exposing the pit. The result was a weak, sick smile like that of a man just asked if he had ever seen a pornographic movie.

Moscow Center is the elite of Soviet bureaucracies. Its members are slick, well educated, and cosmopolitan—or as much so as is possible in the Soviet Union. They look upon the Party apparatus with the same steady, cynical eye with which they view London and Washington. They are the best. A man who sucks on his tooth must be bright indeed to rise in the KGB hierarchy. Volchak was bright. In fact, if he hadn't had the pit he would probably have had Karpov's job, but people couldn't stand him imitating a fish. He might as well have been obese.

"The Premier will be here shortly," Volchak said.

"You were right to use Blue, Volchak." Karpov sat down. He knew Volchak was smart. He respected him but he would never be as familiar with him as he was with Potemkin. It was hard, what with Volchak looking like a fucking carp swimming in the Volga.

Volchak shrugged, his tongue going round and round. "We designed it for a time like this. The Premier said we must know what the Americans know. I agree. Better than us calling them. Let them call. If they don't know about manna, so much the better." Volchak thought it was a stupid idea, overly precious and risky. But what could he do? Nothing. The Premier, who fancied himself more clever than the Americans, supported it. Volchak had no choice.

Karpov thought it was nonsense, too, but said nothing. "Laurence will call as the Premier predicts," he said.

Volchak smiled. "A good plan." His tongue paused, then continued.

Karpov felt suddenly anxious. "That is Blue's beauty, of course. It's nonsense. Gibberish. Blue says nothing at all and everything. It forces the Americans to make the first move."

Volchak's smile remained. The smile, like Ural Blue, said nothing at all and everything. "Poor Laurence," he said.

Volchak, you little bastard, Karpov thought. "Our advantage, Comrade Volchak."

"What if this manna thing is all just nonsense? What if it's just Langley's idea of a little fun? How do we really know?"

Karpov paused, then looked Volchak straight in the eye. "Because we got it from a Cuban giving it to Fidel Castro, that's why."

Volchak shifted in his chair. "How do we know he was for real, I mean the Cuban? Maybe the Americans doubled him. What if he was doubled? How do we know? How can we know? He's dead now. Castro had him killed."

"He had him killed to shut him up."

Volchak turned his palms up. "Maybe Fidel found out the kid had been turned. You find someone's been turned, you take him out. Everybody knows the rules. Double, and you're dead if you get caught. No other way."

"We can't take a chance," Karpov said. "Not with something like manna."

Volchak nodded. "I agree, Comrade. We can't take a chance. But it's a good question, don't you think? What percentage of what we get is real and how much is fake?"

"We get most of it out of the New York Public Library." Karpov laughed.

"Not that, I mean covert stuff—honeypots, bribes, political nuts—that's what costs. That's where the risks are. All that spy stuff. How much of that information is legitimate? As much as five percent?"

"I don't know," said Karpov. He and Volchak had been over this before. Volchak was counterintelligence. It was Volchak's business to be suspicious.

Volchak's tongue stopped. "Five percent? Do you think that's too high?"

"I guess not."

"I don't think we have any idea," Volchak said. "Neither do the Americans or the British. We're basing policy on this information. The question, Comrade, is: Does the good resulting from decisions based on accurate information outweigh damage of decisions based on disinformation? We should be asking ourselves. Does it? Why aren't we asking that?"

"We've been over this before, Comrade Volchak. I understand what you're saying but we can't take a chance on this one, not on manna."

Volchak, tongue working and lips pursed, fishlike, did not stop: "All of us are spending enormous sums of money gathering information and even more money analyzing it. We're floating disinformation every day. They do too. And they accept about as much of it as we do, maybe five percent. Philby says so. He watched the Brits, watched the Americans. He knew our lines and when they were floated. Precious damned few did any good. Any doubts at all on a report and they spike it."

"That's what Philby says." Karpov ran his fingers through his hair.

"How much good stuff didn't we act on? Did you ever think of that? All that good stuff ignored because one false line can do so much fucking damage." Volchak's tongue was back on the pit. He leaned forward and the tongue stopped. "I just don't believe this manna business. It's a trick of some kind."

Karpov slapped him on the back and laughed. "Alexei, my friend, you think too much."

Volchak laughed with him. "I suppose so."

If it hadn't been for Volchak's damned tongue, Karpov would have had him over to his flat for vodka long ago. But the tongue was just too much. "Having given them Blue, what do we do now? Which way do we fall?"

"I have no idea, Comrade. The Premier met with the Politburo. You should have been there."

"The consequences are incredible," Karpov said.

"They are that."

"What would you do, Comrade Volchak?"

"I don't know," Volchak said. "A thing like

that would break their back in the short run."

"And maybe ours in the long run."

"That's one opinion. You read the summary, of course."

Karpov looked at his watch. "He'll be here in a few minutes. I read it several times, Comrade. A good job, I think. It is incredible."

"It isn't easy," Volchak said. The door opened and Volchak straightened up.

It was the Premier, Georgi Kagnanovich, bearing the Soviet position in a yellow folder. The Politburo's decision hadn't been easy to come by. The old factions and cliques meant nothing this time. Manna was not a hawks-and-doves issue. The Russian bear had a live one in its paws. Some of the older members had been there with Nikita Khrushchev when that asshole Kennedy had risked World War III over the missiles in Cuba. This was worse than that by far. Ideology spared the Soviets from having to think. It was comforting in that respect. But ideology was of no use on the question of the manna enzyme. It was an awful decision to have to make, just awful.

Karpov was anxious to know what would be done.

Kagnanovich, looking tired, handed him the folder. "We have to talk, Valery Ivanovich."

CHAPTER

6

FIDEL CASTRO COULD HEAR A MAN ON TELEVISION telling how his Christian relief organization had purchased a German-made diesel truck to move corn from Djibouti on the Gulf of Aden to help feed starving Ethiopians. It was a struggle you wouldn't believe, the man was saying. The truck drivers forced upon them by the Ethiopian government didn't know how to drive a truck and ruined three transmissions in their caravan. They had to wait six weeks for new parts, and then nobody had the tools to fix it. Meanwhile—in spite of the best intentions of God—the load of Christian corn began to get mold.

On instructions of the Marxist government in Ethiopia they were forced to go first to Addis Ababa, which was hundreds of miles out of their way. Then, for reasons which were not explained, they were forced to stay in a wretched hotel in Addis Ababa—the toilets did not work and the help was indifferent—while bureaucrats argued as to whether or not they would be allowed to continue. Finally, they were told the government would deliver the grain. They said no. They were told they had to leave the country. They hid the keys to the truck and refused. Finally they were allowed to continue but with a tattered Ethiopian flag flying from a hastily improvised fender mount.

After a hot, arduous journey with an Ethiopian madman for a driver, they had arrived at their destination, a camp where starving people were allegedly gathered for relief. Only when they got there they found the camp had been disbanded by the Ethiopian government and the people driven out in the desert to starve. The missionary said this was because of the pending arrival of reporters and the Ethiopian government didn't want to admit it couldn't feed its people. Then there were more breakdowns due to reckless Ethiopian drivers. It was all impossible, the Christian said.

Hearing this, Fidel Castro was furious. The lying bastards! He leaned around the corner and there was yet another picture of the large-bellied, starving children the Americans liked to show on television. Pictures of these wide-eyed, pathetic children were everywhere in the U.S. They peered out from the covers of magazines and from the front of billboards.

The Americans were perfect assholes in Fidel's mind. They went from one hero and one fad to the next in a rapid tumble: John Travolta, Sylvester Stallone, and Michael Jackson were scrambled in among citizen band radios, Cabbage Patch dolls, and Trivial Pursuit. Americans had gone from being concerned about the killing of harp seals and the ravages of acid rain to wife beating, missing kids, drunk drivers, and starvation in Africa. Each cause had its moment, only to be replaced by another when boredom set in.

Christian do-gooders seemed to be on every radio and television station, begging listeners to give, give, give, so that starvation might be eliminated. Castro wondered how much grain actually reached people who needed it.

Castro stepped into the bathtub and pulled the chrome knob that would switch the water from the faucet to the shower nozzle. It came out cold. "*¡Mierda!*" said Fidel. Shit! He jumped back, considered the single knob that controlled the water temperature.

Fidel Castro could never get used to fancy bathroom fixtures. In Cuba there was a hot and cold handle to the tap and that was that. You want hot and you pull the hot handle— too hot and you add a little cold. But Americans could never settle on something that was simply utilitarian, something that worked. Castro attributed it to the influence of homosexual designers. He squatted naked on the polished tiles of the bathroom in his Plaza Hotel suite, one hand on the confusing knob, the other on the water. It was tough for him to concentrate on the water because he had something else on his mind.

Fidel Castro was going to provide food to the poor people of the world. He, Fidel Castro. Ahh, he grinned. The water was right.

He stood up and looked at himself in the mirror. He could see imagined thousands, gathered to receive the miracle of science delivered unto them by Fidel. The American television networks would be there, ABC, NBC, CBS, as would the BBC, the Germans, the Japanese; there would be the wire services, AP, UPI, Reuters, Agence France Presse, Tass; and the newspapers, *The New York Times*, *The Washington Post*, and the other great newspapers from Latin America and Europe. Later, he would give an intimate interview with Barbara Walters, the serious American woman with the serious questions and the ability to talk without moving any part of her face except her lips. Fidel thought Barbara Walters's lips were curious. He always stared at them as words came out. He wondered why the Americans paid such enormous sums of money to a woman without emotion. How could she talk like that, with just her lips? Did she practice in front of a mirror like a ventriloquist?

Fidel wondered if Barbara Walters ever laughed. He wondered what she was like in bed. Maybe she would swap an hour of her time for an exclusive interview. Fidel admired his image in the mirror and ran a hand over his hairy belly. His fantasy turned from Barbara Walters to the assembled crowd.

"*He venido por los pobres del mundo*," he would begin. I am here for the poor people of the world. "*Por los pobres del mundo*," he repeated. Did that sound right? Yes.

"*Por los niños de las Américas, de Asia, y de Africa*." For the children of the Americas, of

Asia and of Africa. Yes, Fidel forgot about his shower water. *"Nadie volverá a morir de hambre. Nadie, mis amigos."* No one will ever starve again. No one, my friends.

Fidel stepped back from the mirror and stood, chin up. The next line must be dramatic: *"Por la segunda vez, he ido a las montañas."* For the second time, I have gone to the mountains.

"La primera vez, les traje la libertad, un país para los cubanos.

Yéstavez fuí a las montañas de Norteamérica y traje conmigo un descubrimiento que los gringos querían destruir." The first time, I brought you Liberty, a country for the Cubans. This time I went to the mountains of North America and brought back a discovery the gringos would destroy.

"Un descubrimiento, mis hermanos, que significa comida para los miás pobres." A discovery, brothers and sisters, that will mean food for the poorest of the poor.

Yes, that was it. A speech for all time. Food delivered to the poor.

"Una madre no tendrá que llorar por falta de comida para sus hijos." No mother shall ever cry for the want of food for her children.

"Los niños no llorarán durante la noche por causa de hambre. Yo lo he arreglado." No baby shall ever again cry in the night from hunger. I have seen to it.

For all his posturing, Fidel Castro wanted that more than anything in the world. Fidel had seen and known hunger. It was an outrage that hunger should exist. He had a chance now to end it forever.

"El problema de la hambre ya se acabó," he told the mirror. Hunger is finished.

"Comeremos. Todos. He hecho esto por los pobres de la tierra. Comida para todos, no solamente para los ricos." We will eat. All of us. This I have done for the poor people of the earth. Food for all the people, not just the rich.

Fidel Castro, having seen to the murder of Paco Ortiz, the Soviet spy, of Bernard Goldman's son, Bobby, and of the Cuban student Raúl Vivanco, was convinced Cuba and Cuba alone knew of the manna enzyme. He would see to it that the world shared the miracle.

When he had finished, Castro stood before the bathroom mirror once again. This time he took a pair of scissors he had used to trim his beard and set about to remove the growth that had become his trademark since he had emerged victorious from the Sierra Maestra.

Before he left, Fidel wanted to try out one of those black girls who hung around Forty-second street. Fidel had seen them from his limousine one day and had ordered his chauffeur to drive him around the block so he could get another look. The New York policemen riding escort on motorcycles had yelled at the chauffeur and tried to block his path but the driver moved on as though he didn't understand their signals. The hookers were still there. They smiled and waved at the limousine. They had marvelous butts that turned Castro on. Castro wanted to send an aide on a mission to return with two of them. He couldn't, of course, but thinking about it caused him to have an erection anyway.

So it was that Fidel Castro set to work on his beard, first with the scissors, then with a razor made by a Latin American subsidiary of the Gillette Safety Razor Company. There was no mention of Gillette on the Spanish-language package.

When he was finished, Castro looked at himself in the mirror and laughed and laughed until his face was wet with tears. He didn't recognize himself. He looked like a damned fool.

He then tried on the three-piece suit Rodríguez had bought for him. It was a little too small but not bad. Only then did Fidel Castro realize he had forgotten how to tie a necktie.

"*¡Mierda!*" he said. He looked at his wrist-watch. It was time.

Castro had forbidden security guards on his floor. He insisted they made him nervous. So all he had to do was walk outside, take the elevator to the lobby, buy some Life Savers at a shop in the lobby, and stroll past detectives of the City of New York, agents of the FBI, KGB, and the CIA as well as his own Cuban security force.

Nobody paid any attention. Nobody looked twice.

Fidel Castro walked across the street to the sidewalk that bordered the southern edge of Central Park. The weather was lovely and Castro felt good. He had the rest of the day and the evening free in Manhattan. It was the first time since 1959 that Castro had any real privacy. Young people were throwing Frisbees in the park. Two young girls were leaning up against a rump-high retaining wall eating ice-cream cones. There was a man with a cart selling small bouquets of yellow tulips.

"*Dos,*" said Fidel to the man with the cart. He held up two fingers.

"Ahh, such a lovely day it is. That'll be ten dollars," said the vendor. He was an old man with one shoulder higher than the other.

Castro gave him a twenty and when the man began rummaging for change, Castro refused. "No, no, you keep it," he said slowly, in English.

Castro walked to the two girls and with a courtly bow, offered them the flowers.

The girls were no more than sixteen or seventeen years old. The eldest of the two, tall, awkward, and skinny with braces on her teeth, looked embarrassed and giggled.

"*Por favor,*" said Castro.

The youngest of the two put her hand over her mouth and looked at Castro with pale-blue eyes.

"I'm new in town. I'll be leaving shortly. It would please me for you to have the flowers," Castro said.

The girls thought he was a man who could be trusted. He had a look about him. Besides, there was a cop standing not fifty feet away. They accepted the flowers.

Fidel Castro smiled broadly. "*Gracias, gracias, señoritas,*" he said, and turned west. There was a spring in his step and a smile on his face. He found it hard to keep his hand off his face, however. It was simply unreal not having a beard.

At the southwest corner of the park, Castro bought a Spanish-language newspaper from a sidewalk rack. There was a picture of Castro in beard and fatigues on the front page. The cutline under the picture said: "Fidel Castro, murderer, addresses UN."

Castro folded the paper twice, shook his head, and threw it into a trash can. There was something Castro wanted to eat but had never had the opportunity. He continued west and a block later he found what he was looking for: a Jewish delicatessen.

A large man in a dirty apron looked at him from behind the counter. "What'll it be?" he said, and yawned.

Castro examined trays of potato salad, cole slaw, olives, corned beef, and pastrami. "I would like cream cheese and lox on bagel," he said slowly in English. "I am from Latin America and have never had it before. Be generous and I'll pay double."

"Whatever you say." The man grinned. "You're gonna like it a lot. You're here with the UN, I'll bet."

"*Sí*," said Castro.

"That asshole Castro spoke at the General Assembly yesterday. Guy never shuts up. Spoke for three hours nonstop. You'd think he'd put himself to sleep."

"*Sí. Boca grande*," said Castro.

The deli man, in the spirit of international cooperation and a few extra bucks, made Castro an extraordinary sandwich.

Fidel accepted it with wide eyes. He had

never tasted anything so good. Dann and Rivera weren't due in from Havana until the next day. There was no rush, manna was theirs. Right now, Fidel Castro had an afternoon and evening in New York by himself. He was excited. He would try everything.

CHAPTER

7

THE WERE IN THE HORSE BRASS PUB AT Forty-fifth and Belmont, across the Willamette River from the Masonic Temple where Bobby Goldman took an out dart in the heart. Behind them on the wall were framed photographs of Lord Mountbatten beside a bomber whose fuselage had been ripped by flak, and Mountbatten striding across an airfield with RAF officers. Above them, hanging from the ceiling, were pennants of English football clubs: Tottenham Hotspur, Wolverhampton Wanderers, Sheffield United, the Queen's Park Rangers, and others. Bernard Goldman was a tall man, balding, and somewhat stooped with age; he was about sixty. He had kind, intelligent green eyes above wrinkled black bags that had been years in forming. He wore tan corduroy trousers, an inch short in the legs and held up by suspenders. His dark-brown corduroy jacket had patches on the elbows and was frayed at the sleeves.

Eddie Perini poured them each a glass of beer from a pitcher of Henry Weinhard. "If

I'm going to be of any help to you, Dr. Goldman, you're going to have to tell me what this is all about."

Bernard Goldman swallowed. "It's difficult for me to believe Bobby's dead. First Anna, now him."

It was hard to know what to say at a time like that. To say you're sorry is hardly adequate when a man's only son has been murdered. Perini said it anyway. There was nothing else he could say. "I'm very, very sorry, Dr. Goldman. Bobby was a good friend of mine."

The tears started to come again but Goldman managed to stop them. He sighed and wiped his eyes with the back of his hand. "How were you two doing anyway?"

"We were one match away from money."

"God, this is awful," said Goldman. He wiped his eyes again.

"We have to think about you now. We have to think of the future."

Goldman looked at the football pennants hanging from the ceiling. "The future? I can't even see my son. What future are you talking about?"

"Yours, Dr. Goldman. I gave Bobby my word that I would do everything I can to help you. I mean to keep my word."

Bernard Goldman almost burst into tears again. "My grandparents were immigrants to the United States. Have you ever seen those old photographs of Ellis Island in the late nineteenth century? That's where my grandparents came. When I was seventeen years old I came across a book of those pictures in the New York Public Library: Jewish tenements, women working in sweatshops in the garment industry, hollow-eyed children sitting on stoops in the August heat. My grandmother worked in one of those sweatshops. My father knew hunger. Have you ever known hunger, Eddie?"

Perini shook his head. "No hunger I knew wouldn't be relieved in a few hours."

Goldman smiled. "Neither have I. My parents knew hunger though. My father worked his backside off, determined that I would have an education. Education meant everything to him. He wanted me to have what he never had, never could have. He had to scrape and save all the way." Goldman swallowed. "Every time I open a magazine and see one of those poor African children staring out at me . . . I can hardly stand it, Eddie."

"You were good in science."

"I went to CCNY, later to MIT. I became a biochemist. I was good, Eddie, a pioneer in what was to be called the Green Revolution, the application of science to the production of food. For a while, about twenty years ago, there seemed to be hope. The proper application of phosphates and other chemicals promised to feed the world." Goldman stopped and refilled Perini's glass.

"What happened?"

Goldman took a deep breath. "Mostly, I think, it was rhetoric intended to insure the continued flow of Federal money for research. Give us enough money, we said, and we can feed the world. It was nonsense, of course, the Third World is doomed. It doesn't make any difference if Ethiopia is run by Marxists or capitalists. What are you going to do about the weather in Sudan, Chad, and Niger? You can't grow food in dry sand no matter how much phosphates you dump on it. And even if you do have rain. Just where the hell are those poor doomed people going to come up with the capital for phosphates, much less tractors?" Goldman shook his head sadly.

"Look at India and Bangladesh, Eddie. They hack and scrape at worn-out soil with bullocks much as their ancestors did six hundred years ago. Nothing has changed, probably very little will. They have more and more and more mouths to feed. I can recite statistics that are simply awful: infant mortality rates, diseases that are the direct result of malnutrition, stunted minds and bodies. It's awful. We pretend politics matter. It's all a sick, bloody lie."

"And probably not getting any better."

"Getting worse. You wouldn't believe what's happening in parts of Africa and Asia. We're trapped now by limited resources. Food is power, Eddie."

"So what happened? With you, I mean."

"This pub is a lovely place. Six years ago I won an appointment to a first-rate laboratory at the University of Edinburgh. I was happy there. The university supported me in every way possible. Then, two years ago, my wife died of cancer. She had a radical mastectomy but it was too late. Cancer ate her up. Lewis and Clark College here in Portland has an excellent overseas study program. I helped their students in Scotland and when an opening came, they offered me a one-year appointment to replace a professor on sabbatical."

"Good school," said Perini.

"I took the appointment. I needed a change of scenery. As you know, Bobby wangled his appointment with the Trail Blazers so he could be with me. The Blazers management are good people. They are willing to share their knowledge of sports medicine. Listen, what if I told you I discovered an enzyme here in Oregon that could feed the world?"

"An enzyme?"

"I discovered it by accident, Eddie. Blind luck."

"I don't understand. What does it do?"

"It breaks down cellulose and produces sugar. That's the simplest way of putting it but it's far more complicated than that."

"I still don't understand."

Bernard Goldman leaned forward, his elbows on the small table. "You could ask all the scientists in the world to try and find it and they would probably come up empty. No logic was involved, Eddie. It was a fluke. I'm the first to admit it."

"I'm listening."

"What do you know about field burning, Eddie?"

Perini looked at a photograph of Mountbatten. "Not much. I know seed is the main crop here in the Willamette valley. Trouble is that when you harvest the seed you're left with straw that's worthless, so the farmers burn it, hundreds of acres. Only the smoke fucks up the valley in the summertime."

Goldman nodded. "Farmers on one side, environmentalists on the other. A terrible fight. Cattle can't even eat the straw, Eddie. They can't digest the cellulose in the fiber. Cellulose is a form of starch. A man I met here, a professor at Oregon State University, got a Federal grant to see if he could discover an enzyme that would break down the cellulose and produce sugar in the process. Instead of burning the straw, you feed it to cattle. Less smoke. Feed for steers. Everybody's happy."

"Ahh," Perini said. "Good idea."

"Well, I thought if that could be done for cattle, why not people? I began looking into what are called saprophytes, Eddie. Saprophytes produce enzymes that cause organic matter to decay: wood, leather, you name it. If we didn't have saprophytes, we'd be a thousand miles deep in garbage, hip-deep in crap that won't rot. Are you with me?"

"I guess."

"I mean does it sound plausible?"

"Keep going."

"The way it works, Eddie, is the two principal saprophytes are fungi and bacteria. The human gut has bacteria in it that produce certain enzymes that enable us to digest food. Some foods we can digest, others we can't. We have our limits. Sheep and goats have better guts than we do."

Perini took a sip of beer. "Hence jokes about goats eating tin cans."

Goldman brightened. "Precisely. The enzyme I've discovered could be produced in tablet form that would be available to everyone. It would vastly extend the range and variety of food people could digest. Theoretically, that is."

"Human goats," Perini said.

Goldman laughed. "Something like that. If you want to be fanciful I suppose you could walk out into your yard one day, grab a few handfuls of leaves, add a little dressing, and you've got yourself a salad."

Perini considered that. "Sounds marvelous, I guess. But I don't even like brussels sprouts. How are you gonna convince me to eat elm leaves?"

"Look, most wild vegetation is bitter or tough. That tablet business is science fiction. We're not talking about producing new kinds of protein by manipulating genetic structure. All that RNA and DNA stuff you read about is high technology—limited to the most sophisticated laboratories. Manna is nature's own, Eddie. It's out there for everyone. Better to use the enzyme to treat selected vegetation before it's marketed. Cellulose is a carbohydrate. It contains glucose and sucrose—sugars. The enzyme produced by my fungus—which is plentiful if you know where to look for it—is capable of making a tough and bitter plant both tender and sweet, palatable in any number of forms. You could, again theoretically, harvest the Amazon basin."

Perini sighed. "I can't believe you're serious, Dr. Goldman. People don't wanna eat veggie bars. They want Whoppers from Burger King, spaghetti served on a checkered tablecloth, a hot dog at the ball park, peanuts, all kinds of stuff."

"Your problem, Eddie, is you're not thinking."

"I don't understand."

"There are one-half billion people suffering from severe malnutrition right now—one-half billion! One person in eight on this planet has his growth or intelligence stunted for lack of protein. It's getting worse. Think."

"You're talking drought in the sub-Sahara. You're talking boat people and refugees from Cambodia and Laos. You're talking Indonesia, the Philippines, large parts of Africa, Sri Lanka, India, Bangladesh, and all those poor doomed children in South America."

Goldman nodded his head. "Exactly. The more hungry you get the more desperate you get. You get terrorists. You get zealots like the Muslims in Iran."

"You're saying veggie bars'll look good to some people."

"By the end of the century there'll be people on this planet who'll eat almost anything to see them through the day. I'm not talking about an odd curiosity here. I'm talking about an instant ability for Third World countries to feed their people, countries that don't have phosphates and tractors."

Perini turned his palms up. "Well, then you've done it. No more hunger."

"And no checks on population, Eddie. There's another side we have to consider. Do you know about army ants?"

"Army ants? You asked the right man. I

know about army ants. They live in South
America."

"They can eat anything. Anything, Eddie,
so they eat everything."

"So?"

"So plants are the primary producers of
oxygen. They use carbon dioxide and return
to the atmosphere the twenty percent oxygen
that we breathe. Strip the planet bare for
food, and what do you have? Maybe our
weak gut is protecting us from ourselves. We
have to think about that. To be honest, I
don't know what the hell to do."

"Bobby said you call it the manna enzyme."

"That's it. The problem is that I don't
know whether the world is ready for it or
should have it. It's the type of thing which
we should be very, very careful about."

"Who else knows about it?"

Bernard Goldman closed his eyes. "Well, I've
discussed it with my colleagues at Lewis and
Clark—always on a 'what if' basis, not as an
accomplished fact. I suppose it's possible for
someone to have concluded there is more to
it than my imagination. What I would like
now is for some time to be by myself to
think it over."

"Have you any ideas about that? I think
you should get out of Portland."

"Yes. I was thinking of doing a little
fishing at Diamond Lake or at Soda Springs
on the North Umpqua."

Eddie Perini signaled to the waitress for
another pitcher of beer. "I've been there.
Does anybody know you were planning to go
there?"

Goldman thought about that. "No, not that I can think of."

"Good." Perini refilled their glasses. "What do you say you go fishing like you planned. I have an acquaintance I can call for a little help."

"Oh?"

"Yes, a man named James Chambliss. He's deputy director of plans for the Central Intelligence Agency. I know him from a few years back. You're sure nobody knows where you'll be going?"

"I'm sure," said Goldman.

He was sure then, but not so sure an hour later when he was driving south on the interstate highway. He had forgotten to tell Perini about Raúl Vivanco, but it probably didn't matter. Vivanco was a serious student, dedicated to science.

DAY THREE

ANTHONY LAURENCE'S MUSHROOM SAUTÉ

1½ pounds fresh
  mushrooms
3 tablespoons butter
2 tablespoons fresh
  lemon juice
1 teaspoon salt

⅛ teaspoon ground
  black pepper
¼ teaspoon ground
  ginger
2 tablespoons fine, dry
  bread crumbs

1. Wash and slice mushrooms, leaving stems attached. Melt butter in a 9-inch skillet. Add mushrooms and lemon juice and cook over medium heat until mushrooms are tender, stirring frequently.

2. Blend in remaining ingredients. Heat 1 minute. Serve hot as a vegetable. (SERVES SIX TO EIGHT)

CHAPTER

8

IN THE END, SMALL THINGS MATTER. WE FORGET that. Anthony Laurence was director of the Central Intelligence Agency, one of the most powerful nonelected positions in the world. He was a Harvard man, holder of a doctoral degree in political science. Still, there are matters of intellect, matters of hormones. Laurence, no less than other men, was largely ruled by hormones.

It was one of life's pleasures to run his fingers over the soft down on the flat of his girlfriend's back. Her name was Andrea and she had a pair of dimples there. The dimples intrigued him. Better to think of them than the defense establishment, which wanted Company help to squash the Strategic Arms Limitations Talks. It was an understatement to say that Laurence was the center of attention. The President, whose political future was mortgaged on his ability to gain Senate ratification of the treaty, was Laurence's cousin. That's how Laurence had been appointed to head the CIA at age forty-three. The press was disinclined to let the public forget that. Did it matter that he had tried academic life, found it boring, and spent ten years in the field as an agent for the Company? No.

Andrea moved her back in a languid, sensuous circle. Her butt would turn him on she knew; it never failed. Laurence moved his hand lower. She pushed back against him. Andrea also dated a running back for the Washington Redskins. Laurence tried to convince himself that he didn't mind the competition with a 240-pound jock. He tried to see himself as the Arthur Miller side of Andrea and the running back as a poor man's Joe DiMaggio. There had to be some kind of status that went with sharing a woman with a halfback who had a squirrel tattooed on his chest. It didn't work.

The truth was he hated the arrangement as much as his colleagues feared it for security reasons. He wished she would simply choose between them. If she chose the halfback, Laurence could purge her from his fantasies and find someone else. He hated being single. He needed a woman.

"That feels good, Tony," she said.

He watched her rump move. This couldn't continue. The phone rang and Andrea's rump paused in the middle of an erotic contraction of buttocks.

Laurence, whose breathing had quickened at the sight, answered the phone. "Yes?"

"They say the 'Skins are too old," said a man. Chambliss.

"They've said that for years," Laurence said.

"Allen did 'em in," said the man. "It'll take years for them to recover." Chambliss was saying they had something big on the line: Castro or the Soviet traffic.

"They got what they deserve." Laurence was saying he understood.

"Give me a number."

"Ten, maybe fifteen," Laurence said. That should be enough time. He hung up and put on his trousers and shirt. "Why don't you take a little nap, Andrea. I'll be back in a half hour or so."

Andrea widened her thighs and spread them so Laurence could see everything. She grinned and turned over on her side. "I'll be here."

Laurence pulled his Volkswagen Rabbit onto the street and turned his lights on and off twice. He drove aimlessly for several blocks, watching a brown Ford Pinto behind him. He then slowed and allowed the Pinto to pass. The Pinto was replaced by a Chevette. After three more blocks the Chevette blinked its headlights once. Only then did Laurence begin looking for a pay phone he hadn't used before. He chose one by a White Tower hamburger outlet and dialed Chambliss at Langley. He watched a group of black kids in tattered sneakers playing stickball in a lot that had been cleared of a building. Broken bricks were scattered across the concrete stickball field.

"Chambliss here."

"Tony. What happened?"

Chambliss gave him a summary of what

the FBI had learned in Portland and of a call he had received from Eddie Perini.

"The reason for the Russian traffic, do you think?"

"I'd make book on it," Chambliss said.

Tony Lawrence rubbed his lower lip with his forefinger. "Do you really believe that story, James? That has to be bullshit."

"You want to chance it?"

A skinny kid with a good eye laced one high against the side of a red brick town house. "What's Dr. Goldman's first name again?"

"Bernard."

"What's he doing in Scotland. That's Jewish. He should be from the Bronx or somewhere."

Chambliss laughed. "That's precisely where he's from, Tony. He earned a Ph.D. from MIT, taught for a while at Penn State, then accepted an appointment at the University of Edinburgh."

"Tell me again what he's doing in Portland?"

Chambliss cleared his throat. "He's on a visiting appointment at a place called Lewis and Clark College, a private liberal arts school."

"Well, we have the parabolic report on Castro and we have the Russian traffic. Who else knows about this?"

"We don't know for sure the Soviets do—" Chambliss said.

"Wait, wait," Laurence interrupted. "Tell me more about this guy Perini."

"One thing at a time, Tony. Perini is a sportswriter."

"A sportswriter named Perini?"

"Yes, Tony."

"Christ! Now go back to the Cuban student. The Cuban student told Castro, judging from the FBI report from New York."

"The Cuban's name is Raúl Vivanco. Vivanco went to Edinburgh at the request of the Cuban government to study under Goldman. He followed Goldman to Portland. The FBI says he's disappeared from Portland. They have no idea where he is."

Laurence made a sucking sound with his teeth. "But we know where he is, dead."

"That's what Fidel says."

"Okay, so this former-intelligence-agent-turned-sportswriter is at a dart tournament shooting with Bobby Goldman, Bernard's son. Bobby's killed with a poisoned dart, but before he dies gets Perini to promise to help keep Bernard out of harm's way."

"That's it."

"Perini encourages Bernard to lose himself in the mountains while he gets help. He phones you, an acquaintance from his days as a spook." Laurence slumped against one side of the phone booth and saw there was a urine stain on the other side.

"Bobby was with the Portland Trail Blazers, learning how to treat knee injuries. Perini said he and Bobby were waiting their turn, one match from money, when Goldman began telling the story about his father and the manna enzyme."

"Then what happened?"

"Perini shot for the bull's-eye to see which team would shoot first. He lost, turned around, and Goldman slumped to the floor with a dart between his ribs. I've got Perini's call on tape."

"Between his ribs?"

"Between his ribs, right at the heart."

"You can kill a man that way—with a fucking dart?"

"You can when it's tipped with curare, Tony."

Laurence could hardly believe it. "So now what? This Italian sportswriter turns John Wayne or Clint Eastwood or somebody. Death-bed promise. 'Nobody fucks over my pard.' That kind of stuff. Is that what you're telling me?"

"As I recall Perini was an odd one. Had a slightly wacko sense of humor. But I think he's on the level with this."

"Okay, where, exactly, is Goldman now?" Laurence chewed on his thumbnail.

"He's either on or near a place called Diamond Lake, which is by Crater Lake, a national park. Perini can take us there if we want."

"He'll stay there?"

"He'll stay there until Perini retrieves him."

"Fuck!"

"What?"

"Nothing," Laurence said. He saw that he needed shoelaces. Ever since he'd agreed to be his cousin's DCI, small matters like sex and shoelaces got ignored. He didn't like it.

"I think we have to do something here, Tony. Castro will take his time. Judging from the parabolic he thinks he's got all the time in the world. But we have to find out about the Soviets."

"The traffic. I know, I know." Laurence remembered a professor at Harvard who had told him you could tell the difference between the Russians and the Americans by watching the lights in the Kremlin and Washington when there was trouble in some far-off pipsqueak of a country. The Russian lights go out at ten o'clock. They have their contingency plans. If it doesn't blow over they'll deal with it in the morning. In the meantime they'll drink a little vodka. The Americans, though, they're up all night long, worrying, driving some people nuts, and scaring the piss out of others. "Okay, James, here's what we do. No, first what we don't do: we don't lose our heads. We have to learn the consequences of this thing and we have to talk to Perini. You tell Perini to shut his mouth and get his ass here as soon as possible. Do you have a house that's clean?"

"I told Perini to keep his mouth shut after he told me his story. I have him in the air at this moment. And certainly I have a clean house."

"I mean really clean."

"I've got one, Tony."

"Good. Now when Perini gets here hustle him on out to your house. Don't let him out of your sight. I'll call Boston and get William McClure down here."

"The economist?"

"The same. He was a professor of mine."

"What about the President?"

"I'll tell the President." That wasn't quite true. Laurence would tell the President only after he had discussed the consequences of the manna enzyme with McClure. The President had an uncomfortable habit of thinking the same way as the last person he talked to. On a matter like this—in order to ensure the President wouldn't be swayed by some fool— Laurence wanted to have all the facts at hand before he talked to his cousin. He would have to be decisive and convincing. The President considered the Gallup poll the final authority on almost everything. This was not, Laurence was certain, a decision that should be made with an eye on public opinion or the upcoming election.

"Anything else, Tony?"

"Nobody needs to know about this except you, me, and Perini. Nobody. I won't even tell McClure why I want him. He'll come. I'll want the best you can do in the way of a BI on Perini before I talk to him."

"What about the Germans, the Brits, the Japanese, and the rest? They'll be listening on the Soviet traffic too."

"Go with the KGB-GRU foul-up business. That's if they ask. Otherwise, we sit on it."

"I'll bet the Soviets are crapping their pants. Talk about ironies. They're gonna have to eat all that bullshit ideology." Chambliss laughed.

"I suppose I'll have to find out what they know."

"Good luck on that."

"When was the last time you had your place teched, James?"

"A couple of weeks ago."

"Tech it again."

"It'll have people wondering, Tony."

"Tech it and send the techs off to some-place fun, but tech it again. I think we're sitting on something a trifle hairy."

"You're the boss, Tony."

"Unfortunately," Laurence said. He wished he was back in his town house with his hand between Andrea's legs. "Well, I better come in. Later, James." Laurence hung up.

He returned to his town house. Andrea was waiting for him, lazy-eyed and warm under the sheets.

Laurence decided, suddenly: it was time. "Me or Hamill, Andrea honey, make up your mind."

Andrea looked startled. "What?"

"You're going to have to choose."

"I can't do that now." She rubbed her eyes with the back of her left hand.

"I have to go to Langley." Laurence leaned over and gave her a kiss. He caught a glimpse of her breasts before he stepped out of the door and regretted his decision. But he knew he was right to have asked her to choose. The Company would be relieved, if nothing else. He took the stairs to the side-walk and his Volkswagen on the dead run.

CHAPTER

9

THERE WAS AN ADOLESCENT SIDE OF ANTHONY Laurence that would always be thrilled by helicopters and airplanes. As a child Laurence made elaborate balsa models of World War II airplanes. When the perfect-looking plastic models came out he lost part of his youth forever. It wasn't the same, somehow, like when the American and National leagues expanded and changed a simple pennant race into an elaborate system of play-offs.

The Company pilot was a new man but he knew part of his job was to make sure Laurence got his kicks. He was game. Laurence was no sooner buckled in than the bird rose with a swiftness that left him lightheaded.

"Oh, shit!" he said and grinned. "Oh, boy!"

"Helluva day, sir," said the pilot.

"Where are we meeting him?" Laurence asked.

"Near Manassas, sir."

"Oh," Laurence said. He was disappointed. It was no more than thirty miles from Langley to Manassas, site of the Civil War battles near a creek called Bull Run.

The pilot knew Laurence was disappointed. "Game for a little fun, sir?"

Laurence smiled. "Why not?" His stomach crowded his throat as the copter dropped toward Virginia tobacco like a giant, wounded bird. Laurence looked momentarily concerned as the tobacco rose, then grinned again as the pilot halted his machine a few feet from the ground with a mind-jarring whack, whack, whack of the blades.

"Someone might be following us, sir. Evasive tactics," the pilot shouted above the noise.

"You asshole!" Laurence laughed.

The pilot aimed his copter square at a grove of poplars. Laurence braced his feet against the floor and felt his heart thump as the trees grew nearer and he could see details of leaf and bark. The pilot stared impassively ahead until it seemed they were part of the trees. He suddenly pulled back on the stick and took the trees so low the top branches brushed the skids.

Laurence held his head with both hands as they dropped down on the far side of the trees and his stomach rose with the descent.

"Never can tell where those Commies are, sir," shouted the pilot.

For Laurence the ride had just begun when the pilot eased the copter above on a cleared spot next to an alfalfa field. "We're here sir." He adjusted his sunglasses as he settled the machine easily onto the ground. "Did you like the ride, sir?"

Laurence grinned. "I'll put in a word for you. What's your name again?"

"Symons, sir, Richard Symons."

"Thanks for the fun, Dick."

Laurence waited for the blades to stop and the dust to settle before he stepped out to meet the elegant James Chambliss, who waited beside a sleek Mercedes diesel.

"Hey, James."

"Have a fun ride, Tony?"

Laurence wiped his forehead with the back of his hand and laughed. "Pilot said we needed evasive tactics, James. Commies all over this part of Virginia."

"There'll be complaints, Tony."

There always were. "Relax, James, my cousin's the President. What are they going to do? Is that thing air conditioned?" It was ninety degrees and the humid Virginia heat already had Laurence's shirt sticking to his back.

"It's not civilized to have an unair-conditioned automobile in Virginia, Tony."

James Chambliss took a leisurely drive down a winding country road. Neither man said anything, and in ten minutes Chambliss turned down a dirt road and parked the Mercedes in front of a restored, eighteenth-century farmhouse.

"This is it, Tony."

"You had it teched again?"

"It's been teched twice now."

Laurence took a deep breath. "Let's get on with it then. They're both here?"

"Both."

"We've done our homework?"

"Files on both McClure and Perini."

"I won't need McClure's. But you should review it in case there's anything not right there."

"Done."

"Give me a few minutes with Perini's file. After that I want to talk to him, then McClure, in that order."

"Got it."

"Then let's get out of this fucking heat, what do you say?"

Once inside the farmhouse, Laurence settled into an easy chair by the fireplace faced with river rock. Chambliss brought him a folder containing the summary of an FBI inquiry into Eddie Perini, most of it lifted hours earlier from files—now on microfilm—of an investigation of Perini when he was in the intelligence service.

"We're the only two people with need, James."

"You want me to listen in from the kitchen? We've got it wired."

"We may need a Mutt and Jeff. But don't tape anything, not on something like this. Notes only."

"If I think you skipped anything I'll rap on the door and ask if you need more beer."

"I don't think we'll have to do a routine on Perini, but you never know."

When they went good guy–bad guy, Laurence, by virtue of his rank, played the good. He could be very good indeed. He could be sympathetic when he wanted, warm, understanding. With men he usually talked about sports or women; it rarely failed. With women he talked about sunrises, love, and the moment of birth.

Chambliss played the heavy, emulating, he said, the awful Gletkin who bullied Rubashov in Arthur Koestler's novel *Darkness at Noon*. He was good at it: elegant, precise, murderous, with cold gray eyes. Chambliss had been an actor as an undergraduate at Princeton. It was, he said, a challenge to make the outrageous and brutal seem perfectly usual to his terrified victim. The Company didn't torture people but people thought it did, and that's all Chambliss required. One of his favorites was to tell a man the CIA was contemplating the crude, but simple surgical procedure of cutting off his cock with a bread knife. He was believed. He liked to tell women how the Kikuyu of East Africa circumcised their women by removing the clitoris. He once told a comely Polish defector how this was easily accomplished with fingernail clippers. That said, he took a set out of his pocket and began cleaning his fingernails.

That talent, gross as it was, was invaluable to Laurence.

Thus understanding what had to be done, Chambliss retired to the kitchen to keep Uncle Bill company while Laurence prepared for his interviews. "Rap on the door there when you're finished," Chambliss said.

Laurence opened the file marked Perini, Edward Michael. He skipped the case numbers, source interviews, and investigators' jargon and got straight to the summary, which had been done in a hurry and was far thinner than usual.

SUBJECT: EDWARD MICHAEL PERINI, age thirty-five, is a divorced Caucasian male. Both NAC's and LAC's are negative. HE was born and raised in Lewiston, Idaho, where HIS father owned a Western Auto store. PERINI received a bachelor's degree in mass communications from the University of Washington. HE enlisted in the United States Army upon graduation and was sent to the U.S. Army Intelligence School, Fort Holabird, Maryland, where he was trained in counterintelligence. PERINI rose to the enlisted rank of SFC, E-6, before HE was awarded a direct commission as a first lieutenant. HE was assigned to the 749th INTC Group in Washington, whose activities include courier duty and surveillance of DIA-positive intelligence operations overseas. PERINI served honorably but asked to be transferred to the inactive reserves after the required two years of service following HIS commission. HE then secured employment with the *San Diego Union* as a reporter. PERINI married a Chinese American woman, Michelle Joyce Lum. NAC's and LAC's are negative on Michelle Lum Perini. Michelle Lum Perini's politics are unknown.

PERINI was divorced by HIS wife after six years of marriage. HE has a son, Benjamin, by Michelle Lum Perini. HE moved to Portland, Oregon, after HIS divorce and secured employment as a sportswriter for the *Portland Oregonian*. PERINI covers the Portland Trail Blazers.

SUBJECT is a sexually active heterosexual male. HIS current girlfriend is Anjanette Grace Armstrong, née Becker, aka Anjie, age twenty-eight. NAC's and LAC's on Armstrong are negative. Her politics are unknown.

SUBJECT is a moderate to occasionally heavy drinker. HE apparently smokes marijuana with friends but avoids drugs beyond that. HIS most frequent companion is a dart thrower, Richard LNU, aka Dick, a computer programmer. Richard LNU'S politics are unknown.

SUBJECT'S interests seem to be sex, darts, and hats in roughly that order. He is known chiefly for his sense of humor. SUBJECT is said to literally giggle in odd moments at what HE considers to be irony, stupidity, cupidity, and buffoonery in the world about HIM.

SUBJECT'S politics are described by acquaintances as too diversified to classify. HE is said to be mostly uninterested in politics, which, according to a colleague at the *Oregonian*, HE feels are "a fucking circus and a joke."

A check of local credit bureaus was negative. PERINI does not gamble.

SUBJECT has traveled in Northern and Western Europe and in Southeast Asia. HE has, to our knowledge, never been in a Communist country.

PERINI held a top-secret restricted clearance from the DIA at the time of his service. HIS DIA-PSI file is now more than ten years old.

Sources all report that PERINI is honest, loyal, and trustworthy and recommended HIM for a position of trust and responsibility with the United States Government.

Eddie Perini had pale-blue eyes and a well-groomed handlebar mustache. He was about six feet tall and slender. He wore a gray, crumpled Irish country hat. He extended his hand thumb up for the handshake. Laurence, who was accustomed to the traditional handshake, was momentarily confused.

"Ahh, Dr. Livingston, I presume," said Perini.

"Won't you have a seat, Mr. Perini."

Perini laughed. "Nobody calls me Mister," he said. "I work for a living, sports."

"Well, then I'll call you Eddie. I think we may be seeing quite a bit of each other in the next week or so."

Perini rolled one end of his mustache between his thumb and forefinger. "Whatever," he said.

"Can you shoot?"

Perini looked surprised, then considered the question. "Well, if I've had a couple of beers and a chance to warm up. If not I'll pick up a lot of ones and fives."

Laurence closed his eyes. "A weapon, Eddie, not darts."

"Oh!" Perini looked innocent. "I haven't

shot a rifle since I was a kid and went deer hunting in the Blue Mountains. They tried to teach me to shoot a .38 at the Bird but I was awful."

"That's something," Laurence said.

"Say, do you think you could ask your pardner in there if he could send us in a couple of beers?"

James Chambliss opened the door and passed a six-pack of Premium National Bohemian beer to Laurence.

"Do you have any questions, Eddie?" Laurence handed him a beer and a glass.

"Do we feed 'em or starve 'em?"

Laurence looked at the ceiling. "I don't know. We'll be finding that out from the good professor in there with Chambliss."

"He's next?"

Laurence nodded his head yes.

"If I'm going to help I want to sit in on the discussion. I gave my word to Bobby Goldman and I'd like to know what I'm getting into."

Laurence considered that. He needed Perini's help. "No word of this discussion in his presence. What we do after we talk to him is none of his business or anybody else's."

"Need to know."

"That's it, highly restricted in this case." They shook hands and Laurence got up to get Dr. William McClure, winner of the Nobel prize in economics. Laurence paused before he opened the door. "I'll be calling him Uncle Bill. All his former students call him Uncle Bill. If I don't call him Uncle Bill, he won't be comfortable."

"Swell by me," Eddie Perini said.

"Thank you. I think you're going to have to come to work for the Company for a while, Eddie. We'll see to it that there'll be no problems with your employer. You'll be well paid."

Perini rolled the end of his mustache again. "Look, I know you're the director of the CIA and all but I've got the Celtics coming to town and the Oregon Open dart tournament coming up. I've already told Chambliss everything Bobby Goldman told me—several times, in fact. He taped each interview."

"We want you to take us to Bernard Goldman."

Perini looked surprised. "I can show you on the map."

Laurence sighed. "We have competition. You're a trained agent. Without you we'd have to expand need. We'd rather not do that."

Perini apparently knew it was no use arguing. "Listen, what do I call you?"

"Tony, from now on."

"Now that we're buddies and all, would it offend you too much if I said I don't think your cousin's much of a President?"

Laurence said nothing, then, "He does his best."

CHAPTER

10

WILLIAM MCCLURE WAS TWO OR THREE INCHES over six feet tall and weighed 220 to 230 pounds. He had broad shoulders, a muscular, healthy gut, a leonine mane of silver hair, not much in the way of a chin, and a space between his two front teeth. He wore a rumpled, pale-gray double-knit suit. His fly was half unzipped, a testament to his disdain for matters of dress. McClure was an intellectual. He lived in a world of ideas. Style and fashion did not interest him. He stepped through the door from the kitchen with a beer in his hand and a grin on his face. He had been brought from Cambridge to Manassas, Virginia, and had no idea why.

"Uncle Bill, good to see you," Laurence said. They shook hands and McClure sat in the chair offered him, an antique as was the rest of the furniture. "Uncle Bill, you once said that if I ever needed your help on something I should give you a call. I need it now."

McClure laughed. "So I did. It must be

very serious, indeed. You both look so solemn." He looked at Perini.

"I'm sorry," said Laurence. "This is—"

Perini shook McClure's hand. "I don't think Tony intended for you to know my name."

"Pleased to meet you, whatever your name is. What have you been doing, Tony?"

Laurence shrugged. "Oh, this and that, here and there. But now I've got one hell of a decision on my hands and I need your help. The country needs your help."

"My help?" McClure looked surprised. "How can I possibly help the CIA? I told you to call if you need me, Tony. But I won't be using my academic position as a cover for spying on people."

"I haven't booked you passage on the Orient Express or anything like that, Uncle Bill." Laurence told McClure about the manna enzyme.

When he had finished, McClure sat stolidly in his seat for a full minute without saying anything. Then he wet his lips with his tongue and looked at both Perini and Laurence. "You don't mean that, Tony. It's a joke. Bullshit. You're teasing old Uncle Bill."

Laurence didn't smile. "That's the straight dope, Uncle Bill."

McClure looked at Perini.

"That's it," said Perini.

"You're talking about something that has the potential of making all wild plantlife edible, digestible by the human stomach. Is that a fair summary?" He looked at Laurence.

"You've got it, Uncle Bill."

McClure looked at Perini again for confirmation.

"That's what we've been told," said Perini.

"Have you any idea of what you're really talking about here?"

"I suppose we have some idea," said Laurence.

"This is a chimera that looks like a pretty woman. People are hungry, I know, but the reasons for that are complex in the extreme. People don't just eat. They have to have a bowel movement now and then. They have to have space, a place to get in out of the rain."

Laurence said nothing. Perini shifted nervously in his chair.

"It would feed people, I suppose. But to what end? You throw a variable like that into the world economic order and you might not like the results."

"We want you to help us decide what to do," Laurence said.

"Me? No."

"No, Uncle Bill?"

McClure drank some beer. "Absolutely not, not with something on this scale. I'm not God, Tony. I'm a professor of economics."

"Would you rather I let my cousin decide?"

"His cousin has advertising executives as advisers," Perini said.

Uncle Bill laughed. "Well, he was elected President of the United States, not me. His decision, not mine."

"This time, my cousin is not relying on the advice of an advertising executive. He wants to know what you think, Uncle Bill. On something like this the country needs the best minds available."

McClure sighed. "I'll do the best I can. Do you people have any more beer around here?"

Laurence got more beer from Chambliss in the kitchen. When he returned McClure began:

"Well, first off we should know what we're dealing with here: food, a scarce resource. To understand the consequences of manna we have to face the question of resource scarcity. Let me begin with a broad outline of two sides to the issue. Then I'll narrow it down and we'll see how your enzyme fits. Actually there are two controversies: limits to growth and what is called lifeboat ethics. I'll take limits to growth first.

"In 1972, a group of professors at MIT issued a report in which they argued that at the present population growth and levels of consumption this planet will be exhausted of all resources by the end of the twenty-first century. The decline of the city—in living standards as well as population—is an indication of this, they say. It took seventy years for the population to double between the 1880s and the 1950s. But at the present rate it will double again in thirty-three years."

McClure looked at Laurence and Perini. "Look at it this way. Even if we had zero population growth—a steady state in terms of population—pollution alone would be strong enough to destroy the planet. Pollution alone! There is an inelastic demand for resources. Take oil, Tony. The demand can't be adjusted to meet dwindling supplies. People just don't want to give up automobiles, for example; they represent freedom. Do you understand so far? I'm giving you a bare-bones outline."

Laurence and Perini both nodded yes.

"These people are ecologists. They're concerned with environmental morality. Their underlying assumption is that environmental problems go hand in hand with industrialization and the sophisticated application of technology. There is an inherent goodness, they argue, in reducing consumption levels. But it's not easy to convince people of this need for backing off. You should be familiar with environmental arguments presented in one manner or another by the mass media."

"We are," said Laurence. He knew where McClure was going and wasn't sure he liked it. Academics lived in a never-never land of the abstract, of theory and statistical projections. Laurence lived with greed, passion, and human desire.

Uncle Bill smiled. "The other side is the pro-growth side. These people saw to it that your cousin was elected President. They say growth is absolutely necessary for economic development and social mobility. Without growth, influence falls throughout the world. The Third Worlders are pro-growth also. They want a piece of the good life. They know it's there. They can see it in American movies. They don't call themselves underdeveloped countries anymore. They're developing countries. And that's more than a matter of semantics.

"The pro-growth people say the international price system is the best way to govern consumption. They believe that as resources become more scarce, consumption will go down."

"As the price of coffee goes up people will drink something else," Perini said.

"Exactly," said McClure. "You understand now that both these camps ignore any change in attitudes, values, or morals. The debate is over what is going to happen in the future. The advocates of limits to growth would not want the manna enzyme. It would encourage population growth. There would be no check on population. People consume all sorts of resources besides food. And again, what about the pollution?"

Laurence cleared his throat. "This is all very well and good, Uncle Bill, but what about the kids? Have you ever seen a starving child?"

McClure sighed. "You forget I spent two years on an academic appointment at Hyderabad. I didn't say this would be easy. But, ultimately, I think our only hope for survival depends on technology—that means Japan, North America, Western Europe, the Warsaw Pact countries, and the Soviet Union. I'm sure if you ran the data through a computer you'd find the manna enzyme would destroy their economies. We trade wheat and soybeans for bauxite and copper.

"It would deal a terrible blow to the multinationals. They would want it only if they could control it and profit from it. From their perspective, unlimited access to the benefits of the enzyme would be a disaster."

"And the Third World?" Laurence asked.

"Most of the Third World doesn't have enough food. It's labor intensive, women in Taipei weaving baskets, Filipino cottage industry. Third World countries either don't have the land, the machines, the know-how, or the weather. They either trade for food or they don't eat. The Third World would do anything for the enzyme, Tony."

"Keep going," Laurence said.

"That's one debate. The basic issue is centered on growth. The other is about lifeboat ethics. It has to do with the distribution of resources, what we're doing right now with food and all other common pool resources.

"The lifeboat-ethics people feel what they call 'the tragedy of the commons' occurs during resource scarcity."

"Too many sheep in the pasture," Perini said.

Uncle Bill coughed. "Exactly. The lifeboat-ethics people say we should conserve our resources now and save some for people not yet born. They say foreign aid for the exportation of Western technology to underdeveloped nations is feeding a cancer. Foreign aid won't solve their population problems. Tony?"

"Boy, that's dandy."

McClure shrugged. "It's a hard world. About fifteen years ago the Club of Rome said we're just going to have to write off places like Bangladesh. Save what we can. The manna enzyme would make population problems even worse than they are now. The lifeboat people argue that you have no exports, no imports, no anything. You take care of your own and that's it. They argue that you should simply cut off the underdeveloped countries to provide them with an incentive for frugality and building toward a steady state. They believe it has to be done through coercion, not education."

"Shit," said Laurence. "Those people need to get off campus and take a look around."

"I think I need another beer," Perini said.

"You wanted my help," McClure went on. "The other side, the Christians and Marxists, say there's always room to squeeze more people on the lifeboat. This is supported by the Third World bloc in the United Nations which says we should redistribute the wealth. It's a moral argument, Tony, hardly supported by empirical data. The lifeboat people say we have to put up with starving people. There is no other way. Simply put, there is a class of morally repugnant decisions that would force the sacrifice of human life because of the scarcity of resources." Uncle Bill stopped as though he were finished for the moment, then added: "This would be a tough one for the Soviets. The requirements of ideology don't match economic reality here."

Laurence poured McClure another beer. "Tell me, Uncle Bill, what would happen if the question of the manna enzyme were put to public debate?"

McClure laughed. "Well, for one thing it would be a goddamned media circus. On one hand, there would be intense moral pressure to share the discovery and feed the world. I imagine you'd have slogans, bumper stickers, simpleminded aphorisms, working

their way to protesting, riots and all that.
And on the other hand, you would also have
heavy political and economic pressure on
Congress by all manner of lobbies in Washington. Food is something we have that other
people don't."

"Wheat exports," Perini said.

"That's one case, certainly," McClure replied. "You have to understand that the
larger and more developed a country be-
comes the more dependent it is on the
resources of lesser-developed countries. Oil is
the best example. What would happen if our
enormous investment and advantage in food
production and distribution were to become
worthless on the market? You have to ask
yourself that.

"There are three concerns you have to
think about: political security, environmental protection, and economic efficiency. The
manna enzyme would cripple the developed
world in all three areas."

"What about China?"

"China is doing its best to develop its
economy but China also has to feed eight
million people." McClure leaned forward in
his chair. "You have to keep in mind, Tony,
that the manna enzyme would feed people
and would increase population, but little
else. It doesn't deal with coal, iron, copper,
aluminum, you name it. I have no idea what
the new trade arrangements would be like."

Laurence massaged his forehead. "So what
would you do, Uncle Bill?"

"That's a terrible question, Tony. People
are starving out there."

Eddie Perini cleared his throat.

Laurence looked at him. "You want to say something?"

"I thought one reason poor people have so many children is for labor to help the family survive. If more food means higher birthrates, there'd be more children in developed countries. There aren't. In fact, we have low birthrates. I don't understand."

"You're right, in a sense. If you have machines to work a field you don't need children to grub with sticks. But with development—and a full belly—comes leisure, education, a taste for the good life. People achieve satisfaction and status in ways other than proving they can have children. If you simply have a surfeit of food without addressing the other variables, you're courting disaster. Malnutrition is a chief cause of high infant-mortality rates."

"High infant-mortality rates are good?" Laurence asked.

"I didn't say that exactly."

Perini shifted in his chair. "Well, all I had was an introductory course in economics years ago." It was an awful discussion.

"Bottom line, Uncle Bill."

"I'd make sure no one ever used the enzymes," McClure said.

"You're sure?"

"No, I have to sleep nights too. You asked what the risks and benefits are. To be frank, I'm not sure we know them."

Laurence sighed. "The dismal science. Thank you, Uncle Bill."

"The next time you have a question like

that, do me a favor—please ask someone else."

"Uncle Bill, I'd like you to swear on your honor as a civilized and decent man that you'll keep this conversation secret. I want you to forget the enzyme, forget me, and forget my mustachioed friend here with no name."

"I can't do that," McClure said. "I have a conscience."

"I know."

"I'll do my best."

Laurence shook his head. "Not good enough, Uncle Bill. You have to swear never to tell another living soul."

"Done, then."

The three men shook hands and McClure returned to Chambliss in the kitchen. McClure looked back once. "This is an awful business. You can have it, Tony. I'll take Harvard and the comfort of theory." He closed the door.

Perini stood up to take a closer look at the facing on the fireplace. "Well, do we feed them or starve them, Tony?"

Anthony Laurence no longer wanted to be DCI. "We starve them. There's nothing else we can do. If we had time to study it longer we might think differently. If McClure's right, we're courting disaster."

"I talked to Goldman yesterday in a tavern called the Horse Brass Pub. We sat under English football pennants. He's a caring man, Tony. He's dedicated his life and good mind to the relief of human suffering."

"Shit, I don't know what to tell you,

Eddie. McClure was talking about human suffering in the abstract. I can't do that. I also know I have responsibilities. I knew it when I took this job."

"So how do we starve them?"

"We terminate Bernard Goldman. We stop history before it starts. We don't have the luxury of time or hindsight."

"No," Perini said.

"There's no other way."

"Who killed Bobby Goldman?"

"Fidel Castro had him killed. Did Bernard Goldman ever mention anybody named Raúl Vivanco?"

Perini looked surprised. "Castro had him killed?"

"Castro's in New York to make long speeches at the UN. The FBI caught him at breakfast with a parabolic. The idea of killing Bobby Goldman was to keep us capitalists from learning about the enzyme. The Cubans do not know he talked to you before he died."

"How did Fidel Castro know about the enzyme?"

"Raúl Vivanco."

Perini took a deep breath. "Goldman never mentioned anybody named Vivanco."

"Vivanco was a student who followed Goldman to Portland from Scotland. He killed Bobby. He told Castro where Goldman is fishing."

"At Diamond Lake?"

"Castro's security chief says he knows exactly where Goldman is."

"And what if the Cubans get to him before we do?"

Laurence looked Perini straight in the eye. "They'll take him back to Cuba, learn everything there is about the manna enzyme, and kill him."

"He's dead either way."

"Either way, Eddie. Right now the Cubans think they're the only ones who know about the enzyme. They're willing to let him play with bucktails and royal coachmen for the time being."

"But now everybody at Langley knows about the enzyme."

Laurence shook his head from side to side. "That's why we need your help. We used to do our own domestic counterintelligence. It was against the law but we did it anyway. Ever since the Senate investigations in 1975, we've had to play it straight, let the bureau do all the New York and Washington stuff. Mostly they don't know what they're doing—in our opinion at least. Their reports do come straight to me, however."

"What did you do this time?"

Laurence grinned. "I told them Castro was talking about a Cuban operation we've been following for some time. I didn't have to say anything more. Need."

"And when their courier left?"

Laurence held both palms up. "When he left, Mr. Perini, I shredded the summaries."

"Oh," Perini said. He wasn't sure he liked the idea of using shredders on something like this.

"Would you please send Mr. Chambliss in

here for a moment. I'd like to talk to him. Alone, if you don't mind."

Perini laughed. "I don't imagine it would do me any good if I did mind."

Laurence didn't smile.

A few minutes later Chambliss was in the chair lately occupied by Uncle Bill McClure. "Well?" he asked.

"We have some problems, don't we, James?"

"Yes, I guess you could say that." Chambliss had a good mind. He had listened to the conversations with McClure and Perini. He didn't have to rehash the possibilities.

"Uncle Bill thinks the economy of the Western world is at stake here." He paused. "Well, that's not quite it actually. Better to say what we have is a north-south thing. Temperate world haves—tropical belt have-nots."

"That's how I heard it."

"Russians with the haves?"

The Russians have developed a taste for blue jeans and jazz records. They won't want to give that up."

"But not necessarily."

"No, not necessarily."

"Real problems," Laurence said.

"And your cousin?"

"We work around him—for his own good."

Chambliss raised his eyebrows. "You're talking about the President of the United States, even if he is your cousin."

"With me in charge at Langley he has to bend over backward to give the Senate everything it wants with regard to the Company."

"And they want everything," said Chambliss.

"Everything. This is something they just goddammit cannot have, James. The democratic process just isn't set up to handle something like this. That may sound authoritarian as hell but it's a fact."

"On our own then, we terminate."

"We terminate. The problem is how, without expanding need. We have to play it tight."

"Do it ourselves, Tony?"

"Yes."

"Who?"

"Me. Our friend Perini in there."

"I'm not sure that's smart," Chambliss said.

"If something went wrong, it would destroy the agency."

"We've had Watergate, Chile, Angola. This would be too much, Tony. On top of that, what if Castro beats you? We need a backup, something that guarantees Goldman gets taken out even if Castro wins the first round."

Laurence began chewing on his thumbnail without taking his eyes off Chambliss. "You're right there, of course. In the best of all worlds, James, what do you think the Company could use most right now? Set aside the matter of the enzyme for the moment."

Chambliss smiled. "Well, first off we need for your cousin to be reelected next year so we don't lose our damned jobs."

Laurence laughed. "Yeah, there's that."

"Second, we need to run this agency without a lot of ignorant bastards from the provinces playing to the press and trying to tell us what to do. We need some way of getting those assholes on the Hill off our butts. Your cousin isn't any help. As things stand now we can hardly do the minimum of intelligence gathering on the Soviets, the Chinese, and all their clients. It isn't good for the country."

Laurence looked at his thumb again, then back at Chambliss. "I agree."

CHAPTER

11

ON THE WAY BACK TO LANGLEY EDDIE PERINI
got Chambliss and Uncle Bill McClure engaged in a conversation about the National
Basketball Association. Laurence's mind, however, was on Valery Karpov and Charlie
Davis' reference to Hoyt Wilhelm's knuckler
on the afternoon of the Soviet traffic. Laurence's father, a Wall Street lawyer who had
served under Henry L. Stimson and Dean
Acheson, had frequently driven the young
Tony down from their home in Connecticut
to watch the Yankees. His father had said
everybody except the Yankees were bush. The
Yankees had class, they were elegant.

Tony's father told him he could learn a lot
from baseball. It wasn't a bullshit game like
football, fit for Poles and Big Ten universi-
ties. In the big leagues you had to take your
turn at the plate. You couldn't coast in a
group, you couldn't fake it. You took your
turn and if you couldn't hit, if you choked in
the clutch, you got sent to Fort Smith or
Walla Walla. You had to hit to the opposite
field. You had to get wood on the ball on a

hit-and-run. Above all, his father told him, you had to know your pitchers. What did they like on the first pitch? A fastball? A curve? And what if they got behind, then what?

And the pitchers had to have nerve and concentration. You had to know your batters. Hang a curve on Mickey Mantle and it's gone. If you were to model your life on a baseball player, his father said, then pick Whitey Ford. Ford didn't have Bob Feller's fastball or Ed Lopat's junk, but he had control. He had guile, craft. He hit the corners. He knew his batters. Learn from Whitey Ford, Laurence's father advised.

Laurence knew from experience that it was stupid not to review the book before you went one-on-one with Valery Karpov. Laurence also knew that in the end ordinary people wrote the dossiers on Karpov and others, people who make mistakes. Laurence did not, like Whitey Ford, have the luxury of making his own judgments. He had to trust in the judgments of his subordinates. There was nothing else he could do. And he had to pray there was a mole present, heavy-bodied, harmless-looking, smiling the smile animals have, animals that are rabid and piss in your garden. It was then, with Laurence thinking of moles, that Chambliss' Mercedes arrived at Langley.

Twenty minutes later Frieda returned from records with the dossier on Valery Ivanovich Karpov, director of the KGB. And Laurence, in keeping with the lessons of Whitey Ford, sat down to read the book on Karpov. Always know your man, never leave anything to chance. That was Whitey's law. That was how you won ball games. Laurence agreed. He had made it his law as well. The only problem was Whitey's book was fairly simple. What would a guy do with a curve? Would it serve any purpose to brush him back or would he turn mean and knock the shit out of the next pitch?

Laurence was convinced that a dossier on someone like Karpov could be fairly straight-forward, maybe not so elementary as Whitey's book, but still relatively simple. The problem at Langley was that no report, nothing, was ever allowed to be straightforward and simple. Never. If it wasn't phrased in impenetrable jargon and clouded by pretentious nonsense from the social sciences, then it was too elementary for the impressive business of intelligence gathering. There is, in the end, no final answers to be had about the human animal. There is love, hate, passion, greed, and the rest of it. Laurence wanted to know what Karpov had done with his life. That was the heart of a useful dossier.

Valery Karpov's grandfather, Georgi, had been a successful marine architect in the Russian shipbuilding industry in Odessa on the Black Sea. He was related by marriage to a second cousin of the Czar. His brother, Anatoly, a colonel and aide to General Aleksandr Samsonov, was killed after German troops surrounded Samsonov's Second Army on August 29, 1917, at Tannenberg, Poland. Ninety-two thousand Russian soldiers were captured. The debacle might have been avoided had Samsonov not resorted to issuing uncoded orders over open telephone lines. The German officers listened, shook their heads in disbelief, and moved in like sleek Dobermans for the kill.

It was, an agency shrink had noted, "One of those seminal events in the unfolding of the evolving human psyche that very likely accounts for Karpov's passion for security."

What! thought Laurence. Karpov had been trained for the Soviet secret service since he was a teenager. Laurence made a mental note of the shrink's name, David Adams.

Karpov's father, Ivan, a corporal in his uncle's unit, spent the remainder of the war in a German prison camp and on his release, went home a passionate Marxist. He had an aptitude for both mathematics and administration. Trained as an engineer, he participated in the design and construction of six hydroelectric projects built before World War II: the Dnieper dam at Zaporozhye, the power stations at Uglich and Shcherbakov on the Volga, the Tuloma and Niva plants on the Kola Peninsula below Murmansk, and the Svir works at Podporozhyre.

It was here that another Company shrink, Louis Montelheit, tried desperately to justify his high salary and underemployment. Montelheit noted that "Karpov very possibly inherited a tendency toward dominance by the left lobe, suggesting a precise, mathematical imagination, extending games' situations to their logical conclusion. This could well explain his passion for chess."

"Oh, come on!" Laurence said aloud. The Russians have a national obsession with chess. Laurence had little patience for all the "coulds," "mights," and "ifs." He felt like sailing the dossier across the room.

In 1931, Ivan Karpov married Anna Chara, the only daughter of Aleksandr Chara, a Bolshevik commissar in the industrial city of Magnitogorsk. Aleksandr's ability to rise in the Bolshevik ranks during the Stalinist regime was largely due to his caution, the dossier said (without real evidence to support that conclusion, Laurence noted).

"It would be unwise not to regard Aleksandr Chara as a role model for Karpov. Aleksandr was Valery's sponsor in the KGB and Karpov throughout his career has exhibited a conservative tendency remarkably similar to his successful uncle's." Shit! Laurence checked the notation. Montelheit again.

After the purges of 1938, Chara was moved to Moscow, where his managerial skills were used to design logistics systems for the expected clash with Hitler on the West. He took Ivan and Anna with him and, as he rose in influence in the Kremlin, Ivan was put to work designing Russian armaments. In December 1935, Anna delivered her firstborn, Valery. Two years later, she gave birth to a daughter, Valenta, who died of pneumonia six weeks later.

"This tragic loss of a female sibling could very well account for Karpov's inability to sustain permanent attachments with women," Montelheit had noted. How often was losing a sister not tragic? Laurence wondered. And maybe Karpov didn't get along with women because he had bad breath. Laurence wished he had the authority to fire people arbitrarily. Montelheit would go.

The family moved to Leningrad early in the war. There, Ivan was assigned as an aide to Lieutenant General B. V. Bychevsky, who designed the ill-fated Luga Line and the fortifications surrounding the city destined for a nine-hundred-day siege by German artillery. "It was there the precocious Valery learned to survive," Adams noted. "As Erik Eriksen has suggested in his biographies of Gandhi and Martin Luther, the influence of such a traumatic youth should never be underestimated in establishing the parameters of the adult imagination."

Laurence gripped the edge of his desk. He'd have Adams' ass for cluttering dossiers with this nonsense. Parameters of the adult imagination! What was that?

Karpov's mother died of dysentery in January 1942; his father began coughing blood six weeks later and died in early April. There was, curiously, no shrink's footnote and Laurence almost laughed out loud.

After the siege was lifted, young Valery was returned to his Uncle Aleksandr in Moscow. By now his uncle had become a senior official in the Stalinist regime and saw to it that Valery got the best schooling available. Valery had an aptitude for languages, learning English, German, Spanish, French, and Mandarin Chinese. He studied under the master spy Rudolf Abel after Abel was swapped for the captured U-2 pilot Francis

Gary Powers and participated in the debriefing of the British mole Kim Philby.

Karpov's experience overseas was limited. He did spend two years in Delhi in the 1960s, apparently to study the ramifications of the Indo-Chinese border conflict. Karpov became a student in the Yoga Health Training Center, sponsored by the Indian government at Chandigarh, 200 miles north of Delhi. Chandigarh is less than 150 miles from the headwaters of the Sutlej River and the Shipki Pass into Chinese-occupied Tibet. Karpov's guru at Chandigarh was Swami Tarmananda, who later became wealthy demonstrating yoga exercises on American college campuses.

Yoga! Laurence wondered why Karpov, brilliant, calculating, analytical, should get involved in yoga. Of Karpov's interest in yoga, the shrinks made no mention. There were no "possiblies," no "could bes."

Laurence groaned. Whitey Ford would have been disgusted. In any event there it was: Valery Karpov. It was time to find out about the Soviet traffic.

CHAPTER

12

WILLIAM PUMPHRIES, CHIEF EXECUTIVE OFFI-
cer of Arnaud Mobelier, finally took James
Chambliss' telephone call after Chambliss
had worked his way through seven Arnaud
secretaries of various levels, each of whom
insisted Pumphries was either in conference
or would call back. Pumphries was a busy
man and the secretaries had their instructions. Chambliss, however, was not put off.
He had worked in bureaucracies long enough
to know there was a conspiracy of secretaries
at work whose sole purpose was to spare
employers unpleasant telephone calls. Receive
a call without knowing in advance what the
caller had in mind, and you ran the risk of
being honest—care, guile, and cunning were
necessary for advancement. Guilt and cunning come naturally to some men, like breathing, blinking, or having a bowel movement.
Others have to work at it. The latter requires
secretaries who know how to put people off.

James Chambliss would have none of it.
No secretary in Chicago would put him off.

"My name is George Chandler, executive

assistant to Thomas Walker, chairman of the board of United Fruit. This is very important business. If I don't speak to Mr. Pumphries now, at this time, I'll see to it that you're fired."

Chambliss repeated that in measured tones to each of three layers of secretaries. Each time the enraged secretary at the other end checked a roster of executives on an Arnaud list of clients, and gave in—in a mellow if resentful voice.

It took Chambliss forty minutes to reach Pumphries, far too long for a man accustomed to having his orders obeyed instantly.

"Well, hello, George," said Pumphries. He had never talked to Chandler in his life but Chandler's name was on a list in front of him.

"I am not George Chandler. You and I need to talk. This is very, very important and private business. The future of your business depends on it."

"I . . ." Pumphries began. He hesitated. "Who is this?" His face colored.

"To find out all you have to do is go downstairs to the pay phone in the lobby. There's a security guard right there, so you don't have to worry about anything. You'll find a note taped to the bottom of the telephone. The note contains my identity and a suggestion on how it may be confirmed."

"Well, I . . ." began Pumphries. The man hung up.

Pumphries, a round, pink man, sat staring at the telephone. A half minute later he took a walk to the elevator and rode it downstairs. The note was there as he had been told.

"My name is James Chambliss," the note began. "I am the deputy director of the Central Intelligence Agency. I am standing to your rear by the building directory. Call the agency at Langley. Ask for Vera in ident. When Vera answers, give her the number Alpha Foxtrot Bravo Niner One Zero, say it like that. She'll tell you what I look like. She does that and nothing more. She knows nothing else. Make one call only. If you do not phone the agency, I will know it immediately. I have an instrument with me that picks up the sound of the telephone as you punch the buttons. If you punch any other number than the one listed in this note, I will be gone. When you're finished tape the note back where you found it and take a walk toward the lake. Do not use your telephone credit card. If you need change, I have it." The note ended with a telephone number preceded by a Virginia area code.

Pumphries turned and saw a tall, elegant man dressed in a pin-striped blue suit. His hair was graying. He had a small, neat mustache. He looked like Anthony Eden. Pumphries wanted a closer look. He walked up to the man and said simply, "I need change."

The man in the pin-striped suit smiled and gave him two rolls of quarters. "Remember, one call only," he said.

"I understand," Pumphries said. It was like being in a movie. Pumphries returned to the phone booth, punched the number from the note, fed coins into the phone on instruction of an operator, and seconds later was connected with the Langley switchboard. "I'd like to speak to Vera in ident."

"Sure," said the Langley operator.

"Hello," Vera said.

"Could you please identify a man named James Chambliss?"

"Sir?" asked Vera.

Pumphries was momentarily confused. He looked at his note. "I'm sorry, that should be Alpha Foxtrot Bravo Niner One Zero."

Vera laughed. "Well, I always thought he looked like Anthony Eden. Tall, British-looking, neatly trimmed mustache."

"That'll do, thank you," said Pumphries.

He did as the note said: he took a walk toward Lake Michigan.

Four blocks later a Toyota sedan pulled up beside him and Chambliss said, "Get in please, Mr. Pumphries."

Pumphries got in. "What do you want?"

"Wait, please," Chambliss said. He glanced in the rearview mirror. He drove for several blocks, watching his rearview mirror, saying nothing. At last, at a red light, he said, "James Chambliss." He offered his hand to Pumphries, who took it and swallowed. He was frightened.

Chambliss pulled into a parking lot by a Texaco station.

"What could the CIA possibly want with me?" Pumphries asked. He blinked nervously, once, twice. "I thought I read in the papers where you people were ordered to knock off the drug experiments."

Chambliss looked at him blandly. "I'm deadly serious, Mr. Pumphries. It would serve you well to listen carefully to what I have to say."

"Yes, certainly you're serious, Mr. Chambliss. I'm a busy man. I don't have time for games, even with the *CIA*."

"Mr. Pumphries, your clients would want you to hear me out."

"Well then tell me, won't you?"

Chambliss looked outside. Paper cups and empty paper bags were blown by the wind. "Certainly, I'll tell you, Mr. Pumphries. For a price."

Pumphries laughed nervously. "For a price? Am I hearing you correctly? Are you trying to blackmail Arnaud Mobelier?"

Chambliss made a clucking sound with his tongue. "Not Arnaud, Mr. Pumphries. I'm blackmailing the people who grow and sell food." He scratched his wrist. "Actually 'blackmail' is the wrong word. I'm simply selling something. I'm after a substantial sum of money—millions, in fact. You know people who have it."

"You're talking multinationals here. Powerful people."

"I am, indeed."

"Just how much money are you talking about, Mr. Chambliss?"

"I'm talking twenty million dollars, nothing for the rice people or the wheat people, nothing."

"Twenty million dollars? That's preposterous!" Pumphries wanted to laugh but couldn't.

"Not for what I have to deliver and for

what your clients stand to lose. They'll lose their ass. How old were you in 1929?"

Pumphries didn't answer. Chambliss watched an old woman struggle to put a bag of groceries into the backseat of a Honda. "It's inconceivable that any one discovery could have such a catastrophic effect on the world food market. You're making no sense at all. My clients may be wealthy and a few are noted for their philanthropic efforts—donating money to college endowments and so on—but none of them are fools. You'll have to give them one hell of a reason."

"What I propose to do is give you the gist of the discovery. You contact your clients. If they each contributed to a kitty, twenty million would be pin money to each of them individually."

Pumphries thought that over. "Keep talking, Mr. Chambliss."

James Chambliss told Pumphries about Goldman's fungus and the potential of the enzyme the fungus produced. "For twenty million bucks I'll tell you who made the discovery and where he can be found. There are Latin Americans after him now. By contacting the proper mercenaries, you can beat them to him. If you like I can send you a list of mercenaries we have worked with, men who are skilled, experienced, discreet, and absolutely loyal to the highest bidder." He laughed.

"You're bullshitting me!"

"No, no, Mr. Pumphries. This is absolutely straight."

"I'll have to discuss this with the proper corporate executives."

"Phone them. The Latins may be moving tomorrow or the next day. They think the discovery is theirs alone but you never know what will happen in this business."

"Where are the mercenaries?"

Chambliss withdrew a plain white envelope from his jacket pocket. "Their names are deJonette, Cardinal, and Scanlan. This envelope contains summaries of their dossiers, all that you'll need. It also contains their cable addresses and the proper way to word the cables. Don't deviate from the phrasing. There are matters of protocol involved."

"I don't believe this."

"You want to take a chance?"

Pumphries hesitated and took the envelope. He skimmed over the summaries and read a sample cable. "This sounds like a dinner invitation!"

"It's not like recommending a buy order for the Gambian peanut crop, if that's what you mean."

"A feast?"

"Easy job, little danger, high pay."

"The colonel will sit at the head of the table."

"Colonel Scanlan will be in charge. He's not a colonel though. He just calls himself that."

"They'll understand this?"

"Certainly," said Chambliss.

"It says we'll give them their choice of the very best cutlery available."

"What that means, Mr. Pumphries, is that

we'll provide them with whatever weapons or other equipment they may require. That's important to them. You wouldn't invite three gentlemen to dinner, then give them plastic spoons or expect them to eat with their hands, would you? That kind of thing is okay for a Hindu who wipes his ass with his fingers then eats out of a common bowl. We're dealing with class here, Mr. Pumphries. You hire these gentlemen and you're going first cabin. The matter of cutlery is crucial. You should expect to pay them fifty thousand dollars each."

Pumphries said nothing, then cleared his throat. "I'm not sure that I know what to say. Where do you get this stuff, this 'cutlery,' as you put it?"

Chambliss examined the back of his hand as though looking for a flaw in his manicure. "Oh, there are places I can think of. One warehouse, for example, is located just down the road from the Pentagon. It's a carry-out of sorts, Mr. Pumphries, not unlike Kentucky Fried Chicken."

"Oh."

Chambliss gave him the number of a motel in College Park, Maryland, a suburb of the District of Columbia. "Call at eight P.M., tomorrow. Ask for extension 210. I won't answer the first call. Try again twenty minutes later. I won't answer that time either. I'll answer the third call, but only after the phone rings six times. If I answer before then, hang up immediately. Don't call back. I'll get in touch."

"Yes," said Pumphries. He didn't know what else to say.

"Repeat what I just told you."

"What?"

"Tell me your instructions for calling me."

Pumphries did as he was told with one omission.

"I said to call again twenty minutes later. That's not eighteen minutes later or twenty-two minutes later. That's twenty minutes later."

"Well," said Pumphries. He'd been reprimanded. He felt self-conscious.

"Can you get a cab back to your office?" It was as though Chambliss was addressing a patient sick with the flu.

"Certainly," Pumphries looked uncertain.

"We'll be in touch then."

William Pumphries, not knowing what else to do, stepped out onto the parking lot. For the first time in his life he felt the wind from the lake. He knew the wind, of course, and how to walk with his head at an angle so his hat wouldn't blow away. But it was different this time. He felt fat and slow.

He wondered what was happening to him.

There was a lot of work to do. He had to hurry back and phone his clients. They were all over: right there in Chicago, in Minneapolis, in Kansas City, in Los Angeles and New York, in London and on the Continent. The people in Zurich certainly had to be consulted.

CHAPTER

13

BY WAY OF FINAL PREPARATION BEFORE CALLING Karpov, Laurence got himself another cup of coffee and retrieved a yard-long board from his office closet. He leaned the board against the wall, sat back against it, and closed his eyes, his legs spread wide on the beige carpet. At a Georgetown cocktail party, Laurence had once gotten into a bullshit session about concentration and the capacities of the human mind with the Grand Prix racing driver Jim Donahue and the former San Francisco 49ers quarterback John Brodie. Donahue said all great drivers—from Jackie Stewart to Jody Scheckter—had abilities of concentration that were awesome. He said he himself had the ability—when his mind was working at its very best—to recognize individual faces in a crowd when he was driving at speeds pushing 200 miles an hour. And once, he said, he smelled cut grass as he geared down for a corner after a 160-miles-per-hour straightaway.

Why, his mind asked, would he smell cut grass?

Donahue swung wide.

He missed a racer that had swung into the infield, skidded, and come to rest on the track.

Brodie said that at his best, when he was in top form, he was able to concentrate on two wide receivers and two halfbacks running pass patterns simultaneously. He said his mind was able to stand outside itself: the runners ran in slow motion; he was able to ignore the frenzied violence of his blockers battling Roosevelt Greer, "Big Daddy" Lipscomb, Sam Huff, or Ray Nitsche. And when he released the ball he was able to concentrate on the laces turning, turning, as the ball found its mark. It was, he said, a beautiful and exhilarating experience.

Laurence recalled lines from T.S. Eliot's "The Love Song of J. Alfred Prufrock": "In a minute there is time/For decisions and revisions which a minute will reverse." Was it the same, he wondered, for Prufrock considering middle age and himself faced with the uncertainties of the manna enzyme and responsible for his countrymen? He would have to sound casual with Karpov, confident. He would have not minutes but fractions of seconds to read nuances, Russian deceit, and games playing. The conversation would sound natural enough. There would be banter, a joke here and there, a familiarity of adversaries who had talked before and who knew one another at least a little. Laurence, of course, did not trust Karpov, nor did the latter trust him. Trust was a luxury denied them.

Laurence was not John Brodie with third and short. He was not Whitey Ford standing two and zip. He was director of the Central Intelligence Agency, with the economies of the developed world just possibly riding on his ability to handle a sleek Russian he considered a devious, outrageous fucking liar.

When this was finished, he told himself, he would eat a peach. He would return to Andrea and win her from her halfback lover. He would walk barefoot on the beach.

But just now he had things to do. He punched up Moscow Center on the scrambler. Time to put it on the line.

"Yes, Mr. Laurence?" answered an amiable Russian with a British accent. The same Russian had answered in the past. By now he recognized Laurence's voice.

"I would like to speak to Comrade Karpov, please."

The Russian allowed himself a small laugh. "Sir?"

"I know he's probably tired from his trip to Berlin but this is important."

"One moment, Mr. Laurence."

There was a click. Laurence heard a man's voice say something in Russian. A door closed. Then Karpov was on the line. "Hello, Tony," he said in perfect English.

"You people sure have been talky lately, Valery."

Karpov laughed. "Well, Tony, the deal is the GRU had a thing going in Berlin with the East Germans and they crossed with one of our nets. Stupid bastards."

"Uh huh. We know all about that, a British

double we're told. What's happened out there?"

"We pranged the sucker. Is that how you Americans would put it?"

Laurence chuckled. "We'd be a little more civilized than that. You Russians have an Asian streak in you that's a trifle mean. But all that traffic was not about the Brit."

"By the way, where did you go today, Tony, taking off on us like that? The old helicopter routine again. Do you know that at this very moment your lovely Andrea is entertaining a footballer at her place? What do you suppose they're doing there, reading the sports pages, playing cribbage?"

"I hope you had a nice flight from Berlin. I'm told they serve borscht and bad vodka on Aeroflot. How can you take it? Where I was, Valery, was discussing the consequences of the manna enzyme with an economist. We had a nice chat."

There was a silence. "The manna enzyme, Tony? I don't believe I know about that. A new weapon to further confuse the SALT talks I assume."

"You know about the enzyme, Valery. You spent most of the day discussing it with the Politburo."

"I'm not sure I know what you're talking about."

"Don't worry. We didn't crack your patterns. But I'm not guessing. We know about Fidel's student. The soccer player Bobby Goldman told the whole story before Vivanco's poison got to him. Just think, Valery, you could grow alfalfa to feed people."

Karpov laughed. "If I could get the dollars to you, Tony, do you suppose you could buy me some stock in some good publishing houses?"

"Huh?" Laurence was momentarily taken aback.

"Cookbooks, Tony. People will have to know how to prepare grass salads and baked leaf casseroles. Your publishers will get rich."

"It always bewildered me, Valery, how you can be such a murderous bastard and have a sense of humor at the same time."

"It takes both for us Russians to survive, Tony."

"Well?"

"Well what, Tony?"

"What have you people decided to do?"

Karpov said something in Russian. Laurence waited. "There are people starving, Tony. What are we supposed to do?"

Laurence sighed. "It's not that easy or we wouldn't be taping all that traffic today. How many people can we handle, Valery?"

"We asked ourselves that."

"And what did you conclude? Are you going to be heroic, Valery? Food for the poor people of the world? Fatten them up for the struggle against the capitalists?"

"It isn't funny, Tony. We both know the dangers."

"We can't let it happen."

"No, we can't. What do we do?"

"We waste him, Valery."

"Oh? Who's 'we'? You pregnant, Tony, or do you have a turd in your pocket? Are we supposed to trust you? There's money to be made off the enzyme, we both know that. The problem is security, what happens when the secret is leaked as it eventually will be. We know that from our experience with nukes. When there's profit to be had you people develop odd mental quirks."

"If you don't trust me, Valery, you can send someone to help me do the job."

"Help you out?"

"Certainly. Me personally. The fewer people who know about this thing the better. We don't like to be embarrassed any more than you."

"I'm the only one at Center who knows all the details, Tony. Your side?"

"Myself, an economist, Chambliss, and a sportswriter named Perini, who was with Bobby Goldman when he died."

Karpov sucked air between his teeth. "That makes the six of us plus twelve members of the Politburo, and Fidel Castro. You have that place wired?"

"The UN? No. But we've got our people. You?"

"We've got our people," Karpov said. "That's how we found out about manna."

"If we get rid of Goldman and the enzyme, the Third Worlders will make a lot of noise but everybody knows they're full of bullshit. They don't have any power, so they make noise. The idea of an enzyme that turns bitter fruit sweet is incredible. A typical Third World delusion. Who'd believe them? All that posturing in the UN. All the rhetoric. All those speeches."

"So who cares what they say as long as

they don't have the enzyme, eh, Tony? Keep our little game the way it is. This way the rules are clear."

"Precisely. Sticks and stones."

"What?"

"An old saying, Valery, for children. Sticks and stones will break my bones, but names will never hurt me."

"Ahh." Karpov laughed. "There's an expression like that in Russian."

"You're welcome to join myself and Perini to terminate Goldman. That way you'd be sure. We'll need the help, Valery, the Third Worlders will be after him too. The Cubans are. We know that."

"Well, I have to say, this will be a first," Karpov said. "Let me call you back in a few minutes."

"I'll be here, Valery. Hey, it might be fun!" Laurence hung up. He poured himself four fingers of bourbon from a bottle in his desk and waited. It took Karpov twenty minutes to call back.

"Tony?"

"Me, Valery."

"You alone?"

"Just me and a bottle of whiskey."

"I'll be there at five-thirty P.M., tomorrow. National Airport, United Airlines Flight 197. I'll be traveling under the passport of one John McIntosh. I've recently grown a beard."

"Oh?" Laurence laughed. "We'll have to update our photo file."

"Uh huh," Karpov said.

"You'd just started growing it when we last shot you."

"It'll be good meeting you, Tony. We'll drink some of your good bourbon whiskey."

"Bring some vodka, Valery. We can't get good Russian vodka here."

"I don't think we have any choice."

"I don't either."

"We could have fed the world."

"We could have," Laurence said.

"We have to think of the future."

"Yes," Laurence said. "Capitalist children and Communist children."

"Tomorrow then," said Karpov.

"Valery?"

"Yes."

"I don't think that traffic said a damned thing. I think it was nonsense."

Karpov laughed. "Why should we send nonsense? I don't understand."

"You could have just called, Valery. Saved yourself some trouble."

"You Americans have real imaginations, I'll give you that."

"Tomorrow, Valery." Laurence hung up. He wondered whether Karpov was lying. No: the question was not whether but how much. The Russians always lied, the bastards. No matter. Better to know where a bastard is than let him take you by surprise. He didn't learn that from baseball. It had nothing to do with Whitey's law.

It was Laurence's theorem.

He wondered how he had fared with Karpov and suddenly laughed aloud because he knew Karpov wondered the same thing. After all,

Karpov considered him the biggest liar who ever walked the face of the earth. Laurence secured the office, returned Karpov's dossier to records, and went home.

CHAPTER

14

LAURENCE LAY IN BED THINKING ABOUT THE Colorado Rockies. It was quiet at night in the Rockies. There were no sounds, nothing. And there were stars, white stars, more stars than you could imagine if you spent your life in the great urban sprawl that ran from Boston to Washington. How many tens of thousands of gallons of milk did those people drink each day? How many eggs were eaten? Millions in one day? How much bread? How many carrots? How many apples? The logistics of feeding all those people bewildered him. Where did they come from, those eggplants stacked neatly in Safeway stores in January and February? From Mexico? Texas? How did they get all that food delivered before it rotted, brought right down to the corner store? It was incredible! Could it go on this way indefinitely?

Until this day Tony Laurence had never given food much thought. His concerns at Langley had to do with Soviet missile systems and troop movements in the Warsaw Pact countries. The A & P always had tomatoes and fresh fish. If he wanted coffee, cheese, oil, or anchovies, he simply took them off the shelf and paid for them at the cash register. It was true that in recent years the cost of food had risen higher, higher, and higher still, demand outracing supply. A cheeseburger that had once cost four bits now cost two or three bucks. Was this a sign, he wondered, that the days of plenty were coming to an end?

Laurence listened to the city sounds outside his town house. On lower Wisconsin Avenue, in the Georgetown area of fashionable shops and restaurants, the young, single, wealthy, and well-educated of the city were cruising. There were French restaurants where a cup of coffee cost a buck and a half. Later, in the small hours of the morning, they would return to their apartments to toot coke and, finally, to slip naked into one another's arms. There was, after all, the next page of the "Sauces and pickles for special occasions" section of Dr. Comfort's guide to *The Joy of Sex*. Laurence missed Andrea.

A horn honked on the street outside. He remembered the great, awful slums of Mexico City, where people lived in hives made of flattened tin cans, where the ground was sour with ground-in excrement, urine, spit, and mucus. Laurence turned on his king-size Simmons mattress. Flattened tin cans. There was never enough to eat there. Never.

He remembered having eaten a marvelous lunch at a French restaurant on the Kowloon side of Hong Kong colony, and of being driven in a Renault by a newspaper friend to the New Frontiers. They had pulled to the side of the road and stood, with the tourists, to see the beginning of China in the distance. There, 800 million Chinese imposed upon themselves an authoritarian, regimented, colorless, oppressive life simply that they, as a nation, might eat.

Laurence rolled over. His chief objection to Communist countries was that the people never seemed to have fun. Having fun was frivolous; in the Soviet Union and in Eastern Europe fun got in the way of economic development, of building more tanks and submarines. Building tanks was a terrible priority to put before fun. In Communist Asia, fun got in the way of feeding people. But if people were starving maybe fun was frivolous.

Laurence turned in bed. He remembered eating asparagus soup at the Tivoli in Copenhagen. He remembered eating cheese and drinking a cold bottle of Heineken's beer for lunch in Amsterdam. He remembered eating sausage in a bar in Zurich. Fats Domino had sung "Blueberry Hill" on the jukebox. He remembered young Japanese crowding around a McDonald's outlet on the Ginza. He remembered eating raw fish in a Japanese inn in Kyoto that had a sign at the entrance saying William Faulkner had stayed there. He remembered buying exotic fruits from floating peddlers in the klongs of Bangkok. He remembered an obsequious Chinese waiter in Kuala Lumpur who had served him an exquisite meal of shrimp and red peppers piled on rice. He remembered the vast pits in the Malaysian countryside where there had once been tin. What would happen when there was no tin anywhere.

Laurence turned under the covers. He recalled the food concessions at a chicken fight in the Philippines. A slender young Filipino in a blue shirt had walked slowly around the ring, holding his bird high, while the bettors appraised it, food in one hand, money in the other. He remembered drinking a sweating glass of Dos Equis and eating an elaborate fruit salad on the Paseo de la Reforma in Mexico City.

He remembered again the shacks made of flattened tin cans. He remembered seeing children who were starving. He remembered his own daughter's large blue eyes. He ought to have her down to see him again soon. It had been too long since the last visit. Did a Bolivian father or an African father love his daughter any less? He tried to think of his daughter starving and got out of bed.

Laurence went into his kitchen and cracked a cold can of Coors beer. He was hungry. He got out his electric skillet, some bacon, and some eggs. He made himself a bacon and egg sandwich and sat eating it, listening to the sounds of the city outside.

Laurence wondered about Karpov. Was Karpov having second thoughts? He and Karpov were much alike. They were achievers. He, Laurence, had been appointed to head the agency because his cousin was the President. Karpov had been smart, cunning, brutal, and a bit lucky. Laurence looked forward to meeting him; they had become

friends of sorts after they established direct
communications between Moscow Center and
Langley. Karpov was a Communist, was he
not? To each according to his need. He too
had to think of hungry children. Did not
every man, regardless of his birth or the
misfortune of time or place, have a right to
eat? Was that liberal fancy? Or would the
old law, written in blood, immutable, apply
to the very end?

He put the mayonnaise away and retrieved
another Coors and a half-empty jar of stuffed
green olives from the refrigerator. Had Comrade Karpov traveled or were his opinions
dictated by Marxist texts? Had Karpov seen
the tin-can shacks? Laurence had never been
to Moscow. Were there as many people in
Moscow as there were in the District of
Columbia who subsisted on cheap starches?

What right did he, Anthony Laurence, born
of a wealthy and influential family, have to
deny people food? Uncle Bill was a professor;
he lived in the comfortable, perfect world of
theory, of the abstract. It was easy for him
to stand back and objectively outline the
consequences of food and population. Uncle
Bill had a grown daughter and a son and
grandchildren. Had he gone back to Cambridge and thought about the trust in their
eyes?

Laurence opened a third can of Coors.
Laurence had ordered men killed. He hadn't
liked it but it was necessary under the
circumstances. He was, after all, responsible
for the security of 240 million people. What
was a life here or there, given the stakes?

But what he was about to do now was more than waste one human life in the name of national security. He was taking it upon himself to deny the world a potentially unlimited supply of food. Did he have the right? There was no answer to that question. It was too complicated for simple answers. Would he do it?

Anthony Laurence wasn't sure. He went to the toilet and the telephone rang while he was relieving himself of the beer.

"Hello, Grandma," said a woman's voice.

"Grandma isn't here," Laurence said.

"Tell Grandma her little girl would like to speak to her. It's important."

"Will do," Laurence said. He killed his Coors in a single slug, dressed, and headed for his car. He had a slight buzz on.

It took him half an hour to get to Langley. Frieda Sondheim was there, waiting, looking tired.

"What are you doing here?" Laurence asked.

"Driscoll," she said wearily.

Driscoll, thin and nervous, entered from the next room. He looked left and right as though he were being watched. "London wants you, Tony."

"It's the middle of the night, Driscoll."

"Morning in London, Tony."

Laurence looked at Frieda. "Why does she have to be here?"

"I thought you might want her, Tony, what with that traffic today and all."

Laurence sighed. "Go home, Frieda. You too, Driscoll."

Driscoll started to protest. He was certain

this was something important and wanted to be in on it.

"I'll handle it, Peter. No problem."

"You sure, Tony?" Driscoll cleared his throat.

"Go home, Peter," Frieda Sondheim picked up her handbag. Driscoll lingered uncertainly for a moment, then followed her. When they had gone, Laurence instructed the computer to change the pattern on the scrambler. He punched up London.

"Tony?" answered a man.

"My code," Laurence said in a tired voice.

"The P.M. feels it's essential that Great Britain be included in any decision surrounding the manna enzyme."

Laurence slumped back in his chair and put his feet up on his desk. "I don't know what you're talking about, Archie. You'll have to fill me in."

"The manna enzyme, Tony. You don't need filling in."

"What?"

"Traffic between the Kremlin and Bonn. Traffic between Moscow Center and you."

Laurence laughed. "Archie, old man. Valery Karpov and I are pals. One man can't fuck the entire world by himself. It takes two at the very least. Karpov's brutal, cunning, and a fool, straight out of Dostoevski. I'm vain, cunning, and a fool, straight out of Fitzgerald."

Archie Smethurst laughed.

Laurence continued: "Laurence and Karpov, helluva pair, Archie. Once in a while we just chat, the two of us. We're worriers, you know."

"As I understand the manna enzyme, Tony, this thing's not very damned funny."

"Still don't know what you're talking about, Archie."

Smethurst turned formal. "Do I have to remind you of the agreement between Her Majesty's Government and yourselves in such matters as these? Section four, Tony."

Laurence sighed. He'd been had. "Only if you tell me how you got your information. You didn't break Moscow's traffic."

"No, we didn't."

"How, then?"

"Honey."

Laurence groaned. "Honey?"

"The sweetest, loveliest honey you'll ever see."

"Got a guy thinking through his cock?"

Smethurst laughed. "That's it, Tony. A buyer, or more accurately a member of a pool of buyers."

"We've got a seller at Langley?"

Smethurst cleared his throat. "I'm afraid you do. I'm sorry, Tony."

"Our little agreement you mentioned says you people are supposed to let us know when you find out something like that." Laurence was getting angry.

"I'm telling you now, Tony. Why do you suppose I'm calling you? I have a clock on the wall that tells me what time it is in Washington. It's seven A.M. here. I opened the place to make this call."

"By the way, what happened to your man in Berlin?"

"They got to him."

"Did we try to help you?"

"Yes, you did."

"I'm sorry, Archie. This manna business has me on edge. Is your honey secure?"

Smethurst laughed. "Absolutely no problem, Tony. None."

"So what does the P.M. think?" Laurence began doodling with a pencil as he waited for an answer.

Smethurst paused. "The P.M. believes it would be a disaster to hand the Third World something like that."

"Keep the brown buggers starved and there's not much they can do, eh, Archie."

"You know the P.M. better than that," Smethurst said evenly.

"Bottom line, Archie."

"The P.M. says the enzyme could very well ruin the economy of the developed world."

"Worried about the lifeboat."

"The P.M. thinks we'd be scuttled."

"Tough to put it that baldly, Archie."

"It's like scraping chalk against a blackboard. And your cousin? What does he think?"

"Same as the P.M.," Laurence lied.

"The Soviets?"

"Harder for them, Archie. But Karpov says the Politburo sees it the same."

"Do you believe him?"

"The Soviets are worried about word getting out. It would destroy their credibility in competing against the Chinese. But they don't trust me to get rid of the problem without one of them around. We might come up with some devilishly capitalist way of profiting from it. They look upon the manna enzyme as a forbidden fruit."

"It is tantalizing."

"Yes, it is."

"Again, the P.M. wants to know what you're going to do. You can tell us or he can phone your cousin."

Laurence sucked in his breath. "Karpov and I are going to waste Goldman. We may have a third with us, but I'm not sure."

"A third?"

"Yes, a former agent who learned about the enzyme from Goldman's son. But I'm not sure about him."

"He may be the seller?"

"He may," Laurence said.

"Her Majesty's Government asks that it be represented in any such operation."

"We'll take one Brit, no more," Laurence said. "The last thing we need to do is to have to explain ourselves to the world later on. We're gonna have to sit on this thing to our grave. Please, Archie, if you have to expand need, trust Karpov and me to do what has to be done."

"What about the Third World types? What if the leak should get worse?"

"It won't. And besides, the Third Worlders are hysterical. Everybody knows that. Who'll believe them if they claim someone discovered a way to feed the world? Left-wing rags will mouth off for a while but it'll go away like a bad cold. Sip a little port, Archie. Get some sleep."

"And you?"

"Bourbon whiskey and sex."

"Now, as to our representative, Tony. I can't travel. Diabetes, as you know. I'll have to send someone."

"You shouldn't expand need."

"The P.M. knows. I know. An economist knows. And one agent knows."

"Honey's handler."

Smethurst laughed. "Something like that."

"Can he be here by tomorrow afternoon? Karpov's due at four-thirty P.M."

"Certainly."

"Name?"

"Rue Kadera."

"Well, you tell old Rue he better be in shape. We're gonna be hiking around some mountains. Listen, by tomorrow afternoon—I mean today." Laurence suddenly felt very tired.

"I know. Rue's in shape."

"You tell him to be in the Central Liquor Store in Washington at three P.M. Tell him to carry a green or yellow apple and a copy of last week's *Time* magazine. I'll ask him what he thinks of George the Third. He'll say George the Third was a jerk." Laurence laughed a slightly mean laugh.

"And what will you say, Tony, old man?"

"Why, I'll say 'Thank God for Lafayette.' "

"Done, Tony. And thanks."

"Wish us luck, Archie."

"God knows," Archie said.

Laurence hung up. He rang the duty officer in sitters. "I want to go for a ride, Roy. I'll need a key to the Manassas safe house and a car that's been teched. When I'm clear have your man give me a blink. Got it?"

"Got it, Tony."

Roy, knowing Laurence's taste, provided him with a Triumph. Laurence pulled the top down and drove off into the muggy Virginia night. He gave the sitters a run before they cleared him. He then turned onto the beltway for a stretch before he took an off-ramp and headed for Manassas. It was almost 2:00 A.M. when he reached the safe house. He opened the door with a key Chambliss had given him and headed for the master bedroom, flipping on all the lights as he did.

"What the fuck?" Eddie Perini sat up in bed and shielded his eyes from the lights.

He caught Tony Laurence's fist in his stomach and dropped to his side sucking for breath.

"To whom and for how much?" Laurence demanded.

"What?"

"I said to whom and for how goddamned much." Laurence was enraged. He kicked Perini hard alongside the ear with his foot.

"Aw, shit!" Perini turned to protect himself and grabbed the side of his head. "What are you talking about, man?"

"The Brits know about manna. Smethurst says there's a seller in the Company. I know better. That leaves you, you son of a bitch."

"What?"

"The Brits were working your buyer with honey."

"Slow down, dammit."

"You motherfucker!" Laurence hit him again, again, and yet a third time.

Perini got a foot on Laurence's chest and pushed hard. "Jesus! Back off."

Laurence kept coming.

Perini, fully awake now, his ear and the side of his face stinging, lowered his head and charged straight at Laurence. "What the fuck are you talking about, asshole?"

Laurence grabbed him by the shoulder and pushed him up against the wall. "I'm talking about some mother who peddled manna, that's what I'm talking about."

"Oh," said Perini. His body slumped under Laurence's grip. "Not me. You think I'd do something like that? What do you take me for?"

Laurence nearly picked him off his feet. "I suspect everybody, friend, until I know for certain."

"Well, it wasn't me. I can tell you that."

"Get your clothes on. We'll find out."

They got into Laurence's Triumph, saying nothing. Perini's nose was bleeding. He touched it carefully with his fingertips.

"If not me, then who?" he asked Laurence.

"Chambliss."

"Chambliss?"

"I've known him for twenty years, worked with him, trusted him."

"You fucked up my nose and damned near tore my ear off."

"I'll do a lot more than that if I found you peddled the manna enzyme."

Neither of them said anything on the drive back to Langley. Security tried to stop Perini but Laurence bulled his way through. "He's with me. I'm DCI. I run this fucking place or used to." It was 5:30 A.M. He called traffic. "Check the tapes of the Moscow–Berlin traffic today. I want to know if Chambliss pulled them." Laurence waited. Perini rubbed his ear and drank Laurence's office whiskey.

"Yes, he did, Tony. He was down there all night running them through the machine."

"Didn't anybody ask him what he was doing? The DDP doesn't work a graveyard shift like a mill hand."

"His code was on the dock, Tony. You know Chambliss."

"We've got people in traffic whose job it is to unscramble that crap."

"Chambliss thinks he can do everything himself. Anything wrong, Tony?"

"Nothing's wrong."

"Are you sure?" Obviously something was. Laurence wouldn't be asking questions in the middle of the night.

"Chambliss is just working too hard. See you people tomorrow." Laurence hung up. "How's your ear?"

"It'll work," Perini said. "It's Chambliss, then."

"We'll find out tomorrow when we talk to Kadera."

"Kadera?"

"The Brit who'll be joining Karpov, you, and me."

"Ahh," said Perini.

DAY FOUR

VALERY KARPOV'S CHICKEN
À LA KIEV*

3 whole breasts of
chicken with or
without main wing
bones attached,
boned and halved
½ cup chilled, firm
butter
Salt and freshly ground
black pepper

2 tablespoons chopped
chives
Flour for dredging
2 eggs, lightly beaten
1 cup fresh bread
crumbs
Fat for deep frying

1. Place the chicken breasts between pieces of
waxed paper and pound until thin with a mallet
or the flat side of a butcher knife. Do not split the
flesh. Remove the waxed paper.

2. Cut the butter into six finger-shaped pieces.
Place a piece in the middle of each breast,
sprinkle with salt, pepper and chives and roll up,
envelope fashion, letting the wing bone protrude
and making the sides overlap. The flesh will
adhere without skewers.

3. Dredge each roll lightly with flour, dip into
the beaten eggs and roll in bread crumbs. Refrig-
erate one hour or more so the crumbs will
adhere.

4. Fill a fryer or kettle with enough fat to

completely cover the breasts. Heat until hot (360° F.). Add chicken gradually and brown on all sides. Drain on absorbent paper and place a paper frill on the main wing bones before serving. (SERVES SIX)

CHAPTER

15

ON TOP OF HAVING A CONGRESS FULL OF SELF-serving obstructionists, President Mason Devol had an anus that itched. Labor wanted higher wages. Business wanted tax incentives. Nobody wanted to pay a dime more for gasoline. The country refused to produce: one automobile worker in Japan produced forty-five automobiles in one year; one worker in Detroit produced sixteen. It was the same old story. Now Tony Laurence's second in command, James Chambliss, had called requesting a private meeting on "urgent" business. Chambliss!

What did Chambliss want?

Devol sat at his desk doodling geometric designs, circles, and ellipses. He envied other Presidents their afflictions. Dwight Eisenhower had a coronary thrombosis. You can have a heart attack and maintain your dignity. Devol remembered watching John Cameron Swayze on a black-and-white television set solemnly repeating ambiguous bulletins issued by Walter Reed Army Hospital. A heart attack is tragic. The nation waited, wishing Ike well. Lyndon Johnson had a gall-bladder operation and lifted his shirt so reporters and photographers could see the scar on his Texas paunch. Devol remembered that a cartoonist had drawn Johnson's scar in the shape of Vietnam. Gerald Ford had football knees and a linebacker's brain, but that too was okay. Jimmy Carter suffered hemorrhoids. Was there any good reason, Devol wondered, why Carter had to inform the public that he suffered from hemorrhoids any more than he had to tell Barbara Walters that he and Rosalynn slept together in a double bed? Did hemorrhoids have anything to do with inflation or the defense budget?

Devol began an elaborate pattern of interconnecting circles. The chief of medical services at Georgetown University Medical School had been his personal physician. He failed to cure the itching. Devol had to suffer an itching anus at a reception for the West German chancellor, at a meeting with the president of the AFL-CIO, at a breakfast meeting with congressional leaders and, most recently, at a televised address to the nation on the troubled state of the economy. The itching drove him nuts.

The televised address was the very worst. The President knew the importance of looking good on television—there were those who said it had won the election for him. He remembered the image of Richard Nixon—a pious, sanctimonious liar with small eyes and sweat on his upper lip. Devol's doodles turned into sharp squares and triangles. He had been enraged at having to think about his ass when the lines of his speech appeared on the monitor in the Oval Office. At first he had considered sneaking a hand back there for a subtle nudge. Then he wanted to stand up and, dammit, give himself some relief. Dig right in there. He could do nothing.

So he told the chief of medical services where to shove his pink ointment and got himself another doctor. Out of spite, he told the departing physician he was thinking of introducing a bill before Congress to nationalize medical care in the United States.

So there it was: an itching anus. And a new ointment, white this time. The white goo helped some but the itching returned when Devol was under tension. The results of polls, it seemed, were the greatest irritant. There was a time when politicians didn't know what the public thought except for cranks and oddballs who wrote letters. The public, convinced of democratic wisdom, thought a 59 percent disapproval of a policy made it bad policy. Devol learned to give the 59 percent whatever they wanted.

A mellow beep sounded once and a green light lit over his door. James Chambliss was ushered in by the assistant to the President's appointment secretary, a well-scrubbed young man who was awed by power.

"The Deputy Director of the Central Intelligence Agency, Mr. President," said the young man. He looked at Chambliss, a minor power, as though Chambliss had his penis exposed. "James Chambliss, sir."

Devol dismissed the young man with a wave of his hand and looked at Chambliss slowly, from the top of his head to his feet. People were usually intimidated at having an audience with the President. Devol regarded them slowly to further cow them.

"Mr. President," Chambliss said. He extended his hand. His grip was firm.

Devol felt a twinge of anxiety sprint through his gut. Chambliss seemed nonplussed. Chambliss had known Laurence for years. Laurence had demanded that Chambliss be his deputy. Devol cleared his throat. "Pleased to meet you, Mr. Chambliss." He cleared his throat again. He had never talked to Chambliss without Laurence being present.

"Thank you for seeing me, Mr. President. I know you're very busy."

Devol gave Chambliss the smile he gave for photographers. "I certainly don't mean to be rude, Mr. Chambliss, but I make it my practice to ask my appointments to speak succinctly and clearly. You told my people you have urgent business. I want the bottom line. I'm sure you can understand my problem."

"I do, indeed, Mr. President. I want your cousin's job."

Devol's eyes widened. "I assume you mean Tony Laurence's job."

"Director of the CIA. I assume this room is clear."

"Clear?" Devol laughed. "Anybody would have to be out of his mind to bug this place after Richard Nixon. You can be sure of your privacy, Mr. Chambliss."

For the first time Chambliss betrayed anxiety. He paused, then told the President Eddie

Perini's story about Bernard Goldman and the manna enzyme.

"This is the truth?"

"Yes, sir, it is."

The President said, "You're telling me Tony consulted McClure and on his own decided to kill Goldman. Without telling me."

"On his own," Chambliss said.

"Why are you telling me this?" It occurred to Devol that his cousin might have been doing him a favor.

Chambliss smiled. "I don't want to come off sounding phony now, but the truth is I have my limits. I don't think that's how this country should be run."

"Which is why you're using it to get Tony's job."

"Well, there's that too," Chambliss conceded. "We're talking about a discovery that could feed everyone."

"But play hell with the farmers in Auburn, Nebraska. That's what McClure said?"

"Yes," Chambliss said. "He said it would destroy the economies of the temperate world."

"The temperate world didn't vote me into office. I care about old farts in Nebraska with big green tractors, mortgages, and fields of corn. They elected me to represent them. Now tell me again why Tony Laurence decided not to tell me about this."

Chambliss swallowed. "Do you want the exact words, Mr. President, or will a paraphrase do?"

"Unless you have a photographic memory, an accurate paraphrase will do."

"Your cousin said it was the DCI's duty to protect a President from things he might be better off not knowing."

Devol's anus began to burn. He shifted on his chair and sucked air in between his teeth. "And just what is it you propose, Mr. Chambliss?"

"I think the decision to terminate Goldman is the correct one. But I also think there's a way we can accomplish the same thing and earn, say, twenty million dollars for your campaign chest. That is, if we can strike a deal, Mr. President. May I be candid about your cousin?"

"Please do, Mr. Chambliss."

"Tony Laurence was a good man in the field. I don't think there's any doubt about that. But he's not the man for DCI. I can do his job a hell of a lot better than he can. I'm tired of being his gopher."

"Let's hear your scheme, Mr. Chambliss."

"There are, as you know, multinational corporations with productive capabilities equal to Canada or France whose economic base would be threatened by the manna enzyme. We can't take a chance on that but they wouldn't know how we're thinking for sure. They think an American President would swap his soul for a good Gallup rating. Twenty million would be nothing to them, a trifle, for the opportunity of making absolutely sure their investments are protected."

Devol laughed. "How in the world, Mr. Chambliss, would you go about contacting the corporate heads of multinationals with investments in food production and distribution? There must be dozens of them, hundreds, for all I know."

"There is a man, Mr. President, who knows who they are and how to get in touch with them in minutes."

"And that would be?"

"William Pumphries, president and chairman of the board of a firm called Arnaud Mobelier, a Chicago-based company that sells tight, accurate, confidential information on futures and commodities for vast sums of money. Only a comparative handful of corporations in the world can spring for Arnaud's rates."

"Pumphries, I take it, would be our mark."

"That's one way of phrasing it, Mr. President."

"Now you tell me just exactly how you propose to convince these philanthropic gentlemen that you're telling the truth. We both know I can use the twenty million and I agree that we're talking pocket money for these people."

Chambliss looked confident. "We tell them that if I'm not telling the truth and they feel they've been had in any way, they can get the Mafia to take me out."

"Kill you?"

Chambliss smiled. "Certainly. The Mafia and these people have heavy investments in some of the same firms. The contacts are there. If manna is bogus, it's my neck."

Devol was impressed. "You do want to be director, don't you?"

"I've got the cards. When I've got the cards I bet the limit. Put me in charge of the agency and I'd play them just as well against the Russians."

"And how would I be included in your proposal?" the President asked.

"You wouldn't. I'd tell them I want the money. It's as simple as that. They'd believe me. They understand greed."

Devol leaned back in his chair. "To be honest, Mr. Chambliss, I don't understand why you didn't go for the money to begin with. Why are you here?"

"I want to run the agency myself. I've been working there for ten years and I've got a hell of a lot of ideas stored up. With the contacts the DCI makes, I figure I could make a nice little sum before I retire."

Devol knew that was true. He extended his hand to Chambliss. "You deliver the twenty million bucks and report here alive and you're the director of the CIA. Mention one word of this conversation to anybody and I'll deny it with my hand on a Bible before the television networks, tears in my eyes. Inside of a year you'll be a dead man. Do you understand?"

"Yes, Mr. President, I understand."

"I mean do you really understand?" Devol looked Chambliss straight in the eye.

"I do."

"What will they do, the multinationals?"

"They'll either waste him or they'll snatch him and try to control the use of the enzyme. If they decide on the latter we run the risk of the enzyme eventually making its way to the Third World. Just now, however, either course would be preferable to letting Fidel Castro take it back to Havana with him."

"I see." Devol punched a button under his desk and the door opened. The assistant to the appointments secretary appeared, looking obsequious.

CHAPTER

16

OWING TO A LACK OF TAX AND LAWS ALLOWING the advertising of loss leaders, the District is one of the least expensive places in the United States to buy alcohol. And the Central Liquor Store, on Eleventh Street just off Pennsylvania Avenue, has the reputation of being the cheapest place in the District to buy booze. When you throw a party in Washington, you go to Central. The only problem is parking, but even if you have to spring for the lot across the street, the Central is a deal.

Laurence and Perini scored at a meter in front of a porn shop a block and a half away. The porn shop advertised the latest in "sexual devices." From the front of the porn shop the Redskins' punter could have hit the new FBI building.

Laurence and Perini paused in front of the shop. "Nobody's complained about my device yet," Perini said.

Laurence seemed surprised. "It seems to work?"

"Unless I drink myself blind. Yes, it seems to do the job."

Laurence was beginning to like his odd companion. "I've been told mine would begin to falter with the coming of middle age. I haven't noticed it."

Perini narrowed his eyes and looked about him as though he were the center of a conspiracy. "Rumor, my man, spread by twenty-one-year-old paw artists and quick comers. They're envious."

Laurence and Perini took a Borax walk, doing the best they could with the time they had. When they were convinced they were clean, they doubled back to the Central. They split two blocks from the store. Perini floated. Laurence went inside. The Central wasn't large but there were bottles to the ceiling with islands in the middle with cases of whiskey stacked high. Clerks in yellow smocks mingled among the customers in the narrow aisles. The customers—lawyers and bureaucrats wearing neckties and shined shoes—stared at labels and prices.

The apple and the *Time* magazine would not appear until exactly 3:00 P.M. If they appeared earlier, Laurence would leave. He stationed himself by an island of cognac and brandy. It was 2:52 P.M. Eight minutes to go. There was no sense trying to guess who Rue Kadera was. The Central was packed, as usual.

Laurence contented himself with watching a young woman browsing among displays of Johnnie Walker, Chivas Regal, Old Bushmill, and Jack Daniels stacked perilously high to

make room for islands of Drambuie, Beef-
eater, Courvoisier, Martell, Bacardi, Hud-
son's Bay, Dry Sack, Burgundies and Bordeaux
of every imaginable house and vintage. She
was short, not over five foot three. She wore
dark slacks and a blouse open two buttons
down that attracted the peripheral vision of
male customers who for no apparent reason
began lingering over displays of liquor they
never drank and knew nothing about. When
she moved there was a shifting under the
lower button that was heart-stopping to men
with normal rations of hormones.

She weighed 112 to 115 pounds. She was
soft and rounded rather than lean and hard
according to the fashion dictated by television casting directors and magazine photographers. She walked with a sensual shifting of
a rump that was remarkable in that it was
full and firm without giving way to disconcerting fat on her thighs. But what most
struck Laurence, whose life had more than
once depended on his ability to watch and
weigh people, was a presence that was unaf-
fected, lively, and spirited. She did not slump;
she liked herself. Her elegant little spine
curved sharply inward at the base of her
back and swept upward to her shoulder
blades without a hint of defeat, regret, leth-
argy, or indecision. She was a jewel. She
turned briefly toward Laurence and revealed
a wide face dominated by very large, round
brown eyes and a mouth with lips an actress
would have envied.

Laurence watched her, thought briefly of
Andrea, and sighed. It was 2:58 P.M. He

turned his attention to men with baskets of
bottles waiting in line to be checked out. One
of those men would remove an apple and a
Time magazine from his basket. Laurence
waited, wondering which one it would be.

The girl with the eyes strolled over to
Laurence's island and began looking at
brandy.

Laurence smiled. "Hello," he said. He looked
past her for Rue Kadera. The young woman
was lovely but the last thing he needed was
her there with her cute butt. He had to make
a contact with a British spy.

"I must say, the price is right," said the
woman. She had a rich, low voice.

Laurence wished she would buy her brandy
or whatever and move on. "Pearson's on
Wisconsin is good too," Laurence said. He
began moving away from her toward a dis-
play of gin. The British were gin drinkers.
Maybe Kadera would be there. Port too, and
Madeira. The Brits liked sweet wine. Kadera
was late. Laurence looked at his watch. He
was wondering what could have gone wrong
when he heard the crunch of an apple.

The girl with the eyes was chewing pen-
sively on a yellow apple, watching him with
an amused look. She had a trim nose, straight
on the ridge, and carried a copy of *Time*.

Laurence looked at her stupidly and blinked
once. He almost forgot his lines. Smethurst
had laughed on the phone. Was this why? A
woman agent! "You were looking at the gin
over there. Are you British by any chance?
What do you think of George the Third?"

The girl laughed, showing very white teeth. "Why, you must be confused," she said.

Laurence panicked momentarily, wondering what had gone wrong. Nothing like this had ever happened to him.

"I was by the rum," she said. "This is gin here. I think George the Third was a jerk."

Laurence was relieved. "Thank God for Lafayette."

"Please call me Rue, Mr. Laurence," she said, and extended her hand.

Laurence cleared his throat. "It hadn't occurred to me that Rue was a woman's name. Were you the case officer for Smethurst's honey?"

Rue Kadera laughed. "Oh, yes. I'm the case officer."

"Ahh," Laurence said.

"And the honey."

"Oh." He could see why but didn't know what to say. He hesitated.

"I can take care of myself, Mr. Laurence."

"Tony."

"Tony then."

"Smethurst must be having some fun."

Rue Kadera looked blandly at him with her brown eyes, then let her gaze stray to the rest of the room.

Laurence was embarrassed. "My God, I'm sorry. Yes, I think we should talk someplace else." He gave her his elbow, she took it, and they left the Central Liquor Store with Laurence wondering if she would tell Smethurst about his mouth. He'd behaved like he was on his first assignment.

Once on the sidewalk, Kadera said, "No, Tony, I won't tell C." C was Smethurst.

Laurence and Rue Kadera took a walk with Perini floating first ahead, across the street, then behind them, walking with a curious, ambling walk, peering into parked cars, and staring at objects on the sidewalk. Kadera had him spotted in two blocks. "I assume the man with the mustache is with us."

"Oh yes. His name is Eddie Perini. He's a sportswriter, covers the Portland Trail Blazers."

"He writes about basketball?"

"Yes, basketball. He was trained by the Pentagon and worked as an agent before he turned to the newspaper business."

Kadera stared fascinated as Perini, aware that he'd been found out, seemed alternately to be imitating the walks of Alfred Hitchcock, Charlie Chaplin, Stepin Fetchit, and John Wayne.

"It's all a circus for him," Laurence said. He finally gave Perini a nod and Perini joined them.

"God, I love this stuff," Perini said. "Floating. Eyes squinting. Reflections in mirrors and windows. Danger. Heart thumping like turds in a blender. Just like the movies." He tugged at his mustache. "My heavens but you British are civilized. All of Tony's women agents look like Nikita Khrushchev in drag."

"Oh?"

"Big, husky broads with mustaches and shoulders like linebackers. Tony here figures the Russians go for 'em that way. Lotsa meat and potatoes. Need a big warm body for those cold Siberian nights, the way he sees it."

"Is that true, Tony?" Rue liked the idea of teasing Laurence.

Laurence glared at Perini.

"Look there, the President's cousin. We're getting him all worked up," Perini said.

Laurence didn't know what to say. He had never really been teased in his life. He knew nothing of the affectionate give-and-take of the American working class. He had been an achiever always, the man in charge. He was director of the Central Intelligence Agency. People told him what they thought he wanted to hear.

"He's probably an okay guy though," Perini said.

"I'm pleased to be with you both, Mr. Perini," Rue said.

"Eddie. When you're off to murder someone the least you can do is to call your colleagues by their first names. Colleagues? Is that the right word here?"

"This is going to be real fun with you along," Laurence said. He had always been a serious man among serious men. Eddie Perini had an offbeat, Bohemian quality about him, a willingness to accept the absurd. Eddie was a free spirit. He would not sacrifice his freedom for power or authority. Power meant absolutely nothing to him. He would write spirited accounts of basketball games but would always consider it a game. He would never be an editor. Laurence envied him.

CHAPTER

17

IT WAS NINETY-SEVEN DEGREES IN WASHINGton. An oppressive gray-yellow pall hung over the city. Eddie Perini's shirt stuck to his back and chest from floating on the sidewalks outside the Central Liquor Store. Washington is a city of black people and the city's blacks went stolidly about their business, skins shiny. Young white women who worked as clerks in Commerce, in Labor, in Agriculture and other government agencies, watched the heat from air-conditioned offices. In the afternoon they would be packed, sweating, in buses, reading paperback romances or watching black people drinking beer and laughing on marble stoops of row houses. By the time they reached Laurence's car, Rue Kadera's blouse was beginning to cling to her back.

"I've never known heat like this," she said as Perini slipped onto the backseat. "What do people do?"

Laurence adjusted the rearview mirror. "The bureaucrats will retreat to Chevy Chase in northwest Washington and to white suburbs in Virginia and Montgomery County,

Maryland. Everything is air-conditioned out there. You'll find lawns, shrubs, and trees."

"And these people. What about them?" She gestured to a group of young blacks with floppy hats, see-through blouses, and platform shoes jiving down a sidewalk to rock music from a transistor radio.

Eddie Perini leaned forward from the rear seat. "The men will collect in neighborhood bars to have a bottle of National beer and cool off after work. The women will wait. The kids there will cruise and hang out and shuck and jive until it gets dark. Then they'll fuck one another and fry their brains with speed."

Rue turned and looked at him.

Perini shrugged. "You wanted to know."

"And there's no end to it?"

"None that I can see," Perini said. "Fifty-one percent of the children born in the District are illegitimate, last stats I heard. If you're a woman and spend your life in the District, chances are one in five you'll be raped somewhere along the way."

"What?"

"One in five."

"Black on white?"

"Black on black. The whites have all left. Schools are ninety-six percent black."

Rue looked at Laurence, who drove and said nothing. She turned to Perini again. "And the economics?"

"You mean do they work?"

"Yes."

"The government's done its best to open slots for blacks but most don't have the skills. The bureaucracy's top-heavy with underemployed Ph.D.'s. The blacks move the paper and run the District government. They came here during World War II and changed Washington from a provincial Southern city to a city of poor and pissed-off people. Some don't have heat in the winter. Some don't eat."

"Don't eat?"

"Well, I suppose most of them eat," Perini said. "But you try eating a diet of greens, pork, and cheap starch."

"A little hyperbole there, Eddie?" Laurence said as he braked for a light.

"Maybe it's me," acknowledged Perini. "But a whole lot of truth. You know it. I know it."

"Bloody grim," said Rue Kadera. The sun looked orange behind the murk.

Laurence was forced to stop the car again as a bus filled with students unloaded in front of the Smithsonian's National Air and Space Museum. "I think we have some business to attend to before we get to Karpov," Laurence said. "We've got a seller in the Company. We need to talk about the leak."

"Plug the leak," Perini said.

"I guess we're lucky you British found a man with a taste for honey."

Rue Kadera watched the children dancing up and down on the sidewalk.

"Yeah, Rue, tell us all the juicy details," Perini said.

Laurence turned in the seat. "Rue *was* the honey, jerk!"

Perini groaned. "Hey, you know me, Tony— all class. I'm a classy guy, Rue."

Rue watched the children being counted by their teacher. "Look at them having fun. That's okay, Eddie, you didn't know. The mark's name was Ralf Havlock. He's a Welshman who moved to Switzerland to avoid British taxes. We were trying to trace a laundry, and Havlock has contacts with the gnomes. I made my move one night at a party at the British Embassy. It was easy, a pair of limpid eyes and a breast brushed casually against his shoulder. He went for it like a shark."

"I can imagine," Perini said.

Rue laughed. " 'Limpid eyes,' that's good, don't you think? Limpid. Anyway, we went to bed that night. Unfortunately, he wasn't a talker. Couldn't get anything on the laundry but Havlock's on the board of directors of a corporation with a heavy investment in soybeans. He told me a story he thought was a joke. It seems there is a firm in Chicago, independent, whose business it is to monitor the international commodities market. Arnaud Mobelier."

"Arnaud Mobelier?"

"Yes. Arnaud is said to be absolutely dependable. Its research is thorough, complete, and confidential. It's also very, very expensive."

Perini laughed. "To you or me, maybe, but not to corporations who swap food around the globe."

Rue nodded her head. "Certainly not to the multinationals. You want to know about beef, chick-peas, or rice, you ask Arnaud. Corn? Pork bellies? Durham wheat? They know. Commodities is a high-stakes game. When you win, you win big, but for every winner there's a loser. Big winners, big losers."

"You pay big to win big," Eddie said.

Rue grinned. "The reason Havlock told me about the manna enzyme was he thought you people were having him on. He said there was no way the number two man in the Central Intelligence Agency was going to fly to Chicago with a cock-and-bull story like that—"

Laurence interrupted her. "Number two man?"

"That's what he said, Tony."

"Chambliss?" asked Perini.

"Yes. Keep going, Rue."

"Well, Havlock said you people were onto an enzyme that could theoretically destroy the international production and distribution of food—and along with it the futures and commodity market—by making all plantlife edible. He wanted twenty million dollars for the location of the man who discovered it." Kadera's large brown eyes blinked once. "Arnaud thought it was a joke at first too but they checked on your man's credentials. When they found out he was for real they began to worry. What if manna were genuine? It would put them out of business."

"They had to regard it seriously," said Laurence.

"Of course, they worried if there was some kind of ploy going on, an entrapment to embarrass them for reasons they couldn't imagine. They think you people are capable of anything. So what would happen, they wondered, if they asked their clients to share expenses and risks? The multinationals have clout."

The bus moved out of their way and Laurence continued east on Independence Avenue. "So they called their clients."

Rue nodded yes. "They called their clients, told them your man's story, and asked them to contribute to a kitty. Those wonderful people who control everything from prostitution to the distribution of food to grocery stores in New York agreed to hit him if he was lying. That was part of the bargain. The Mafia threat didn't bother your man. He took the money and told Arnaud all about Bernard Goldman and the manna enzyme."

Laurence slowed for some jaywalking tourists. "He made a believer out of the food people."

"Most of them, apparently. Havlock still thought it was a joke or he wouldn't have told me. But he didn't think I was any threat—two breasts and a bush, nothing more."

"Smethurst didn't think it was funny."

"Nothing's funny to C. He never laughs. Never. The two of us paid a visit to Number 10 Downing for a little chat. The P.M. called an economist friend and we discussed the consequences."

"You couldn't afford to take a chance any more than Arnaud Mobelier," Perini said.

Rue Kadera laughed. "The P.M. was adamant on that."

A Toyota pulled out of a parking slot. Laurence took the space immediately. He rolled down the window and slumped back on the seat, looking into the steamy Washington afternoon. "We've got almost two hours before Karpov arrives. We have to talk. Chambliss first, then the multinationals."

"What can you do to Chambliss?" Perini asked.

Laurence sighed. "I don't know, Eddie. There's a hell of a lot more questions than that. For example, how long has he been a seller? What else has he sold and to whom? Who's been hurt besides us? The British? The West Germans? All of NATO?"

"Back plumb," Perini said.

"From faucet to well. If the British are hurt they have to know. The same with our other allies." Laurence fell silent.

Perini shifted in the seat. "So you're asking yourself what happens when he finds out?"

"Eddie, he just fucking can't find out. Excuse me, Rue."

"Chambliss would go to ground, defect," Rue said.

"Worse."

"What's worse?" She looked surprised.

"Later he'd defect, sure, but worse if he finds out now."

"What happens if he finds out now?" Perini asked.

"If he finds out now he tells my cousin about the enzyme."

Rue Kadera turned her head to one side. "You haven't discussed this with your President?"

Laurence grinned. "No, and I'm not going to if I can help it."

Rue looked bewildered. "You're making this decision by yourself. Your cousin is President of the United States."

"If word gets out it's my butt, not his. He's in the clear."

"So what do we do about Chambliss?" asked Perini.

"Nothing for now. We let him sit. When this is over you and I will do the back plumbing ourselves and arrange for an early retirement for Chambliss. For health reasons, something like that."

"When this is over I go back to writing about basketball."

"No, when we finish the plumbing you go back to writing about basketball."

"I was just throwing darts, for Chrissakes, and I wind up plumbing the number two man in the CIA. What about Arnaud Mobelier?"

"What would you do about the enzyme if you were one of Arnaud's clients?"

Perini rolled and unrolled his Irish walking hat. "I'd go for the enzyme. I'd form a cartel with those corporations who sprung for Chambliss's fee. I'd hire some brains to tell me the most efficient and culturally acceptable crops to process with it. I'd make a whole lot of bucks." Perini grinned broadly as he raked in imaginary greenbacks.

"And you?" Laurence asked Rue. "What would you do?"

"You'd have an industrial security problem that would be something else. This is not a complicated process like manipulating

DNA. This is out there in nature, out there for the asking."

"The P.M.'s economist concluded we'd be overrun by Third Worlders, I take it."

"That was his feeling."

"He thinks we should get rid of it?"

"This heat is outrageous," Rue said. "Yes, that's our feeling."

Perini shook his head. "Nobody has ever gone wrong in this country by overestimating the avarice of corporation executives. I'm sure German and British executives are no different. With a profit like manna could produce they'd convince themselves they could handle security."

"What if he's right?" Rue asked Laurence.

"If he's right, they'll be competing with the Cubans." Laurence started the car. "We'll see what Karpov has to say."

They rolled up the windows and Laurence turned on the air conditioning. Thus protected from the debilitating heat, they drove to National Airport to meet the head of the KGB.

Valery Karpov looked smaller than he seemed in photographs Laurence had seen of him. He had black hair, a high forehead, black eyebrows, and a well-trimmed black beard. Laurence had spent his life among powerful and well-known people: writers, entertainers, politicians. There was always a shock when a myth or legend appeared in the flesh; mortal, they were curious figures, unrelated somehow to people you saw on television or in a movie theater. It was almost shocking when Laurence first met and shook hands with an American President, the one before his cousin. So it was when Laurence first spotted Karpov, wearing a natty fedora and carrying a leather attaché case. Laurence knew Karpov also must be thinking that Laurence—the implacable, scheming, cunning enemy—was a real person.

Karpov was accompanied by a tall man with slightly hunched shoulders, suspicious eyes, and thin lips. Laurence wasn't surprised. Although Karpov hadn't mentioned bringing anyone with him, Laurence knew he would.

"How was the flight?" Laurence shook Karpov's hand.

"Fine, fine," Karpov said. "This is Vasily Rubashov."

Rubashov watched a crowd surge down the corridor. "Your airport's crowded," he said.

Laurence offered Rubashov a hand. "Pleased to meet you."

Rubashov looked at Karpov and shook Laurence's hand weakly.

"We have three airports around the capital," said Laurence. "Dulles, Baltimore-Washington, and National here. National's the closest, so it's overused. It's hard to get people to try the others."

"Capitalists never plan," Rubashov said.

"We muddle through," Laurence said.

"Where do I pick up my luggage?" Karpov asked.

"Down the hall here. Good to meet you. We should have met long ago."

"I think so," Karpov said.

Rubashov followed Laurence and Karpov, watching the surge of businessmen and lobbyists with interest. Laurence led them to the luggage area, where suitcases tumbled off a belt onto a revolving circular pickup around which the passengers from the commuter flight had gathered. The passengers were part of an army of men in neckties encamped in Washington to ensure that the public purse remained bloated and accessible to them and their friends. The three men said nothing while they waited for the Russians' luggage to tumble from the belt.

"Very efficient," Karpov said.

Rubashov looked at him. "We could have helped the workers unload. All this money, wasted. Are your farms this efficient, Mr. Laurence, or do overworked Negroes grow the food for all these men in neckties? There's mine." He slipped through the crowd to collect a leather bag from the tray.

"*Svoloch!*" Karpov muttered.

Laurence leaned toward him. "What's that mean?"

Karpov smiled. "Translated, maybe asshole, maybe motherfucker. Depends on the circumstance."

"This time?"

"Just asshole. He gets worse."

"You didn't have a choice?"

"None without expanding need. I should have expanded need by one and had Rubashov shot."

Laurence blinked.

"A joke, Mr. Laurence."

"I understand. There are people who work for me I'd like to shoot too. Right now we have to get ready to catch another plane."

CHAPTER

18

WHILE ATHOS, PORTHOS, AND ARAMIS MAY have been the three best blades in the service of the King's Guard, Louis XIII was small bucks compared to the clients of Arnaud Mobelier. When you're talking everything from breadsticks to cornflakes you don't rely on romantics with feathers on their hats. The only honor among corporations is profit and expansion—anything less is quaint at best. Honor is dollars and cents. As for the manna enzyme, well . . .

D'Artagnan need not apply.

William Pumphries should not have been surprised that James Chambliss drew the names and cable addresses of deJonette, Cardinal, and Scanlan from his jacket pocket as though they were dates who did it on the first night out.

There are professionals and there are politicals. When the manna enzyme is at stake, the men you want should be dispassionate and careful. Professionals do a job. Politicals believe in causes. The distinction is crucial.

A professional has no loyalty except to the

employer of the moment—no commitment to truth, to justice, to any ennobling idea of a better world. When an annoying wart must be excised—such as Patrice Lumumba in the Congo—there are people who can make the hit and not be traced. Politicals are marked by the crazies, zealots, and religious fanatics of the world, followers of the IRA, the PLO, the Red Brigade—people who believe there is something to be gained by swapping a civilian dictator for a colonel, or a colonel for a Marxist. Politicals live and die by the abstract; they are prepared to enter battle carrying any weapon they can get their hands on.

While professionals may be callous and cynical, they are not foolhardy. The best—in keeping with their status and reputation—will enter battle only with the best and most appropriate weapons available. As Chambliss knew well, deJonette, Cardinal, and Scanlan would probably request as starters an American-made Ingram M10, which can be silenced and fire 9mm cartridges at 1,200 rounds per minute, or the American-made M21 sniper rifle that can prang someone from 300 yards. There is the quiet, British-made Sterling Mark 5, the German-built Heckler & Hoch MP5SD2, used against the Black September terrorists in the 1972 Olympic Village murders. A good choice for sniping, assault, or even grenade launching is the Colt XM177E2 or, perhaps better yet, the Israeli Galil assault rifle, which fires 650 rounds of 5.56mm cartridges per minute at

3,000 feet per second. The Galil was used in the freeing of the hostages at Entebbe.

When the young man delivered Jan deJonette's cable, deJonette was in the middle of doing coke. He tipped the young man, read the cable, smiled, and rearranged the coke with a single-edged razor blade. One of the pleasures of doing coke was arranging and rearranging it in patterns with a razor blade. The coke was bright white on the mirror; it was aesthetically pleasing. DeJonette leaned to within inches of the mirror and, being careful not to breathe on it, chopped it finer and finer. He was in no hurry. Anticipation was part of the ritual. DeJonette pushed the coke left and then right with the blade. He moved the blade in an arc and left a half-moon on the mirror. He pushed it into one, two, three, four lines then back to two, then one. He chopped it some more, then leaned back on his chair to appreciate the red-tiled roofs of the villas below him. It was a bright white, hot day in Capetown. The sea and the sky were pale blue. There was no humidity. Later, he would go to one of the resort hotels with his Porsche and his money. He would pick up a girl with delicious nipples and firm ass and return to his villa; failing that he would simply hire one.

DeJonette was an object of curiosity in the world of professional soldiers, a world whose members are routinely acknowledged to be misfits, malcontents, and psychopaths. He was an intellectual—or at least he had begun that way. Jan deJonette had earned a doctoral degree in psychology from the Univer-

sity of Brussels. As a youngster, he had won
a scholarship offered by the Belgian government to the sons and daughters of Belgian
soldiers. It surprised no one that when he
was twenty-six deJonette received an appointment at the Sorbonne in Paris. He
spoke Spanish and German in addition to
Walloon and French, immersed himself in
Arabic, and at age twenty-eight was in the
mountains of Bolivia with the French scholar
Régis Debray interviewing Che Guevara and
his comrades. DeJonette was interested in
the mind of the guerrilla. What was it, he
asked the readers of French scholarly jour-
nals, that motivated the terrorist? There was
religious passion, economic injustice, hatred
so old that its cause was forgotten. DeJonette's
articles grew increasingly bitter: history was
a lie; the principal actors were liars or fools.

In 1973, the economist Robert Heilbroner
published a provocative essay in *The New
York Review of Books* called "The Human
Prospect," in which he forecast that terrorists—scrambling for the scraps of dwindling supplies of world resources—would one
day hold the world at bay. The saddened
Heilbroner concluded that given the circumstances the only solution in the end was a
regimented, Orwellian world not unlike that
of China. One month later, *The New York
Times Book Review* examined—in a front-
page essay—a book called *The Mind of the
Terrorist*, written by a man named A.J.R.
Wedmore, which was, the reviewer noted, a
pseudonym. It was a definitive work, he said,
awesome in its perceptions. Wedmore knew

his terrorists. The real author was Jan deJonette, who had lived, loved, and killed with terrorists in Latin America, Africa, and Asia. On the Sunday of the review in the *Times*, deJonette was on the West Bank with Arabs shooting up an Israeli settlement. He never returned to the Sorbonne.

DeJonette—the Professor to his colleagues in the mean streets of Marseilles, Macao, and Montreal—had once gotten high on ideas, on notions of an ordered, more perfect world. The intellectual struggles of academe, he concluded, were so far removed from genuine passion as to be laughable. So deJonette took refuge in the baser thrills: in dope, in sex, in murder. Sex made him high. He either found that or bought it. Dope was on the market also. Sex and drugs are common enough pleasures, enjoyed in one form or other by most people. Murder was simply exquisite; there was no other word for it. It was made even more grand for deJonette because governments, malcontents, and psychopaths all over the world paid him handsomely to risk his life, inducing in the process a lovely surge of adrenaline throughout his body.

DeJonette separated part of the coke and laid it out in two thin, neat lines. He contemplated it, pushed the mirror aside, slid Pink Floyd into his tape deck, and turned the volume nearly as high as it would go. He took a small white tube from a packet on his desk and did both lines, first the left nostril, forefinger closing the right, then the right, forefinger closing the left. He leaned back

THE MANNA ENZYME   171

and felt the lower registers of Pink Floyd's
marvelous moog wash across his body. These
were deJonette's fifth and sixth lines; it was
good coke. It was expensive but the price
was nothing for entertainers, professional
athletes, jet-setters, and mercenaries.

DeJonette swallowed once, then again, feeling the coke in his sinuses. He wet his
forefinger with his tongue and ran the finger
across the powdery residue where the two
lines had been; he ran the finger across the
gums above his front teeth. The coke tasted
sour.

When deJonette got high, he liked to remember times past. He remembered cutting
an African politician in half with a British-
made Sten Mark II. DeJonette had been in
the pay of a man he assumed to be from the
KGB. He didn't ask questions—Russian
money spent just as well as American. He
remembered that the politician—a thick-
lipped, yellow-eyed black man who covered
himself with medals and called himself a
field marshal—had pursed his lips in surprise before deJonette pulled the trigger.
DeJonette couldn't miss with a Sten at four
feet. He regarded the field marshal as an
animal who spoke French.

DeJonette had taken the field marshal un-
awares when the black man was touring the
provinces in a Rolls-Royce to cheer up people who were starving. The state radio talked
incessantly about the trip. Even tribesmen
who had no radios were rounded up, required to wash, and forced to line the two
parallel paths in the dirt that served as a

road in the interior. DeJonette picked a town where there were enough Europeans for him to achieve some anonymity and waited.

Three months later, in the pay of the French, he murdered the field marshal's left-wing successor. The left-winger's name, deJonette remembered, was Mgubu, and he hardly seemed different from the first. As far as deJonette could tell their rhetoric was the same. He wondered why the Russians or French cared. No matter.

The shooting of Mgubu didn't require a lot of finesse. DeJonette rode a bicycle to the hotel where the field marshal was staying. The bicycle had a basket on the handlebars that carried an Ingram M10 folded neatly in a paper bag. The African's bodyguards were smoking and shooting dice at the entrance to the hotel. DeJonette slipped behind them unnoticed. He assembled the M10, fitted it with a Sionics noise suppressor in an alcove, and murdered Mgubu in bed while Mgubu's mistress watched, wide-eyed. DeJonette motioned the mistress onto her stomach with his hand, which she did. He took her in the anus while she moved her rump in small circles in an effort to please him. DeJonette wasted her with the Ingram also and murdered the guards on his way out. No one saw him; he rode his bicycle back to a European bar where he drank gin. Mgubu's mistress and the killing excited him. He hired two black prostitutes to spend the night with him. He saw to it that they earned their pay.

DeJonette separated more coke with his razor blade and formed two more neat lines, one for each nostril. The Mgubu hit had been fun. He smiled at the memory.

He almost forgot his cable. He read it again. The language smacked of Langley. The Americans weren't bad sorts. He'd do it.

He had a first name but R. Cardinal never used it. An initial was enough for him. R. Cardinal, he called himself, pronouncing it slowly, lingering on the R. It was pretentious and theatrical but people waited until later to laugh. R. Cardinal lacked the social graces. He thought only of himself and was impressed. As some men are born without feet, without hands, or without eyes, so apparently was R. Cardinal born lacking any capacity for human compassion.

As you could learn from dossiers in London, Bonn, Moscow Center, Langley, or Peking, R. Cardinal's first name was Ronald. Cardinal thought Ronald sounded British public school and possibly homosexual, so he never used it. Cardinal was six feet tall, slender, and had a mop of curly brown hair on his head that looked like a transplant of pubic hair. When he smiled his eyes narrowed and his parted lips revealed two large front teeth, so that he inevitably reminded people of a grinning rodent.

Cardinal carried his curly head at a proud angle, chin up. More than one impartial R. Cardinal watcher had concluded he was a chronic sufferer of gaseous intestines. A British agent once remarked, spitefully, knowing that R. Cardinal was eavesdropping, that his problem was even lower down.

"The reason he looks that way is his arsehole, poor bugger. A homosexual, I'd wager. Hemorrhoids. Christ, can you imagine anything as awful as that? Objects up the old hole. Ouch! I can see him grinning. Rather ratlike what with those front teeth, wouldn't you say?"

R. Cardinal, believing he was covert, could say nothing. He was enraged.

The agent's friend wished they were in a position to see how Cardinal was taking it. "That's rich, Roddy. Had his fudge packed, eh?"

Cardinal's chin moved even higher.

"Fudge. Packed right in there." The first man laughed.

Cardinal got even by murdering both men three weeks later. It wasn't part of a contract. He did it for fun, like some people work crossword puzzles or eat ice cream.

Cardinal's father was Italian, from which, it was said, he inherited his love of violence. His mother was Danish. When his parents were killed in an automobile accident while on vacation in Nice, R. Cardinal inherited a tire recapping company in Genoa and a flat in Copenhagen. He sold the tire recapping company and moved to Denmark.

He took Pumphries's cable to the Tivoli, the amusement park in the heart of Copenhagen. There, looking slightly ridiculous eating asparagus soup with an imperious tilt to his head, he studied the proposition. The soup was good, so was the cheese and Carlsberg beer. But Cardinal—code-named Leper by the CIA—wasn't thinking of food. He was being asked to team with Jan deJonette. In the business eleven years, Cardinal had often heard of the legendary Belgian, but had never met him. They had both worked for the Russians, the British, the Americans, as well as the PLO and ad hoc terrorist groups.

"It's either you or deJonette, depending on who you ask," a Moroccan freelance had once told him, retelling largely apocryphal tales of prowess with automatic weapons.

"They say I'm better with explosives," R. Cardinal had replied, slightly miffed.

The Moroccan freelance had a sense of humor but he hadn't survived as an assassin by being stupid. He didn't laugh. One did not laugh at R. Cardinal. Instead, he picked his nose, wiped it on the wall, and said, "They say it's even money with the explosives, R. Either way, I steer clear of guys who blow people up." He looked serious, blinking once, twice. He took a hit on his hashish pipe.

Cardinal smiled at the compliment: even money with an automatic rifle between himself and deJonette. The Moroccan was okay but he had brown skin and oily sweat on his nose. He smoked hashish. Cardinal didn't know how the Moroccan could be very smart, being brown and all. His sweaty nose was disgusting: Cardinal was accustomed to pale, dry Danes. He would have preferred that the compliment had come from a European, an East German maybe. East Germans knew what it was to be tough.

Cardinal's new employers, knowing the rivalry between himself and deJonette, had avoided touchy questions of pride, seniority, and reputation by putting Colonel Mikki Scanlan in charge. Mikki Scanlan. R. Cardinal smiled his rodent smile. The people who sent the telegram had a very important job in mind. They wanted the Pelé and Johan Cruyff of professional soldiers in front of the net; they had them in deJonette and Cardinal.

Mikki Scanlan was something else again.

Scanlan had apprenticed with the IRA. He first used drag as cover in a Belfast gay bar where he murdered a porcine British officer who used a cigarette holder. The Brit had come by his sexual tastes in a public school. The IRA, however, was too confining for Scanlan's tastes. He moved to Amsterdam, where his Dutch mother had returned after his father's death, and went freelance. He became an airline pilot, the better to hijack airliners, and once buzzed Tel Aviv in a DC-10. The Israelis could do nothing; there were more than 150 people on board, including the Polish national women's basketball team. That buzzing alone made Scanlan's reputation. After that his prices went up and he began calling himself Colonel. Everybody went along with the fiction. After all, why not?

Mikki Scanlan, having agreed to take the Goldman job, needed pocket money for the trip to New York. He put on an outfit he had recently bought in a Piccadilly boutique, found himself a sleazy Amsterdam bar, and waited. He eyed himself in the mirror behind the bar. It was a handsome mirror. Mikki took a lipstick out of his purse and gave his lips a touch-up. It was time, Mikki knew, for the guy next to him to make a move.

The man, in his early forties and paunchy, cleared his throat. "Say, do you speak English?" he asked hesitantly.

"Why sure, honey," Colonel Scanlan said, and smiled.

The man's left cheek twitched nervously. He made an involuntary sucking sound with his pink lips. "What do you do?" he said in a hurry.

"Why I do a whole lot of things. You'd be surprised, Mister? . . ."

"Well," the man paused. "Dooby." His hand moved to his chin.

"Mr. Dooby. Do you have a first name, Mr. Dooby?"

The man, who was British, relaxed somewhat. "Rigby. Rigby Dooby. I'm an accountant for a hospital in Brighton."

"That's nice," said Mikki Scanlan. He couldn't believe anybody could have such a fucked name. Christ! He showed Rigby Dooby some thigh. An accountant!

Dooby couldn't decide if he wanted his hand on his chin or on the bar. He couldn't take his eyes off Mikki's thigh.

"Ah, do you, do you . . . ?" Mr. Dooby was uncertain as to how he should proceed and left the sentence unfinished.

Mikki saw he needed help. "Like I said. I do a whole lot of things." He gave Rigby Dooby a smile that was without ambiguity.

Dooby's breathing quickened perceptibly.

"Ah, I was thinking of sex." He took a deep, nervous breath. There, he had said it.

"I thought that, Mr. Rigby Dooby. I think I should tell you, though, I only go once a night and it's expensive."

"Whatever," said Dooby quickly.

Mikki Scanlan adjusted his bra, which was too tight under the arms. "Let me see your wallet."

Stupidly, Dooby gave it to him, thinking for some odd reason that he had to prove his identity.

Mikki lazily eyed the thick wad of pound notes. "I have a lovely room," he breathed. "With equipment."

"Equipment?" Dooby looked eager.

"For whatever your heart desires, love. Satisfaction guaranteed." Mikki slipped off the bar stool and led the way, doing his woman's walk. Rigby Dooby followed, his eyes on Mikki's ass. They walked past seamen's bars and crowded cafés smelling of Indonesian food until Scanlan turned, at last, up a dimly lit side street.

"Are we close?" asked Dooby.

Scanlan turned suddenly, grabbed Rigby Dooby by the collar and pinned him high against a brick wall. Dooby hung there like a great corpulent doll. "Having a good time, Mr. Dooby?"

Dooby said nothing. His mouth was open, his eyes wide. He let out a fart. "Excuse me," he said politely.

"Are you here with your wife?" Scanlan asked.

"Yes," said Dooby, whose face was swelling from trapped blood and lack of oxygen.

"How old is she?"

"Uh, thirty-six now."

"Good fucking?"

Dooby made a small sound.

"Take me to her. First, give me your money."

Dooby did as he was told. Later, with his hands tied behind him, he watched as Mikki Scanlan raped his wife. Rape made Mikki high. It was his seventeenth rape, something like that. He had lost count.

Mikki Scanlan, teamed with Jan deJonette and R. Cardinal; it was a dream trio, and he was in commnd. Mikki knew there would be great stories afterward. It would be legendary. Scanlan cut Rigby Dooby's throat while his wife watched, paralyzed.

"Please," she begged. Her breasts were too large. They hung pathetically on her ribs, covered with Scanlan's sweat.

"If women didn't have cunts there'd be a bounty on them," he said.

"Please."

Mikki Scanlan cut her throat too.

CHAPTER

19

FIDEL CASTRO WAS LARGE ENOUGH AS IT WAS. Stuff him and his two comrades in the rear seat of a Plymouth and it was just too much. But the cabbie wasn't about to let anyone ride up front with him. They were big mothers, he noted, Latinos. Puerto Ricans, probably. Carmine Petrocelli's cab had been ripped off three times in two years. He had a wife and two kids to support. He took no chances.

Fidel Castro sat stolidly in the middle, watching the row houses of Queens slide by on the way to Kennedy Airport. The lawns, shrubs, and two-car garages of the American Dream were nowhere to be seen. Castro saw hard-edged concrete housing projects in the distance. The freeway was crowded with traffic. The drivers, most of them alone in a Japanese- or German-made car—the better to beat the high price of gasoline—hurried to families and mistresses waiting in Nassau.

On Castro's left sat his old friend Jaime Rivera. Rivera was a stout, round-bodied man with a puffy face, swollen jowls, and thin blond hair that needed washing. He

180

laughed constantly with a disconcerting snort as he sucked air past the openings of his sinuses.

Jaime Rivera, trained as a lawyer as was Castro, had been with Fidel from the beginning, since the assault on Moncada Barracks, since the voyage of the *Granma* from Tuxpan on the Mexican coast, since the Sierra Maestra. Rivera was cautious, a brake on Fidel's excesses.

On Castro's right was Arturo Dann, a hard-nosed Marxist intellectual. Dann had been with Che Guevara when Che was killed in Bolivia. He was a broad, lean man with shoulder-length black hair parted in the middle. Known as the most radical of Castro's inner circle, Dann was much in demand as a speaker in Third World countries, partly because he had been a confidant of the martyred Che, partly because of his ability to stir crowds with outrageous speeches. It wasn't simply that he was theatrical. Dann had a feel for language. He was a poet of sorts, and people recognized it. There were those who envied his friendship with Castro and who claimed his speeches were a joke on Dann's inferiors, people who thought like sheep. If they believed Castro would have cared, Dann's enemies would have told Fidel how his friend loved to bed down Marxist groupies overwhelmed by the idea of sleeping with a man who had been there, in the Sierra Maestra, in the beginning. Even worse, they might have told Castro that Dann insisted that such young women be made available as a price for his performances.

Once, on a visit to a rally in Nicaragua, Dann received a howling, cheering ovation for calling the United States "a punctured prophylactic fucking the prostituted body of this hemisphere!" Afterward, he went to bed with two Nicaraguan girls at once. Dann lay back, eyes closed, and welcomed their tongues. The alliteration is what did it, he later told Castro, referring to the speech, not the girls, whose names were María and Marta.

Castro would have enjoyed hearing about the girls. He was himself a boring speaker, known for long, tedious efforts. He was tired of hearing about Dann's great speeches. He was envious of Dann's charisma on the podium.

They were together now, the three of them again. When they were, Dann and Castro did most of the talking. Rivera preferred to listen.

"I wouldn't want to live here," Castro said.

"No," Dann said.

Rivera tugged at his underwear with his left hand.

"I remember the big Buicks they used to drive," Dann said. "Big Lincolns and Mercuries, Cadillacs with hoods fifteen feet long. Mama had to have a station wagon. Do you remember the ads in the magazines? A skinny woman always, no tits or ass, and those kids, perfect things, smiling all the time."

"And the man." Castro laughed.

"*Sí*, the man. In a suit with a little hat, the tie all clinched down and everything. Straight nose. Perfect teeth."

Rivera grinned. "Dad's leaning against the lawn mower, beaming."

"Not with a suit. You're getting the ads mixed up," Castro said.

"You're right, *sí*. He's wearing a sweater and trousers. No denim, and sneakers."

"Leaning against the lawn mower?" Castro asked.

"Yes, and the wife has a look of joy on her face. Her arms are outstretched and she's looking at a great juggernaut that gets four miles a gallon."

The cabdriver, who had shown no inclination to talk, turned his head briefly and looked at Castro. "Madison Avenue baastids. Fuckahs suck!" He ran his hand over his head.

"*Sí*," said Castro. He wanted to hear what the cabbie had to say.

"You guys P.R.?"

"We're from Costa Rica. Coffee."

"Really? I knew a chick from Costa Rica once. Jesus!" He started to say something more but thought better of it and fell silent.

"Well?" asked Castro.

The cabdriver looked embarrassed. "You guys bein' from the same country and all best to keep my fuckin' mouth shut."

"You were about to tell us she was good in bed," Castro said.

The cabdriver laughed. He was visibly relieved. "Now that you mention it, I was gonna tell ya she gave great head. Great, soft strokes. Fuckin' near blew my mind."

Castro, Dann, and Rivera all laughed.

"Always thought it was because she practiced on bananas," said the cabdriver. He was getting into it.

Castro, Dann, and Rivera all laughed again. Castro wanted to smash the cabbie's skull. So did Dann and Rivera.

"In the Sierras it was only bullets," Castro whispered into Rivera's ear.

"*Sí*, you could fight bullets," Rivera said softly.

They said nothing then. They watched the buildings in the distance.

Finally, Dann cleared his throat. "It was 1955, wasn't it, the first time? Not counting the UN trips later."

Castro smiled. "Yes, 1955, here for money to fight Batista. You were with me."

"So was I," Rivera said.

"Yes, you also. But that wasn't my first time in America, you know."

"No?" Rivera looked at Castro in surprise and turned his head at an angle.

Castro held up a finger. "You forget, my friend, that Mirta and I honeymooned in Miami in 1948."

Rivera and Dann laughed, then fell silent for the remainder of the ride.

At the airport the cabbie said, "Costs a few, gents," and motioned to his meter.

Dann paid the bill, shaking his head.

"Things're fuckin' tough all over," said the cabbie.

An hour later they were strapped three abreast in a Boeing 747 that circled north then west over Long Island then ascended over New Jersey, headed for the blackness

over Pennsylvania, and beyond that O'Hare
Field in Chicago. When the stewardess came
by with a refreshment cart, Dann bought
four miniatures of rum, four of bourbon, and
four of scotch. The rums were for Castro, the
bourbons for Rivera. Dann kept the scotch for
himself and happily opened his complimen-
tary package of smoked almonds.

Castro watched Dann pour his miniature
over ice in a plastic cup. "Gringo!" he hissed,
and laughed. He didn't care about Dann's
vices. Dann had been one of the twelve in the
Sierra Maestra when they ate red beans and
drank pond water laced with cow piss. They
sipped their miniatures, ate their smoked
almonds, and watched the lights of an occasional town below until, one after another,
tired passengers doused the reading lamps
on the bulkheads above them. Castro, Dann,
and Rivera switched theirs off but remained
awake.

It was Dann who spoke first. "On the
Granma the food was soaked the second
hour out."

"Playa Coloradas," Castro said.

"November twenty-fifth, 1956," Dann said.

"Raúl should be with us," Castro laughed.

Dann took a sip of scotch. "And Che—
Che'd have a helluva time."

Castro looked at Dann. Che was dead and
Raúl had cancer. "Che took too many chances.
I knew it would kill him in the end."

Dann finished his fourth bottle of scotch.
"I wonder if I can just walk back there and
buy some more."

Castro had long ago tired of talking about

Che, who was fortunate enough to die a martyr while he, Fidel, had to go on with the struggle of running a country so poor it had to depend on the Soviet dole. "The *Granma* was on the Tuxpan River. I had to borrow money to buy her."

"She made it," Dann said.

"And that gringo from UPI reported that Raúl and I had been killed. Batista's doing, the liar."

Rivera, who had said nothing, crushed an ice cube between his molars and observed, "*¡Cabrón!*"

Castro and Dann laughed.

"We should have Colonel Bayo here to help us out, tell us about the mountains, how to move at night and sleep in the day, how to hit quickly and disappear." The bourbon had given Rivera a slight glow.

"How to convince a *New York Times* reporter we had a company of men when we only had twelve," Dann said.

"Eighteen then, I think," Castro said.

"Whatever."

Castro looked out of the window at another small town far below. "People said I should have listened to Bayo a little more. Maybe it would have gone easier for us. We're going to mountains again. We know mountains." Castro liked to talk big. He always had. He had talked big before the debacle at Moncada Barracks on July 26, 1953, the inspiration of the July 26 Movement in the cities that in the end made his victory possible. They had assembled at a chicken farm near Siboney, just outside Santiago. There were 167 of them, including two women: three were killed; 68 captured and executed; 32 served prison terms, including Castro, who served 22 months on the Isle of Pines. It was there where Castro, who as a lawyer was able to stand in his own defense, gave his famous *La Historia Me Absolverá* speech, the expanded and rewritten version of which was to become the manifesto for the revolution against Fulgencio Batista.

Fifty had escaped the raid on Moncada Barracks. Dann was among them. Although he was a brave man and fought well, he always felt guilty for his good fortune.

"*Sí*, mountains are mountains and we know mountains," he said.

CHAPTER

20

As soldiers for centuries have cleaned their weapons carefully before battle, so as not to die by misfire, so deJonette snorted coke if it was available and convenient. If not, he took amphetamines. He took speed so as not to die by mistake, the risk of a tired mind. Professor deJonette did not buy street speed. He bought his amphetamines from a London chemist who ran a mail-order business for the right people. The chemist sold pink pills half the size of an aspirin tablet. The pills had a small crease on top. DeJonette called them Bujus after an Ibo with whom he had fought in the Biafran war. Buju lisped, revealing the tip of a tongue startling in its pinkness. On top of that he never slept: hence, Bujus.

The amphetamines filled deJonette's brain with a buzz at first. Later, his mind raced and soared. He couldn't study or concentrate but he was able to think faster, move more quickly, and go without food or sleep for days if necessary. He used cocaine for sex, usually, reserving speed for work.

DeJonette shaved with a straight razor, which he sharpened on a leather strap, a skill he learned from his father, who was a sergeant major in the Belgian Army. There was a certain pleasure in running the cutting edge along his jaw. Besides, the razor had twice doubled as a weapon. Both victims were sleeping; deJonette laid their throats open with neat, quick strokes. He shaved with his straight razor, showered, excised a blackhead from his left shoulder, and waxed his mustache, which swept upward at the ends. There were those who said he should pose for a whiskey ad but they never said so to deJonette.

He dabbed a modest amount of Aramis cologne on the hollow above his collar bone, studied a map of the state of Oregon, and took a Buju. He relaxed, yawned as usual, and waited for the buzzing to come. He would take another Buju after they had arrived on the West Coast. Now it was time to meet Cardinal and Scanlan at Kennedy Airport. A Langley rep would be there with the weapons they had requested. DeJonette would rent a car and find a place to park near the airport. There, he would assemble his weapons—he had requested an Israeli Galil assault rifle and an American M21 for sniping—check the mechanisms, and break them down to be packed in his Samsonite traveler for the trip to Portland in the hold of a Boeing 727. DeJonette knew better than to use a john stall for this chore; the vice cops often had the stalls staked out, looking for queers and fruitcakes strayed from gay bars.

Mikki Scanlan's preparations for the flight to Portland were more elaborate than deJonette's, because he shaved, lacked breasts and had a narrow pelvis. Well, there was the presence of his plumbing too, but Scanlan wore skirts whenever he could so that was taken care of. Scanlan was a homosexual—he dreamed about men—but talked incessantly of tits and ass so he could call himself a bisexual. His use of drag, he said, was merely effective cover. Nobody argued with him. What was the point? The word, though, was that it was wise to keep your back to the wall with Mikki Scanlan around.

It took Scanlan a full two hours to fix his face in the morning. That was just his face. He had to fit the pads that gave him hips and a proper butt. Then there were the pantyhose, foam-rubber breasts, C-cup bra, and the rest. That might have been excessive if Scanlan had a boyfriend but he didn't. He was a loner. He liked putting on makeup. It gave him privacy, time to be by himself. He regarded the application of makeup as an unrecognized art form.

Mikki Scanlan viewed himself as an artist.

The biggest problem was his face; Scanlan had a beard that rasped after four hours. The problem in the morning was to shave as close as possible, then fill the pores with foundation. Scanlan used Natural Glow, a brand advertised in *Cosmo*. He began by washing his face with a nonallergenic soap. An experienced drag queen had given him instruction in his IRA days: "Regular soap is just too rough, Mikki. It just won't come off your face. Ooooh!" The drag queen had made a face.

Natural Glow came next. He used the maximum so as to fill the pores where the whisker stumps waited. By midafternoon Scanlan would have to wash his jaws again and redo that portion of his face. After Natural Glow came Cover Up, which he used to fill the cracks around his eyes. Then Scanlan applied highlighter—high on his cheekbones and above his eyes on the outside corners. This also was on the advice of the drag queen, who explained to him the strengths and weaknesses of his face. Scanlan had bluish eyes, which he liked to appear almond-shaped. That required plucking his eyebrows, which he now did, and curling his eyelashes with a special curler. He then gave shape to his eyebrows with a pencil and applied highlighter both above and below his eyes with a padded applicator.

Having done this, Mikki Scanlan leaned back in his chair, dug at his crotch, squinted his eyes, and regarded his handiwork so far. He smiled, leaned forward again, and outlined the shape of his woman's lips with a thin brush such as might be used by an artist for detail work. He then applied lipstick with a small brush. The thin red border kept the lipstick from running. Mikki Scanlan did not want to be tacky.

Eyeshadow followed his lips; he applied the eyeshadow to the natural curve above and below his eyes. He blended the eyeshadow in with his fingers, wiping his hands on a towel periodically. He then applied mascara to his eyelashes and eyeshadow on the top of the skin covering the bottom of his eyes. He followed that with eyebrow pencil on the skin just below his eyelashes. He then highlighted his cheekbones with blush and blended in his morning's effort with a soft pad.

He was finished. Mikki Scanlan leaned back once again to admire his work. He put on his foundation garments and a chic woman's suit. He was ready for the flight to Portland.

R. Cardinal's morning was far simpler than either deJonette's or Scanlan's. He simply got up, showered, shaved, and spent ten minutes admiring himself in the mirror. Cardinal was proud of his jaw. He had one where many people didn't. He believed jawless people were weak. They had no chins, so were dumb. The worst of them had Adam's apples that bobbed up and down when they swallowed. R. Cardinal was disgusted by them. They were inferior people who had somehow survived. He turned his face to the left and to the right. Yes, he had a handsome jaw. Cardinal looked at his digital wristwatch. It was time to rendezvous with deJonette and Scanlan. DeJonette had a jaw. He was okay. It didn't make any difference whether Scanlan had a jaw or not. Scanlan was something else.

R. Cardinal arrived early, as had deJonette, so he could run a weapons' check and satisfy himself that he was not being tailed. It was impossible to move automatic weapons past customs—he left that to the arms people who supplied the malcontents of the world. So he had to trust Chambliss' arrangements. But Cardinal didn't know Chambliss. He wouldn't have trusted him if he had. He didn't trust anybody. He had once heard, in a Hamburg whorehouse where his profession was taken as casually as women who have sex with dogs, that a West German named Hans Kramer had tried to assassinate a Greek colonel with a British Sten provided by rebels in Athens. The whore who had told him the story, a blonde whose hair was brown at the roots, dabbed politely at eyes that were not moist, and said she was once engaged to marry Kramer.

She paused for effect.

Cardinal waited.

"My life would have been different," she said softly.

Cardinal's chin moved slightly higher. The woman's body was too thin for his taste. He liked nice butts. If she didn't finish her story he would have to beat her.

"The weapon jammed," she said. "The colonel's bodyguards killed Hans."

"He was a fool," Cardinal said. He ran a hand down the prostitute's breast and squeezed.

The woman winced. "He was good at his work."

"He was a fool," Cardinal said again. Cardinal always checked his weapons carefully. He unzipped his pants.

Cardinal was reminded of the whore by a magazine at the airport. A model in *Hustler* magazine had the same hollow look in her eyes as the woman in Hamburg. She had one hand draped languidly over her crotch as was the fashion in skin magazines. Cardinal recalled the story of Hans Kramer, put the magazine down, and checked the estimated departure time of his flight, which was listed on a television screen mounted above the magazine rack. There was time for the remaining magazines. There would be women with oiled bodies, women masturbating, women in lesbian poses. The editors knew the fantasies: they hired the best photographers; they found the sleekest women. Cardinal was looking for the skin in *Penthouse* when he spotted deJonette at the far end of the rack.

DeJonette was browsing through the *Times* and laughing softly to himself. Though Cardinal had never worked with the Professor, he knew what deJonette looked like. He knew that deJonette had once taught at the Sorbonne, had become a mercenary as a result of his research on the psychology of the terrorist. There were those who still wondered whether deJonette was with them or watching them. As Cardinal himself wondered, the Professor looked up from the *Times* and winked at him. "Wonderful magazines these Americans publish, eh, Mr. Cardinal? The color is first-rate."

Cardinal appeared momentarily startled.

"No worry, we're clear," deJonette said.

"You're sure about that?"

"I'm sure."

Cardinal put his *Penthouse* back on the rack. DeJonette was different. Cardinal wondered what had gone wrong in the course of his research. "It's time we should be going, I suppose," said Cardinal. He glanced up at the television monitor.

DeJonette looked up also and smiled. "Yes, I suppose so," he said. He put the *Times* back where it belonged. "See you there, Mr. Cardinal." He paused like he wanted to say something more but didn't.

Cardinal followed deJonette across the terminal and down a long corridor to the gate where their flight was to depart. Cardinal had his place in the world, his reputation, the freedom to take what he chose without guilt. He was cunning, not subtle, but he wanted to know about deJonette. He suspected deJonette of analyzing him, or worse, of laughing at him. If the latter was true, Cardinal would kill him. Now they had a job to do. Cardinal was a professional. The job came first.

Mikki Scanlan was the last of the three to arrive at the departure gate. Mikki turned a lot of male eyes. His walk was lovely, the result of having practiced for hours in front of a mirror as an adolescent. The trick was to walk with the right knee in front of the left, left knee in front of the right until it came naturally. The hips followed, moving this way and that. Mikki could hardly walk like a man anymore. He had bought a smart woman's suit with his Rigby Dooby money, and a dress that clung suggestively. He did

not want to be coarse or tacky. The stakes
were high. He was in charge.

The three of them settled into their seats
without acknowledging the presence of the
others. They waited, adjusting their seat
belts, as the pilot received his instructions
from the control tower. They listened as the
stewardess explained emergency procedures.
The pilot taxied the plane onto a runway;
they waited again to take their turn in line.
Finally, the plane rose into the blackness of
the night and deJonette, Cardinal, and
Scanlan looked down on New Jersey and
Pennsylvania as Castro, Dann, and Rivera
had an hour before. It was Mikki Scanlan,
the man in command, who spoke first: "We
should talk, I think."

"Yes, I should think," said deJonette, who
sat by the window.

Cardinal sat in the middle. "The cable was
vague."

"It was also too clever by half," added
deJonette.

"Langley," Cardinal said.

"Yes, Langley."

Scanlan looked across the aisle, then turned
in his seat. "I assume Langley wrote the
cable. They certainly provided the hardware."

DeJonette looked down on the lights of a
small Pennsylvania town. "So then, our man?"

Scanlan took a small compact out of his
purse and checked his lipstick. He rolled his
lips once and wiped some excess lipstick off
with the end of his little finger. "A man
named Goldman, Professor deJonette." There
was a silence.

"You say Goldman?" Cardinal said.

"I wasn't told much. Where he is."

"Well, what exactly were you told, Colonel?" deJonette asked. "I don't lay my cock on the line for people who play games. I know what you know or you can complete your little adventure with Mr. Cardinal here."

"I agree with the Professor," Cardinal said.

Scanlan sighed. "His name is Goldman. He's a biochemist with a chair at the University of Edinburgh. He's on a visiting appointment at a private college in Portland, Oregon. He likes to fly-fish. He's in the mountains there hiding while the CIA makes up its mind what it's going to do. He's at a place called Diamond Lake, in the southern part of the state."

"What is he? A fin, a peddler, what?"

"You have a good question there, Professor. Judging from the tone of all this, I don't think he eats people. I don't think he's an entrepreneur either."

This was extraordinary. DeJonette was intrigued. "A biochemist, you say?"

Scanlan nodded yes.

DeJonette ran two fingers down the bridge of his nose. "What you're saying, Mikki love, is that a private, supported by Langley, has hired the three best fins in the world to chew a Scot teaching in Portland, Oregon. Now why would they do that?"

Scanlan shrugged.

"Yes, Mikki, why would they? May I call you Mikki?" Cardinal suppressed a grin.

Scanlan was charming. "Yes, darling, you may. The answer is I don't know why. I do

know we take him out in Havana if we miss
him in Portland.''

"Havana? Whoa!" Cardinal rubbed the side
of his face with the palm of his hand.

"Havana, Mr. Cardinal.''

DeJonette cleared his throat. "A biochemist. I don't imagine you know what private
we're working with?''

Scanlan shook his head no.

"Langley's watching or it wouldn't have
arranged the hit.''

"They're watching," said Scanlan.

"The question is why are they staying out
of the water?'' deJonette asked.

"Yes, why indeed. I don't know why I wore
these pumps. They kill my feet on long
flights.''

"If Havana's pulling a snatch, then Moscow Center must want him out for some
reason.''

Cardinal, who had said little, looked puzzled. "Why is that, Professor?''

DeJonette was patient. "Because the Russians've got the Cubans wired. If Goldman is
worth all this commotion and attention from
Langley, then the Russians would either want
him for themselves or want him out. Do you
follow me? Comrade Karpov is a competitor.
If he can't have the cake himself he'll piss on
it out of spite.''

"I see," said Cardinal. He didn't entirely,
but wanted to be known as more than a
technician.

"Moscow Center is not on our itinerary,"
deJonette said.

"Oh!" Cardinal said. He understood. Or

did he? "Why don't the privates let the Russians take care of him?"

"A good question," deJonette said. He looked at Scanlan for an answer.

Cardinal turned his head slightly.

DeJonette was having a good time. "Laurence and Karpov would never play the same game, of course, not really. You have to understand, Mr. Cardinal. Cops want to arrest people. Bureaucrats want larger budgets to waste. Generals want to fight people. There comes a point where Laurence serves himself, not the President. The same is true of Karpov. It's impossible for either of them to enter into a pact for the benefit of both."

"Impossible?" Cardinal asked. Both he and Scanlan knew deJonette was spaced on drugs but they wanted to hear him out. He was brilliant. They knew that by his reputation, his bearing, the assurance with which he spoke. He was of them in the sense only that he was a professional. That and no more.

DeJonette rubbed his eyes. "They believe in nothing, not freedom, not justice, not the State, none of that. They respect only power. They will do anything to gain it. Anything to keep it. As you know I was an academic as a younger man. The game then was to publish so that I might impress my colleagues." DeJonette smiled. "I was good at it but I didn't have any new ideas. Not really. I thought I could learn something in the mountains so I joined Régis in Bolivia. The Bolivians are doomed." DeJonette fell silent.

"What was it Goldman has discovered, do you think?" asked Scanlan. "Why do the

Cubans want him? Why does Langley want
him out?"

"I don't have any idea," said deJonette.

Scanlan spread his fingers on his thighs.
"The privates don't want to risk a Russian
failure."

"Or the Russians agree with Langley,"
deJonette said.

"When was the last time you saw Moscow
Center afraid of the water?" Cardinal asked.
"They're liars, the Russians are. They can lie
and lie and lie and not give a damn whether
anybody believes them or not. I know. I've
worked for them. They'd hit him themselves."

DeJonette sucked on an ice cube. He was
wondering if he needed another Buju. The
conversation was fun. "Let's assume, for the
sport of it, that Langley and Moscow Center
are both watching this, otherwise why the
three of us, why Havana after Portland and
not Moscow?" DeJonette looked at Scanlan.
"If Laurence and Karpov, then Smethurst
too. They all watch one another take a leak.
Perverts."

"Yes, I can follow that. Add the Brits,"
said Scanlan, ignoring Cardinal, who had
started to speak.

"What is it that a biochemist in Portland,
Oregon, could possibly know that would
have Laurence, Karpov, and private playing
the same game? What?" DeJonette was wondering if he had missed something.

"An alchemist, maybe he's an alchemist
who can turn bananas into gold," Scanlan
said.

"Or cigars," Cardinal said.

"Who's backup?" deJonette asked. "Laurence and Karpov always plan for the worst."

"Maybe they'll send Volchak," Cardinal said. He laughed. None of them had ever seen Volchak but they had all heard of him.

"Volchak and Chambliss," said Scanlan. He laughed too.

CHAPTER

21

THERE ARE FEW THINGS MORE UBIQUITOUS ON the American landscape than the motel. The tradition of fine hotels is European; they are of the city, which Europeans regard as civilizing. Americans, owing to geography and history, have tended to the road. The motel is theirs. The signs of the old days of cheap and unlimited gasoline remain yet, rising high above freeways and turnpikes, beckoning motorists to Holiday Inns and Best Westerns.

The Red Lion Inn on the banks of the Columbia River just north of Portland was a first for Valery Karpov. Perini and Rue Kadera, who had slept all the way from Washington in a snarl of arms, legs, and torsos, checked into a room of their own. Karpov and Rubashov examined the suite they were sharing with Laurence with a mixture of awe and bewilderment: there were the water glasses, covered with paper to assure their sanitation; there was the toilet lid, taped shut to assure the guests that

it had been cleaned; there was the coffee pot
and neat little packets of powdered coffee.

Perini said they all needed to relax for a
while. "We'll be back in a jiff," he said as he
led Rue Kadera to the door.

"God, is he randy." She grinned.

Rubashov tested a bed. "Far too soft," he
said.

"A capitalist bed?" asked Laurence.

Karpov grinned.

"This is not a worker's bed," Rubashov
said.

"I've got an idea Eddie and Rue might be
awhile," Laurence said. "You two like a
Coke?"

"Certainly," Karpov said.

"Coke rots the teeth," Rubashov said. He
seemed deep in thought.

When Laurence returned with Cokes from
a machine in the hall, Rubashov still looked
pensive. "What are they doing?" he asked.

"Who is that, Comrade Rubashov?"

Rubashov didn't like Laurence calling him
Comrade. "Your Mr. Perini and the British
lady."

Laurence turned to Karpov. "You're his
superior, Valery. Do you want to tell him?"

Karpov ripped the paper off a water glass
and poured himself some Coke. "I imagine,
Comrade, that they're getting to know one
another."

"We're on a mission," Rubashov said.

Karpov lay back on his bed. "We agreed
we needed to rest, Comrade. Rest."

Rubashov said nothing.

The three of them waited for more than an

hour, their imaginations and hormones racing, until Perini and Rue Kadera returned, grinning and looking slightly foolish. Perini had with him a black canvas bag that had British Airways printed on the side in white letters. He unzipped the bag and removed a blue plastic tube on a polished teak base. The tube had an aluminum pipe near the bottom that stuck out at an angle. Karpov looked at the tube and took a sip of Coke without saying anything. Rubashov picked it up and weighed it in the palm of his hand.

Laurence looked puzzled. "What's that, Eddie?"

"Bong."

"Bong?"

"Bong. Be right back." Perini went into the bathroom and returned with the bottom of the bong filled with water.

"What's a bong?" asked Laurence.

"You smoke?"

They all knew what he was talking about except for Rubashov, who smoked cigarettes and an occasional cigar but never out of a blue plastic tube. Laurence had always wanted to try marijuana but being DCI deprived him of experiences most people took as a matter of course. He had been to parties in Georgetown, where he knew pot was smoked—but it was always in the next room, by people trying to protect him, never in his presence.

"Sure," he lied. He felt suddenly excited, anxious. He had expected to smoke a joint someday but the bong was different, more exotic, more forbidden.

Eddie Perini laughed. He knew from the

look on Laurence's face that Laurence was lying. Perini understood, however. If word got out that Anthony Laurence had smoked dope, it would destroy his career. "And you, my dear?" he gestured to Rue Kadera.

"Joints," she said.

"Joints waste pot," Perini said.

Karpov looked interested. Marijuana. Karpov was a cosmopolitan man. He had read newspapers and magazines from virtually every country of the world. They were delivered to Moscow Center by Tass correspondents, embassy officials, and KGB operatives. "Marijuana," he said.

Rubashov stood and gave Karpov a reproachful look.

"Sit down, Rubashov," Karpov said.

"But, Comrade . . ." Rubashov looked anxious.

"Sit down, I said."

Rubashov sat.

"You may continue if you please, Eddie."

Perini grinned. "Tell you what, Valery Ivanovich Karpov. May I call you Valery Ivanovich?"

"Please do."

Rubashov looked angry. In Russia it was a privilege of intimacy to call another by his first and middle name. Rubashov had never dared to call Karpov Valery Ivanovich.

"Well, Valery Ivanovich, it's always been a fantasy of mine to smoke dope with the head of the KGB—international understanding and all that, cross-cultural communication. Me, Eddie Perini, sportswriter and fuckoff without equal, smoking dope with my friend

Valery Ivanovich. As I said, friends, this is a bong." He held it in his left hand with a flourish. "You don't waste smoke with a bong. One hit's a laughful. No waste. Smoke a joint and the damned thing keeps burning as you pass it around. I've got some good buds here, Colombian. Lots of THC."

"THC?" Karpov held out his hand for the bong, which he took and examined closely. Karpov was a careful man and that was why he had risen so high in the Soviet hierarchy.

"Tetrahydrocanabinol, I believe, is the two-dollar term. It's what gets you high. The trick is to keep the smoke in your lungs as long as possible to soak up the old THC. Smoke from a joint is hot, Valery, burns hell out of your lungs. But hah! Pass it through water and you've got yourself some cool smoke." Perini slid next to Rue. She looped a thigh over his, grinned, and put a hand on the back of his neck. Karpov passed the bong to Laurence, who also examined it carefully. Both Karpov and Laurence were envious of Perini, who was free, free to share a bed with Rue Kadera if he pleased, free to smoke pot if he pleased, free of power, free of responsibility.

Perini took Rue's hand, gave it a squeeze, gave her a wink, and leaned back with a broad grin. "Gentlemen, the blue plastic is the barrel, the aluminum number is the stem. That little hole on the side is the carburetor. Shall we proceed?"

"We proceed," Karpov said.

"Certainly. We're among friends," Laurence said.

"We're among friends—" Perini said.

Rubashov interrupted, "An example of decadence. The people of South America could be growing food to feed their children. We don't drug ourselves in the Soviet Union. I want no part of it."

Karpov thought about the amount of vodka the Russians consumed. "That's fine, Comrade Rubashov. You do what you feel is right."

Rubashov regretted making such a dumb pronouncement. He wanted to try marijuana too but was unable to do anything without prefacing it with the appropriate rhetoric. The ability to preface everything with the currently approved rhetoric was necessary if one wanted to rise in the humorless and suspicious Soviet bureaucracy. He hoped he would be asked again so he could accept with a statement about advancing the spirit of détente.

Perini pulled a clear plastic bag from his British Airways bag. He shifted Rue so she had both her legs over his and he was able to work with both hands on the coffee table. He crushed several marijuana buds with his fingers and raked the seeds to one side with the edge of a matchbook cover. The cover was decorated with a naked woman on a zebra. Perini took a pinch of pot and filled the small bowl at the end of the aluminum stem. "Ahh, the KGB and the CIA. Moscow Center and Langley, innocents both. Watch closely, friends."

Karpov and Laurence watched. Eddie Perini put his finger over the carburetor hole, applied a lit match to the marijuana, and inhaled it in one long, measured draw, the top of the bong around the outside of his mouth. The water churned in the bong. When the last of the marijuana was burned, he lifted his finger from the hole and the smoke zipped into his lungs.

"You, love?" he asked Rue without exhaling.

"Certainly." She gave his thigh a squeeze.

"I'll give you six weeks to stop that," he said. He had yet to take a breath.

He refilled the bong and Rue Kadera, agent of Her Majesty's Secret Service, took a hit.

Perini exhaled. "You?" He motioned to Karpov.

Karpov smiled. He felt self-conscious as he put his mouth on the inside of the bong and his finger over the hole. His desk-bound colleagues at Moscow Center would be envious.

"Let it burn," said Perini as Karpov inhaled slowly, steadily. "Lift the old finger."

Karpov lifted his finger and felt the smoke rush into his lungs. He had taken too much and wanted to let it go.

"Hold it, Valery Ivanovich."

Karpov held, then released the smoke slowly.

Then it was Laurence's turn. When he finished he said, "Nothing happened."

Perini shrugged. "Well, then I guess we better have another go at it, eh, Rue? High in a Red Lion Inn with Tony Laurence and Valery Karpov."

Rubashov wanted a turn and everybody

knew it but they said nothing. He had made his serious little speech.

They each took three hits before Perini set his bong aside. Laurence felt a slight warmth wash across his face. Karpov grinned. Perini slipped his arm around Rue Kadera's waist and drew her close.

"Has anybody here ever seen anybody malnourished?" Perini asked.

"All people have enough to eat in the Soviet Union," Rubashov said.

"I have," Perini said. "In Mexico City." The correct word was starving. Malnourished was a bullshit euphemism. He wondered why he'd used it.

"You?" Laurence looked at Karpov.

Karpov's face was awash with a lazy glow. "Yes." He remembered India. Then casually, as though it were nothing, he leaned against the wall and slid both ankles around his neck. It was an act of contortion he slipped into naturally, without effort.

"There were serfs who starved before the Revolution," Rubashov said.

"Rue?" Laurence asked.

"I've seen hunger." What she hadn't seen was anybody contort his body as Karpov was now doing.

Perini smelled Rue's hair. "It's not easy to talk about hunger." It was hard not to stare at Karpov. Rubashov looked earnest but bewildered. "Another hit?" Perini asked. Nobody said anything. He began sorting seeds again.

Laurence went first. "The bottom line is how do we know for sure what would happen if we let him go," he said without exhaling. "We can't go back. What if we're wrong?"

Karpov adjusted his mouth inside the bong and took a hit. "We're asked to be gods."

"The party has decided in this matter, Comrade Karpov," Rubashov said. He leaned forward, his mouth open.

"Shut up, Rubashov."

Rubashov's mouth closed.

"I'm hungry," Laurence said.

Perini laughed. "You've got the munchies."

"Munchies?"

"Pot makes you hungry."

"Ahh."

"I've eaten my dinner," Rubashov said. "There are children starving in Cambodia."

"Pizza!" Perini said.

Rue sat up. "Pizza sounds great!"

"First, the Yellow Pages. We'll have one delivered." Perini began searching through the phone book. "Ahh, here we are, place not far away. What'll it be, friends?"

"Pizza?" Karpov asked. He had never eaten pizza. He unwrapped himself.

"Pizza. The phone book says they'll deliver. I say we go for their special, whatever that is. Anchovies okay?"

"Not for me," Laurence said.

Perini dialed a number. "My name is Eddie Perini, and I'm on my way through town to murder a man." He paused, listening. "That's it, the Blazers writer. Only the season's over now and I'm traveling with the head of the CIA and the KGB and a beautiful British agent. We've been smoking dope in the Red Lion Inn and have the munchies. We'd like a couple of your largest and most lavish pizzas, please, but hold the anchovies."

He listened on the phone and laughed. "The Russian's name is Karpov. You might have read about him in the papers. He's been bonging." He laughed again. "That's right, the one across from Jantzen Shopping Center. That's not too far, is it? Tell them to load it now. Charge us double, the Kremlin's paying." He winked at Karpov.

Perini hung up. "Guy says I either have to be high or have one hell of an imagination. We could have had food delivered from the restaurant here but this is more fun." He felt Rue Kadera shift her rump against him.

"What is pizza?" Rubashov asked. He decided he was hungry after all. He looked outside. It had begun to rain.

CHAPTER

22

So there it was: Fidel Castro, minus beard and fatigues, was returning to the mountains with his comrades of more than a quarter of a century. It's one of life's curiosities that a dedicated, cold-blooded Marxist, a murderer if you believe the worst of the gringo rhetoric—a man able to put even his most committed followers to sleep with six-hour speeches—should want to visit the dance floor of a disco in Portland, Oregon.

It all began with Miami television in 1959, and Fidel's anxiety over the infamous American stupidity. The Russians had wonderful stories: You never knew what the Americans would do next. How could you plan? The Latin Americans had some good stories too: Listen, they said, you could work a deal with the gringos. It could be done. Sure, they had all the cards and you usually got screwed in the ass. All you had to do was go along with a little semantic shuffling to make sodomy sound elegant and you had a deal of sorts. Peasants never knew the difference. Then at the last minute some overweight senator in double knits would queer the deal because some twit hadn't supported his corn bill. It was one damned thing after another when you tried to work with the Americans.

When he was out there in the Sierra Maestra eating food with sand in it, Castro was a hero of the American press. Everybody loved him. A man of compassion, it was said. When it was all over and he began shooting people and shut down the most fun city in the Western Hemisphere, well, they fucking near went nuts. ¡Mierda!

Fidel was worried at the time. Not a lot, but worried still. When he heard the American Secretary of State, Christian Herter, was to appear on a program called *Meet the Press* to discuss Cuba, Fidel asked some engineers if they could equip a television set to receive signals from Florida, ninety miles away. Besides that the Chicago White Sox had won the American League pennant and Castro wanted to watch Luis Aparicio in the World Series. Yes, he was told, it could be done.

When Mr. Herter appeared to answer questions from a *Times* man who smoked a pipe, a television reporter who had problems with grammar, and a determined newsmagazine writer with a cold in his nose, Fidel watched on a black-and-white set. That wasn't the only program featuring interviews of public officials. Castro was both intrigued and amused at the parade of people who appeared on *Meet the Press*, *Face the Nation*, and *Issues and Answers*. There was the learned Senator J. William Fulbright, chairman of the Senate Foreign Relations Committee, urging his countrymen to be civilized and to show restraint at the unfolding of events in Cuba. There was Senator Lyndon B. Johnson, Senate Majority Leader, a man with small eyes and big earlobes who talked with his hands and insisted the country should not put up with Castro. There was Senator Barry Goldwater, Republican of Arizona, who had a firm, square jaw and urged military intervention. And there was Vice-President Richard M. Nixon, who appeared with sweat on his upper lip to chide the Democrats for ignoring Communists ninety miles from Florida.

Fidel watched them all. He was bewildered and amazed that so many people could have so many completely different and absolutely crocked, ignorant opinions about Cuba. On those and other news programs, Fidel watched the Americans ask themselves the most embarrassing, dumb, repetitious, and pointless questions imaginable. He could hardly believe it! They examined every part of themselves on television, bent double in pain so as not to miss the anus. It was fun. Fidel smoked cigars and enjoyed himself. He was still watching in amusement fifteen years later when Richard Nixon was taken under by the Watergate scandal. Castro considered Nixon to be the biggest asshole gringo who ever lived but if a newspaper publisher had done to him what Katharine Graham did to Richard Nixon he'd have fed her to the fish.

The whole thing was awful in 1959, but he watched fascinated. Then he began to turn the knob. In those early years he watched shadowy men boxing in the snowy picture that carried across the ninety miles from the Florida Keys. In those days the networks telecast *The Wednesday Night Fights*, which Fidel liked. In the summer there was baseball with Dizzy Dean and Pee Wee Reese. Then, when he was bored, there were *The Lucy-Desi Comedy Hour* and *The Ed Sullivan Show*. Ed Sullivan was on Sunday nights. If Sundays are boring for most people they're positively wretched when you're Premier of Cuba. Castro always watched Ed Sullivan.

But Fidel was hooked, nevertheless. He even did Ed Sullivan impressions in those early years. His English was terrible but he wasn't bad. He liked impressionists—Frank Gorshin in the early years and later, Rich Little. It wasn't easy to be addicted to American television when you were a Marxist. But still, it helped him relax. After a day of touring communal farms to shake hands with Cuban workers in cane stubble, Fidel went home and watched *Route 66*. After long hours of making speeches on how the economy was progressing, he watched *Wagon Train, Gunsmoke, Bonanza* and *Wanted—Dead or Alive*.

But Fidel Castro's favorite was Dick Clark's *American Bandstand*, which in those days was telecast every afternoon. No one knew. No one. At 4:00 P.M., Eastern Standard Time, when the sons and daughters of the gringos got home from school and settled down in front of the old black-and-white, feeling their pimples gingerly with the tips of their fingers, Fidel watched with them from Havana.

And there on the screen was Dick Clark with his pompadour and perfect teeth. Fidel watched the delicate spines of slender teenage girls twisting gently above perfect, tight butts. Twenty years later, they would look the camera straight in the lens and make erotic humping motions with their pelvis. He watched intense young men with dark, Italian eyes dancing with chins held high, eyes focused just above the part in their partners' swaying hair, which in those days was usually worn long, Joan Baez–style. It was, for Fidel, a lovely thing, music, the joy of youth. The politics of their parents aside, they were having fun.

And along the way, maybe curiously, maybe not, Fidel Castro became an afficionado of popular music. Bored with the attentions of yes men, he danced by himself in front of his set. He wasn't bad and knew it. He followed the names and faces of the musicians, not because he was a fan in the usual sense of the word but because he was curious about the mindless idolatry of teenage celebrities. It was, he felt, one of the most appalling of the gringos' wretched excesses. The Big Bopper, Gene Vincent, Bobby Rydell, Little Richard, Bobby Darin, Gene Pitney, the b's and y's and i's rattled his brain in those first years. Fidel knew they were making hundreds, yes, hundreds of thousands of dollars while he was forced to ration rice, red beans, and bananas. He thought of the phosphate a hundred thousand dollars could buy and was hypnotized by *American Bandstand*.

Baseball, he liked, not football. There was

too much talking on *Perry Mason*. Fidel didn't understand it. He watched *The Honeymooners* for a while. He wondered if a sly Marxist might not have conceived of the drama of Jackie Gleason, a bus driver and Art Carney, a suspender-snapping sewer worker. He watched it for a while but gave it up, disgusted. He turned to other channels in search of the character of that American monolith that hovered above his island like an egg-sucking dog. Were American men as ineffectual as Robert Young in *Father Knows Best*? Were American NCOs as loony as Phil Silvers' portrayal of Sergeant Bilko? Could an American cowboy be as dumb and naïve as Dan Blocker's Hoss Cartwright?

Fidel Castro wondered.

He wondered also what those graceful young people on *American Bandstand* were thinking of as the camera paused then moved on to sweating black men with saxophones, drums, and small mustaches. Did the dancers think of themselves and themselves only? Is that what made their fathers build banks, railroads, steel mills? Just greed, aided by coal, luck, land, and circumstance?

Fidel was convinced that artists were of the left. Artists challenged. They pushed out and explored. Were the Dick Clark musicians artists? Artists suffered. Children suffered. Fidel knew that without a doubt. He had seen it. He had lived with it. He had dedicated his life to easing the suffering of Cuban children. But American children did not suffer, at least not the young ones who rode the television signals from Miami.

Fidel watched as the singers donned blue jeans, carried signs, and talked Marxist jargon in the 1960s. Were they really radical? Fidel didn't think so. The singers sang radical lyrics that made no sense. Dick Clark joined the young people of Philadelphia, dressed in their finest, in applauding in the right places. You had to have the right places memorized because the electric guitars drowned out the words. Fidel couldn't imagine what the Americans expected in Vietnam, taking pimple-faced, dancing teenagers out of Philadelphia and handing them M-16's in rice paddies.

He was still watching Dick Clark when the Americans withdrew in 1973, looking awkward and embarrassed like a poodle bitch caught pissing on the carpet.

Which is why, as their Boeing 747 taxied through the rain to the terminal at Portland, Castro was moved to tap Rivera on the shoulder.

"Yes?" Rivera asked.

"If we can do it, I'd like to go to that place you were reading about, Krakatoa Kate's." He held up a copy of United Airline's *Mainliner* magazine.

Rivera laughed. Snort, snort, snort!

The snort grated on Castro even though he had been with Rivera for more than twenty years. He punched his friend on the shoulder. "Laugh, *carajo*, and you'll wish you hadn't."

"No reason why not, we're the only people who could possibly know about Goldman," Dann said. For the first time in over two decades they had privacy. They had spare time. Why not go for Krakatoa Kate's that, judging from the *Mainliner* story, looked like an especially amusing capitalist outrage.

CHAPTER

23

THE CUBANS WERE THE SECOND GROUP TO AR-
rive at the airport in Portland—they were
behind Laurence and Karpov but almost two
hours ahead of Colonel Scanlan and his
friends. The Cubans were the last on their
plane to step onto the folding ramp that led
to the terminal. Rivera went first, followed
by Dann, then Castro.

They left the ramp, crossed a waiting area
surrounded by sagging velvet-covered ropes,
passed through stainless-steel posts marking
the exit, and entered a carpeted corridor.
The walls were soft blue and cool gray with
an accent of maroon. They passed a young
man with earrings and a portly woman with
a wilted lei on her sagging bosom. A severe-
looking man in a three-piece suit stepped out
of a rest room, sour-faced and tugging at his
fly. They walked beyond a cocktail lounge
with an artificial fire in a cardboard fireplace, the cardboard molded to look like
brick. The people inside sat on red vinyl
barstools and watched pools of water form
on the concourse. An airliner taxied by, the

screaming of its jets oddly muted by the
glass walls. They passed a souvenir shop
with wire racks of paperback novels and
piles of newspapers. They came upon a ticket
counter that stretched fifty yards in either
direction.

It was a strange place for Fidel Castro,
who was used to stopping his car to let a
Rhode Island Red cross the road or because
he wanted to watch the simple beauty of a
girl chasing a pig in a field.

They paused near a young man kneeling
before a suitcase on the floor. A young
woman watched him, giggling.

"Excuse me," Dann said. "We're looking
for the Hertz Rent-a-Car outlet. Could you
help us?"

"Left my camera in the suitcase," the
young woman said. "We're from Boise, going
to Hawaii on our honeymoon."

"Maui," the groom said, struggling through
underwear in search of a Kodak Instamatic.

"I'm sorry," Dann said.

"I think I saw them one floor down," the
young woman said. "The rental places."

Dann thanked her and they rode a stainless-
steel escalator one floor down. The rental
counters were at the far end of the terminal.
The Hertz clerk was a pretty brunette. A
slender teenager with blond hair hanging
down in dirty ringlets sat on a folding chair
nearby. He had bulbous eyes, almost no chin,
and looked bored. He dug at the armpit of
his polyester blazer.

"Excuse me," Dann said. "My name is Mr.
John Dalmo of New York. I have a reserva-

tion here for an economy car." Dann pulled an American Express card from his wallet.

"Mr. Dalmo?" said the girl.

"Yes, Dalmo."

"Were you given a receipt with a number on it?"

Dann gave her a piece of yellow paper. The girl looked at it and punched a series of numbers on a computer terminal. Castro watched the details of Dann's false name appear in green on the screen.

The girl smiled. "Yes, Mr. Dalmo. A Ford Escort—will that be satisfactory?"

"Yes," said Dann.

"Robert!"

The young man with the dirty hair got up from his folding chair. "Yes, ma'am."

"You can just tell us where to go," Dann said.

"That's what Robert's for."

"I'm a valet," Robert said, pronouncing the *t*.

The girl gave Robert a form. Dann followed him to pick up the Escort.

Castro and Rivera watched people come and go in Volvos, Toyotas, and taxis. Their reflections looked back from the glass walls. Rivera and Castro had been young men once, lean, not thick. There had been Batista, torture, casinos, whorehouses in Havana, an economy dominated by Americans. The three of them, Castro, Rivera, and Dann had gone for days without eating or sleeping. When they did get food it had dirt in it, or there wasn't enough, or Batista's troops were so close no one wanted to swallow. Castro remembered the American journalist who visited him in the mountains.

"What will you do if you should win, Señor Castro?"

Castro had looked surprised. "We will win."

"What I mean is, will you have a democratic form of government?"

"It will be a government for the people."

The journalist's pencil paused. "What governments do you admire?"

Castro had not been sure at the time what he would do once he was in power. He would do what had to be done for the Cuban people. "I admire governments that are fair to the people. You may report to your readers those are my intentions," Castro had said softly in his bad English.

It was one of those accidents of history. The journalist, a careful, pipe-smoking man, much impressed with himself, was widely honored and respected, a confidant of American Presidents. He puffed on his pipe, looked thoughtful, and made a note to himself. He later wrote in a nationally syndicated column:

"Castro looked me in the eye and said that he admired governments such as America, governments that are fair to the people. 'You may report to your readers those are my intentions,' he said firmly. I may be wrong but I don't think Señor Castro is another two-bit Latin revolutionary. He's a serious, dedicated man, correctly enraged by the staggering excesses of the Batista regime. If we take a wait-and-see attitude, I think this one will turn out right."

Castro had once read that this journalist

had learned to write as a sportswriter. That made him wonder why anybody would want to write about sports. There had been some Americans, believers, who did wait and see. But when Castro began executing people, it was all over.

The journalist with the pipe later reported, in responsible, serious phrases, that he had "gravely misjudged" Castro. "Castro obviously changed. What happened to him we may never know. We can only wonder and do what we can to stop the Russian bear pawing at our underbelly."

Castro had laughed out loud when he read that. He executed eight people that day. Stupid gringo, hadn't Castro told him he was for governments that are fair to the people? *¡Mierda!*

Dann soon appeared with the Escort, a white car with blue racing stripes on the sides. As Rivera got into the backseat, Castro looked closely at the stripes and saw they were decals.

"German made," Dann said. The clutch was tight. Dann spun the front wheels on the pavement as they set off in the wet, black night. "Different than the first time, eh, Fidel. Carbines then, wet fatigues, and machetes."

Castro grinned. "It is different and the same, *mi amigo*. We're older now, but the same men. Mountains are mountains. Justice is justice. Gringos or Batista's pimps, what's the difference?"

"People eat in Cuba," Rivera said from the backseat. "Everybody reads now."

Castro reached over the backseat and gripped Rivera's knee. "We did that, *amigos*. We may have big butts now from sitting, and bellies from eating too much, but we're the same."

"The *muchacho* with the pimples said to follow the green signs," Dann said. "We take I-5 South." He braked the Escort to a stop at Eighty-second Avenue and turned left as the first of the green signs indicated.

Castro fell silent. He watched the signs and names: you could have fried chicken at the Colonel's, a Big Mac at McDonalds, or a Whopper at the Burger King. If you needed groceries there was a Safeway, an Albertson's, and a Thriftway. He counted three stores that sold stereo equipment, tapes, and records—Terrible Trumble's, Angie's Rip City Sound, and Little Willy's. The bars and taverns all had odd names: Faggot's, The Partly Stuffed Polish, Three Women in a Tub, I'll Remember You, Hole in a Shirt, Noble Pub, The Revolutionary Respite. Castro stared back over his shoulder at the latter.

"All this," Castro shook his head. "Bacchus Photography. What's that?" There was a nude girl painted on the front.

Dann laughed. "A whorehouse, Fidel."

"A whorehouse? It says photography."

"Brothels are against the law in America, except maybe in Nevada. You go in there, see, and rent a camera for twenty dollars, pay another thirty for a half hour of a nude girl's time, and once you're alone with her you negotiate the price for taking care of your erection."

Castro looked amazed. "Why don't the police go in, agree on a price, and arrest them?"

Dann stopped for a red light. "Because once you bring up the subject of sex the girl will ask you if you're a cop."

"So?"

"So you can't lie and still make the arrest. It'd be thrown out of court."

"*¡Mierda!*" Castro said. "How can you run a country like that?"

Dann slowed the Escort, took a left, and swung right again onto I-84 for the run to the heart of Portland, a city of bridges and hills, firs and parks, flanked in the daytime by the startling white of Mount Hood and the active volcano, Mount Saint Helens.

Castro spotted a young man walking along the edge of the freeway. "Let's pick him up. See what he has to say."

"*Por qué no?*" said Dann. He braked the Escort to a stop as the young man turned to face them, thumb up.

"Hey fuck, thanks," he said as Castro leaned forward so the young man could join Rivera in the backseat. "I got this Fiat, real shit-box, think the transmission went out on it. Name's Dutch." He ran the fingers of his left hand through his curly hair. "I'm trying to make it to Lewis and Clark College. You guy's going south?"

"We just got in at the airport," Dann said. "Never been here. What's Lewis and Clark College?"

"A private school at the south end of town."

"Ahh," said Castro. "Where are you from, Dutch?"

Dutch grinned. "Nevada."

"Do they have brothels in Nevada?"

"You bet," said Dutch. "They've got every damned thing you can imagine in Nevada, and then some. Where you guys from?"

"Costa Rica," Castro said. "We're with a business that exports coffee to the United States."

"Well, shit, okay!" Dutch said. He had assumed they were beaners from L.A. Costa Ricans had to be all right.

"You ever been to a disco, Dutch?"

Dutch laughed. "Well, yeah, but I don't like to waste my time with that crap. Like to get on with it, massage the old meat."

Castro leaned forward and took his wallet from his hip pocket. He turned and held out two crisp new one hundred dollar bills to Dutch. "You take us to a disco? We've only got this one night."

Dutch laughed and took the bills. "Hell yes, man! You want me to drive? Pull this sucker on over. Man, these bills're gonna go right up my nose. Right straight up my nose!"

Dann slowed the car. "Up your nose?"

Dutch grinned. "Yes, sir. Nose candy!"

The Cubans didn't understand but said nothing. Castro took his own large nose in his hand thoughtfully.

Dutch was warming up. "You wanna go to a disco, we're fucking well gonna go to a disco. Maybe you guys can swap some coffee for a piece of ass." He laughed. "Unlimber the member. Dip the wick. Handle the candle."

"On the airplane we were reading about a place called Krakatoa Kate's," said Dann.

The car had stopped. Dutch got out and traded places with Dann. "Krakatoa Kate's, my man, is the very wildest."

Dutch was likable, exuberant. Castro liked him.

"Listen, I didn't get your names," Dutch said.

"José," said Castro. He shook hands with Dutch.

"Hosing José!" Dutch leered.

"Raúl," said Dann. They shook.

"Reaming Raúl!"

Rivera paused, wondering if he could stump him. "Pablo," he ventured.

Dutch didn't hesitate: "Pokin' Pablo! You guys are all right. All that caffeine in your systems, I'll bet you can flex those rods all night." He was thinking, Christ, wait'll the guys at the dorm hear this. Three old farts, greasers, one of 'em looks like Fidel Castro without a beard, give me two hundred bucks to take them to Krakatoa Kate's. Two hundred bucks! Crisp numbers, not a wrinkle on 'em.

"What is this place called Krakatoa Kate's?" Dann asked.

Dutch, pretending he was Juan Fangio out of respect to the company, dug at his crotch with gusto and geared down for an off ramp. "Well, Kate's has this sound system that will blow your fucking mind, gents, I shit you not. Some fucking loony designed it and an asshole with more bucks than good sense paid for it. Guys in double knits who love themselves in the mirror go down there. It's fun though. You want to be around when time began, you'll be there at Kate's."

"When time began?" Castro asked.

"Uh huh, when time began. When God wept alone in the void. Kate's got it on tape."

"On tape," Dann said.

Dutch laughed. "Be damned if I know how they did it. All I know is there're women there." He made an obscene sucking sound with his mouth. He ran the Escort through its paces as if he were demanding that it prove it was German-made, and turned, at last, into a vast parking lot. There was a shopping mall across the street. Castro had never seen so many automobiles.

"*¡Mierda!*" he said.

"Yeah, helluva sign, eh?" He was looking at an immense neon volcano. "Krakatoa!"

Castro hadn't seen the sign. He was still staring at the cars. He sat back in his seat as though pinned by the surreal garishness of the neon volcano. "*¡Dios! Qué es*, Dutch?"

Dutch understood. His roommate was a Spanish major. "That, my man, is Krakatoa, a volcanic island between Java and Sumatra."

"*¿Por qué?*"

"Why is it here?"

"*Sí*," Castro said.

"Probably all the fuss caused by the erup-tion of Mount Saint Helens. Krakatoa vomited the very bowels of the earth in 1883, killed 35,000 people."

Castro, Rivera, and Dann followed Dutch into Krakatoa Kate's. It was there that Fidel Castro had an intuitive rush in which he understood that a capitalist entrepreneur in Portland, Oregon, straining at the furthermost reaches of irony, had the soul of Dante, of Hieronymus Bosch. There was no leather in Kate's, no wood. The interior was fashioned of stainless steel, glass, and vinyl. There were four sunken floors around which spectators sat watching the dancers below. The floors were surrounded by mirrors in which the dancers, in narcissistic contemplation, could watch themselves moving to the driving rhythm of the music. There were circular banks of colored lights overhead with thousands of bulbs, green over one floor, red over another, yellow over a third, blue over yet a fourth. Above the lights were Kate's speakers, capable of delivering sound of such force and intensity as to deliver the leaden heartbeat of the cosmos, of washing through the human body in sensuous waves of energy.

Dutch found four empty seats at the red floor. "We're in luck, gents. Show's coming up."

Castro and his companions sat, looking up at the lights and the speakers, then down at the floor.

"Incredible!" said Castro.

A waitress with a push-em-up bra and low-cut blouse appeared by Castro's side. "Yes?" she asked.

Castro paused and looked at Dutch.

Dutch gave an extravagant gesture with his hand. "My good friends here are coffee merchants from Costa Rica. Make it Bacardi light, on the rocks."

"I'll buy," Castro said. He pulled a fifty-dollar bill from his wallet.

Dutch leaned Castro's way with his hand cupped to his mouth. "Christ man, will you look at the bush."

Castro hadn't noticed the young women, sitting in groups of three and four, divorced most of them with children at home. They laughed among themselves and sat hopefully, afraid of the future. The dream had failed them. They waited, most of them unsure for what.

"Look at the ass in here, will you?" Dutch said.

"*Sí*," Castro said.

Dann and Rivera said nothing.

"They have this sound-and-light show before the music. It lasts about fifteen minutes and is fucking something," Dutch said. As he spoke, Kate's was plunged into darkness.

There came first the sound of a baby crying. Fidel listened in the darkness as the crying receded into the distance and was replaced by the howling of a wolf. Castro, in his mind's eye, could see the wolf alone with the wind on the tundra, howling at the stars, white in the blackness of the arctic night. The howling faded to silence. The red lights above Castro lit with startling suddenness, lights of such power as to wash heat across Castro's face. The lights formed geometric patterns—circles, squares, zigzags, rectangles, triangles, ellipses, waves—that raced around the circle above the dance floor and above the spectators, raced left, raced right, raced left again. Next a low rumbling sound whose power surged through Castro's body and became in turn a screaming babble of humans facing the apocalypse. The lost baby could be heard above the pathetic wailing. The speakers caressed the interior of Kate's with horror. The geometric patterns leaped and danced, reversing themselves above the spectators who sat, open-mouthed, staring into the heat of the light bulbs, listening to the yawning terror of Krakatoa.

Then there was a scream that was maybe human, a woman perhaps, maybe animal, a feral cry shocking in its intensity and duration. Then there was nothing, silence. The lights continued above, the patterns reversing themselves in spastic runs at madness.

Then the wolf again, alone. The baby was gone. The wolf faded, replaced by the crashing of a surf of such violent intensity that it shook the room.

"*¡Mierda!*" Castro said. He realized, suddenly, that the surf also had disappeared and there were dancers on the floor going through intricate stylized steps. The red geometry above was joined by black light that made white teeth and sweaters glow. The dancers did not smile. They rarely touched. They admired their profiles and gleaming teeth in the panels of mirror that surrounded the floor.

Castro leaned toward Dutch. "*Gracias,*

amigo, for bringing us here." He'd never seen anything like Krakatoa Kate's.

Dutch grinned. "Play your cards right and you can pick up a piece," he said. He was thinking what woman would want to go to bed with a large-nosed greaser like old Hosing José. But he felt he had an obligation to pretend José was no different than anybody else. After all, José had come across with two hundred smackers for cocaine. Dutch inhaled deeply.

Castro thought he said something. "I don't understand."

Dutch laughed. "I said these women are hard up or they wouldn't be here. Probably fuck a donkey."

Fidel Castro didn't understand Dutch. He did understand, more than ever, the importance of finding the scientist Bernard Goldman.

CHAPTER

24

THE PIZZAS, WHEN THEY CAME, WERE MARVEL-
ous. Karpov hesitated, watching Perini pick
up a piece and eat it with his hands, before
he too helped himself. Rubashov watched
Karpov, waited, and was the last to get a
slice. They were generous pizzas, heaped
with pepperoni, sausage, Canadian bacon,
onions, mushrooms, and green pepper.

When they were finished, Perini sat back,
satisfied, twisting his mustache. "What do
you say we have a little fun?"

"Fun?" Laurence asked.

"Place named Krakatoa Kate's," Perini said.
"Be an experience for you all."

"A capitalist's idea of fun is to take advantage of working people," Rubashov said. He
wiped some tomato sauce from his lip.

"What's your middle name, Vasily?"

Rubashov looked at Karpov. The latter
wondered what Perini had in mind. "It's
Leonidovich, isn't it, Rubashov?"

Rubashov sat erect. "Yes, Comrade Karpov."

Perini put his arm around Rubashov's
shoulder, and grinned when Rubashov flinched.

"Well, Vasily Leonidovich, my friend, has no one in Moscow Center ever told you the best way to defeat your enemy is to understand his weaknesses, his excesses?"

Rubashov looked at Karpov again. He wanted Perini to remove his arm.

Karpov shrugged. "He has a point, Rubashov. Listen to him."

"At Krakatoa Kate's, Vasily Leonidovich, you will see firsthand what has gone wrong with us capitalists. You won't have to trust *Pravda* and *Izvestia*. We both know they're full of shit."

"They print the truth," Rubashov said. He yanked his shoulder from Perini's grasp.

"I say we go," Karpov said. He enjoyed Rubashov's suffering.

"Second that," Laurence said, who was red-eyed and sleepy from the pot.

"Sounds like fun," Rue Kadera said.

Perini was already putting on his jacket.

They found seats at the floor with the red lights. They were late for the first eruption of Krakatoa, so they watched the dancers and waited. Rubashov stared openmouthed at the mirrors and the lights above that zipped back and forth in time to the bump, bump, bump of the music. A young man in a tuxedo played the tapes from a plastic bubble set in the ceiling. His features were without flaw. He was handsome but betrayed no character. He apparently had no sense of humor, no sense of the ironic, and had no great likes or dislikes. He played tapes without zest or energy. He looked down on the dancers and spectators with bland, bored eyes.

Perini nudged Rue and nodded toward the young man in the bubble. "Good-looking sucker, eh? Bet you'd go for him in a big way."

Rue looked disgusted.

It was then that Eddie spotted a Latin-looking man across the circular dance floor. He had seen him somewhere. He was certain of it. "The man in the middle, over there. Have you seen him before?"

Rue knew who he was talking about. "I know what you mean. He looks familiar."

They both watched the Latin, who was staring, fascinated, at the dancers on the floor.

Eddie Perini couldn't get the man's face out of his mind. Not then, not later when he was sitting on the toilet, staring first at a high line on the wall labeled "Bill Walton peed here," then at a *Newsweek* magazine that had been left on the tile floor.

"Castro at the UN," said the *Newsweek* headline.

Perini ripped off the cover, curved his hand around the beard, and grinned. The large, soft eyes, the long nose, the fleshy ears. They were all there. Fidel Castro was sitting across from them in Krakatoa Kate's!

Perini returned to his seat beside Rue Kadera, placed the *Newsweek* cover in front of her, and whispered in her ear, "Put your hand over the beard, love, and check our friend again."

Rue did as she was told, and grinned. "I know it's crazy, but I think you're right."

"Try Laurence," Perini said.

Laurence was looking at her. So was Karpov. "Hand over the beard," she whispered to Laurence. "The man across from us, the one there in the middle."

Laurence made the comparison and looked astonished. "The ears give him away, and the nose." He slid the magazine cover to Karpov. "We need Moscow Center's opinion. The man across the way, Valery."

Karpov looked at the cover, looked across the floor, looked back at the cover. "It can't be!"

"The ears and nose, Valery, and his eyes."

Karpov frowned. "It couldn't be. What happened to his chin?"

"The beard. You've never seen his chin before."

All five of them gathered around the magazine and stared at the cover. When they looked up, Castro and his companions had gone.

"I've got to go to the john. Then I think we'd better get on with the business at hand," Laurence said. "We've got some driving to do."

Laurence was gone ten minutes and when he came back Karpov said he, too, had to relieve himself.

"My God, they're worse than having my nephews along," Perini said.

Rue Kadera laughed. She wondered when she would get her chance to make a phone call. Fidel Castro in Portland, Oregon. Smethurst would want to know. She was along as a courtesy to Her Majesty's Government. She'd have to wait her turn at the "toilet."

As they were leaving Krakatoa Kate's, Karpov put his arm around Rubashov's shoulders. "Comrade, I want you to remember this place. Let it be a lesson to you."

Rubashov was the last one out the door. He paused before leaving and took one more look at the music and lights. He left puzzled, wondering which lesson Karpov meant. He thought about asking him but decided not to.

It took Scanlan, deJonette, and Cardinal three hours to drive from Portland to Roseburg. The one hundred and ten miles from Portland to Eugene was virtually a straight line through the darkness—relieved only by green interstate highway signs. The signs informed them of exits to communities named Mollala, Sublimity, and Sweet Home. Eugene was the only town of any size. After Cottage Grove, the highway curved through and over a series of valleys and ridges. Douglas firs loomed high and gloomy on both sides of the highway.

Around the bend of one curve they saw five sets of eyes that reflected ruby in the headlights. The deer were paralyzed by the light, frozen, unsure of their fate.

It was 1:00 A.M. when R. Cardinal left the freeway at the second Roseburg exit. "Roseburg," he said.

Scanlan looked at his tiny wristwatch. "What do you say we find a bar and have a drink? We need to stretch our legs."

"That's fine," deJonette said.

"We should be able to find out if the lodge at Diamond Lake has rooms."

Cardinal said nothing. He slowed as he approached downtown Roseburg. "There's a place—The Tall Timbers Tavern. What do you think?"

"Fine by me," Scanlan said.

As the car slowed, he saw a banner on the outside of the tavern that said there was a "live" country and western band inside. Live was in quotes.

"Did we expect a dead band?" deJonette said.

The door to the bar was propped open by a chair to let in some fresh air. Mikki Scanlan stepped inside first, followed by deJonette and Cardinal. The band, consisting of a lead guitar and singer, a bassist, and a drummer, played on a small stage with twelve-inch mirror tiles behind it. The singer, a hard-looking man with large hands and jet black hair set in a pompadour, sang a song about a truck driver with a true love in Boise.

Colonel Scanlan made his way to an open spot in a crowded semicircle of tables surrounding the dance floor in front of the band.

"Excuse me, hon. I'm sorry." Scanlan breathed his sexiest best, Pierre Cardin cologne wafting past the noses of men who felled trees for a living.

DeJonette's mind buzzed from the Bujus, but he was fascinated by the faces in the tavern. They lived hard lives and had tired wives at home. The wives watched soap operas all day and gossiped on the telephone with their girl friends. Their kids tipped cups of milk over and had to have their meat cut for them.

Cardinal went last, looking aloof and distracted.

Scanlan looked about him and saw that the patrons of The Tall Timbers Tavern drank their beer from brown stubby bottles. Scanlan touched deJonette's shoulder, letting his fingers linger for the briefest of moments. "Oh, be a dear, Jan, and see if you can flag us a waitress," he said in a soft voice. He was thinking Ava Gardner, and coming close.

DeJonette laughed and waved for a waitress. "These are wonderful American types, don't you think, Mikki? Right out of American movies."

"Why, yes, they're loggers, honey. All those muscles, think of it. I adore strong men. And no AIDS in this hick town, I'll bet. A girl could take it all night long and not worry."

"I like this kind of music," Cardinal said. "I was once at a bar in Zurich that had T.E. Lawrence memorabilia on the walls and country music in the jukebox."

"Willy's," deJonette said. "A Russian named Yershov likes that place. They drink Japanese beer there."

Cardinal looked surprised. "You worked for Yershov too?" Cardinal liked being with Scanlan and deJonette. In the judgment of their peers, they were the three most treacherous mercenaries in the world. An all-star team of killers. Cardinal felt a man had to have pride in his work to look at himself in the mirror each morning. Pride gave a life meaning.

"Hasn't everyone? The czar's gold spends the same as everybody else's," deJonette said.

Cardinal blinked. "They're Communists."

"What? Oh, yes. Communists, we're told."

"Oh, aren't you the clever one, Jan." Scanlan had never worked in a team before. He either commanded others or took contracts by himself. He was touched by the intimacy he felt with deJonette and Cardinal. He too felt pride of craft. The three of them had survived where few others had dared to step. They were the best. "You know one day they'll get us, don't you think?"

"You'll never hear the shot that kills you," Cardinal said.

"Oh, that's old, R. Can't you come up with something witty? Listen to Jan. Jan, say something clever, won't you? Something very Oscar Wilde." Scanlan was aware that he was being watched and appraised by the lumberjacks and truck drivers around him. He was flattered. Scanlan had a way about him. He could be precise, logical, and absolutely unemotional one moment—a killer in lipstick—and a seductress the next. He slipped easily from one persona to another.

Cardinal looked slightly sullen. "It's true. You'll just be dead," he said, knowing he sounded even more stupid the moment the words left his mouth.

The waitress arrived and deJonette said, "Three bottles of whatever's local, please."

"Henry Weinhard's?"

"That's fine."

Scanlan said, "You're so masterful, Jan, honey."

"The French didn't think it was true, what R. said about you not hearing the shot that kills you. The way the French figured, since it takes several minutes for a brain to lose consciousness without blood, then it's possible for a guillotined head to be alive for a few minutes after the blade. A man could contemplate his severed body in the moments before silence."

Mikki Scanlan looked shocked. "Brrrr. Jan, honey, don't be so morbid. Do stop. Make him stop it, R."

An earnest-looking lumberjack leaned in Scanlan's direction and said, "Did I hear you say you're from out of town, ma'am?"

"I'm from Europe, hon." Scanlan gave the lumberjack a special smile, letting his lips fall into a sensual slack.

"Europe?" The young man looked impressed.

"Amsterdam, actually," Scanlan breathed. He was thinking Susan Hayward.

The lumberjack scooted his chair closer to Scanlan, who now oozed sex. "Amsterdam? I seen a program about Amsterdam on TV. They showed these guys in screwy costumes carrying balls of cheese around on stretchers. People with cameras were crowded around taking their picture."

"A cheese festival. Was it at Edam?"

"That could have been it. I don't know. Would you like to dance?"

"R?" Scanlan draped a languid hand toward Cardinal, asking R. Cardinal's permission to dance with the young man.

"I . . ." Cardinal didn't know what to say.

"Do have a good time, Dominique," deJonette broke in.

"Oh, thank you, Jan." Mikki Scanlan allowed himself to be escorted onto the tiny dance floor. The band was on a break but the jukebox played on and people still danced; the music was best when the musicians were in their dressing rooms smoking joints. Scanlan pressed close to the young man as Andy Williams sang "Moon River."

The young man, woozy from Scanlan's eau de Paris, said, "My name's Dale Swingle. I live on down to Riddle."

"I'll take a man with muscles any day," Scanlan said, pressing tighter. "Say, do you know if they have a hotel at Diamond Lake?"

"They have a lodge up there but I don't think it has much in the way of rooms."

"So you think we'd be better off finding a hotel here in Roseburg?"

"Motel," Swingle said, stressing the *m*. "Roseburg doesn't have much in the way of hotels. But we've got plenty of motels, Best Western and all of them. Say, I'm driving up there tonight myself. My uncle lives in a ranger house at the top end of Soda Springs Reservoir. You fish?"

Scanlan breathed into his ear. "Do I fish? Honey, you'd be surprised at some of the things I do."

*   *   *

It was 2:00 A.M. when Eddie Perini turned into Rod's Tavern in the village of Glide on the North Umpqua River. Rod's was closing, but Perini managed to rent two small cabins that sat behind the tavern. There were ten cabins in all. Eight were occupied by fishermen. Perini and Rue Kadera took one; Laurence, Rubashov, and Karpov shared the second, which had a single bed and a bunk bed. Laurence took the single bed. Rubashov took the top bunk, Karpov the lower. Laurence set his travel alarm for 6:00 A.M. and they rested before heading for Diamond Lake.

It was a simple enough stopover. But the next morning Valery Karpov wouldn't wake up. Both Rubashov and Laurence tried to shake him awake. Nothing.

When Laurence checked his pulse there was none.

Rubashov looked sick. "His heart."

"His heart?"

"Comrade Karpov had a bad heart."

"Oh shit, just what we need." Laurence checked Karpov's pulse again. There was none. He placed his ear on Karpov's bare chest. Nothing.

"His heart," Rubashov repeated.

Laurence had had it with Rubashov. He could have slugged him. "Listen, you stupid bastard, I don't give a damn how he died. The head of Moscow Center is dead in this fucking cabin and I'm stuck with his corpse. I don't want to hear it about his damned heart."

"We'll throw his corpse in the river," Rubashov said.

"Sure, we throw it in the river to wash up in Roseburg, or whatever the hell that place is called back there."

Rubashov looked at the corpse as though he still couldn't believe it. "The fingerprints match the passport in his pocket. It's British. The passport is real. The clothes are right. If they check they'll find there is a John McIntosh. Everything fits."

"You're saying if we try to bury him we're apt to get caught. Throw him in the river and there's a chance he'll never be found."

"That's what I'm saying, Mr. Laurence."

Rubashov made sense for a change. "The river it is, Comrade."

Rubashov carried Karpov out of the cabin on his shoulder. There was a fog on the river. With Laurence watching, Rubashov dumped the corpse of Valery Karpov into the cold water of the Umpqua. It drifted downstream around a bend, and out of sight.

When they returned, Perini and Rue Kadera were waiting by the car, ready to go.

"Where's Karpov?" Perini asked.

Laurence told him what had happened.

"Dead?"

"Dead. A heart attack, Rubashov thinks. I don't know. All I know is he's dead on our turf. He's on his way to the Pacific Ocean right now. We've got a job to do. Comrade Rubashov here is the representative of the Soviet Union."

"I'll do my best," Rubashov said.

Laurence wished he could phone Chambliss again. "Karpov is dead and that's that. There's no use rehashing it and it's too late to call the coroner."

They got in their car and continued up Route 138 to Diamond Lake.

DAY FIVE

RUE KADERA'S
MOUSSE AU CHOCOLAT*

1 cup (6-ounce pack-
  age) semisweet
  chocolate pieces
5 tablespoons boiling
  water

4 eggs, separated
2 tablespoons dark
  rum

1. Put the chocolate pieces into the container of an electric blender and blend on high speed six seconds.

2. With the motor off, scrape the chocolate from the sides of the container with a knife. Add the water and blend on high speed ten seconds. Add the egg yolks and rum and blend three seconds or until smooth.

3. Fold the chocolate mixture into the stiffly beaten egg whites. Spoon the dessert into individual serving dishes and chill one hour before serving. (SERVES EIGHT)

CHAPTER

25

MASON DEVOL KNEW ALL PRESIDENTS HAD their problems, but why, dammit, did all the most preposterous seem to land on *his* head? It was like knowing the odds for catching cancer or having a heart attack. You know the statistics but you never think it will happen to you. It happens to the other guy. When it happens to you, you don't believe it at first. Then you get pissed off and resentful and take it out on your wife or whatever God it is you pray to.

Why, Devol asked himself, was it impossible for an American President to govern the country for a four-year term without having to endure some positively bizarre crisis. Was it too much to ask? Was it asking so much to be able to do your job without having a bunch of dumb blacks burn their neighborhood down, without getting sucked into somebody else's war, without having a national guard commander fuck up a simple campus riot, without having the oil run dry, without having paranoid Muslim fanatics hold your embassy people hostage? Jesus, why? Ike had

come the closest to making it: he had Suez
to contend with, and Powers and his U-2. He
was bum-rapped for having a boring presi-
dency, but was that so bad? He made it
through two terms, didn't he? Christ, look at
the others: Wilson endured World War I,
only to have Lodge rob him of the League of
Nations; Harding had Teapot Dome; Hoover,
the Crash of '29; Roosevelt, a bunch of jerks
on the Supreme Court; Truman, the atomic
bomb; Kennedy, the Bay of Pigs; Johnson,
the Vietnam war. Then there was that sleaze,
Nixon. All Presidents after Nixon had an odd
feeling in their stomach even thinking about
him. Devol supposed he ought to include the
Cuban Missile Crisis in his list; Kennedy had
to survive that too before Oswald took his
head off in Dallas.

That latter incident was what bothered
Mason Devol just now.

It was said—with more than enough evidence to convince Devol—that Oswald was
getting even for a botched plot of Bobby and
Jack Kennedy to prang Fidel Castro for the
error of blundering into the Soviet camp. Tit
for tat. Fidel got Kennedy, it was said. Well,
that wouldn't have bothered Mason Devol a
whole lot; it was, after all, Jack Kennedy
lying six feet under at Arlington, not him.

But here, sitting across from him at the
polished Presidential desk, looking bland and
imperturbable in his undertaker's outfit, was
James Chambliss telling him that Fidel Castro was somewhere in the continental United
States traveling incognito. Fidel Castro. Traveling incognito! My God, it was like the

fucking Marx Brothers. All Castro needed
was a plastic nose and horned-rimmed glasses.
Shit, what next?

The day had started innocently enough:
the Arabs were jacking their asking price to
forty dollars a barrel, forty bucks; the Italian
President had been kidnapped by unidenti-
fied Sicilians; the Brazilians were once again
threatening to withhold their coffee from the
world market; some punks in West Germany
were claiming to have an atomic "device" in
their possession. The television people went
along with the "device" euphemism for reasons Devol could not understand. A bomb is
a goddamn bomb! An asshole is an asshole!
Devol remembered the media going along
with the Symbionese Liberation Army horse-
shit when Patty Hearst was grabbed; since
when were five malcontents an army? Since
when? It was like fuzzy wuzzies in Africa
calling themselves field marshals. Now this,
Fidel Castro incognito.

As Devol saw it, time and history had long
ago proven anything possible. Nobody re-
members Lyndon Johnson's 89th Congress.
All they know is he couldn't recognize the
sound of a toilet flushing in Asia. Devol was
determined always to be the first one out of
the water. He listened constantly for a warning gurgle. He knew that if anything could
go wrong, it would. He knew from experience that it was in the White House that
truth outran fiction. It couldn't be nuttier if
a comic wrote the script. It was impossible
for any ordinary mortal to maintain any
kind of perspective in these circumstances.

All that talk about issues and platforms, monetary and fiscal policy, leadership and congressional relationships, all that was bullshit.

Devol knew a term as President was a white knuckler all the way. It was like riding a roller coaster—all you could do is hold on and trust that the engineer wasn't drunk or a practical joker. A smart voter went for the guy who knew how to hang on and look good on television afterward. The television bit was important: you had to look like a President. Presidents don't sweat under the lights.

"Mr. President?"

Devol snapped out of his reverie. "Once again, please, Mr. Chambliss." This was the second visit in two days for Chambliss. My God!

"We have a report from extremely reliable sources, Mr. President, that Fidel Castro, minus his beard, is traveling incognito in the continental United States with two companions. A man resembling Castro and purporting to be Castro returned to Cuba on a chartered flight from New York. Our sources in Havana tell us that Castro is officially listed as ill with an intestinal virus as the result of drinking the water in New York." Chambliss paused and smirked. "The duties of Señor Castro are officially being handled by Rolando Paz until Castro is up and about." Chambliss rolled the R in Rolando. "However, the rumor in Havana is that Castro is not sick at all. Nobody knows where he is."

"I take it Raúl Castro is too weak to run the government."

"Radiation treatment, Mr. President."

"You're telling me we know where Castro is."

"We do indeed, Mr. President."

"Where is he?"

Chambliss cleared his throat. "We don't know exactly, Mr. President." He paused. "Not *exactly*."

Devol normally handled games players well but Chambliss in particular was a slicko. Devol wondered how he was being taken. He wondered if he really was stupid, as *The New Republic* had said in so many words a month earlier. "You don't know '*exactly*.' Would you care to tell me what that means, 'exactly'?"

Chambliss was not put off by the sarcasm. "Our source wants a paycheck."

"What kind of paycheck?" It was amazing how everything finally came down to a paycheck. No matter where he turned somebody had his hand out. Marx may have been wrong about almost everything else but he was right about greed.

"He says one million dollars."

Devol sighed. "He does, does he? Well what if you told him to shove it up his ass and break it off? What does my cousin Tony say about all this? And, while you're at it, why isn't he here instead of you? The Company isn't yours quite yet."

"Mr. Laurence is on the West Coast."

"On the West Coast. You have communicated with him, I take it." Devol started to say something but thought better of it. He wanted to hear Chambliss' line.

"Mr. Laurence wants to know if we should take Castro out, Mr. President."

Devol told himself not to shout at Chambliss. The best way to control a situation like this was to keep calm and rely on a President's ability to bully and intimidate. "Take him out? Take him out? Tony Laurence wants me to decide here, now, in this room, whether or not to assassinate Fidel Castro? I say again, why in the hell, Mr. Chambliss, is your superior not in this room with you if he has reason to believe Fidel Castro is on our soil, at our mercy. What could possibly be more important on the West Coast?"

"Mr. Laurence is on the West Coast, sir, on the Goldman matter we discussed yesterday." Chambliss shifted in his chair.

Devol was pleased to see him squirm. "Are you familiar, Mr. Chambliss, with the arguments about the motivation and control of Lee Harvey Oswald?"

"You mean am I familiar with the theory that Oswald was an agent of the Cubans sent in revenge for a botched attempt on Castro's life?"

"I'm asking exactly that."

"I'm one of the chief proponents of that theory, Mr. President. I believe there is overwhelming evidence that it's true. It isn't all that popular an idea at the agency as you might imagine. We were responsible for the failed attempt on Fidel's life."

"Knowing all that, Mr. Chambliss, I ask you a third time to tell me why I'm talking to you and not Tony Laurence? The manna enzyme can damn well wait."

"We have reason to believe Castro is on the West Coast, Mr. President. If we are to eliminate him we have to do it in the next twenty-four hours. After that, we believe, he'll be back in Havana."

Devol began doodling. "Who else knows about this?" Those bastards from Langley never tell the whole truth, Devol thought, not at once anyway. You had to drag it out of them. They didn't respect you if you didn't. If a President wasn't smart enough to play the game then that was tough. Devol may not have been a Rhodes scholar but he knew how to play games. That's how he got to be President.

"Our source, Tony, you, and I are the only ones who know, Mr. President."

"The four of us?"

"That's all, Mr. President."

"And Tony's recommendation?"

"Tony thinks we should prang him and make sausage out of his corpse." Chambliss smiled. "Or whatever."

Oh shit, Devol thought to himself. "Just what is it that Castro's supposed to be doing on the West Coast?"

"You want to know the truth, sir?"

"What the hell else would I want? Some cock-and-bull story?"

"Mr. President, remember we told you it was the Cubans who were after Goldman. Well, sir, it's not just any Cubans. It's Fidel Castro himself. It was easy for him to do. All he had to do was shave and buy a ticket on a commercial airline."

Devol looked incredulous. "Fidel Castro?"

"Yes, Mr. President." Chambliss nodded. "You remember it was the failure of the sugar crop in 1970 that drove the Cubans completely into the Russian camp. Castro understood he was striking a pact with the Devil, but he had to do it to feed his people. The Russians agreed to pay him twelve cents a pound for sugar worth seven."

"Oh, boy!" Devol took a deep breath. "Okay, assuming I believe this story of yours, who would take over on Castro's death—other than Raúl, of course."

"Our medical people tell us Raúl's cancer will kill him inside a year. We're looking at Rolando Paz, sir, an old line Fidelista."

"I've heard it before, I know, Mr. Chambliss, but I would like to hear the line on Paz again—just to refresh my memory."

"Paz is one of an influential group of Fidelistas and Raúlistas who were ousted from the Political Bureau by Soviet-backed Popular Socialists in 1972. They regained power in 1975 but were forced to rethink their attitude toward the Soviet Union. It was either back off or risk being purged again. The Soviets didn't like paying a nickel a pound over market for sugar to support soreheads in the Political Bureau. Paz has always been the most independent of the Fidelistas. The Soviets fought his appointment as president of the National Assembly but Castro saw to it anyway."

Devol tried not to appear impatient. "The only thing that really matters, Mr. Chambliss, is what he thinks of us."

"He believes Cuba's future would best be

served by opening up diplomatic relations and trade with the United States. He's had to be careful, of course. He's surrounded by Soviets. We believe Castro would like to do the same thing but he's trapped by his rhetoric and by his dependence on the Soviet dole. You don't preach hate for twenty years then simply turn it off one morning, like a tap. And while the Cubans would benefit economically by trade with the United States, it would take time to make up for the loss in Soviet aid. Paz may be able to do it, not Castro. That's why Fidel moved him, just under Raúl, in power."

"And when Raúl came down with cancer?"

"The Russians got nervous. After all it was Raúl, as the man in charge of the Cuban banking system, who pushed the Cubans toward the Soviet bloc in the first place. The revolution hadn't been Marxist in the beginning; it just turned out that way, partly because of our stupidity, partly because of Raúl."

"The Soviets don't like Paz."

Chambliss smiled. "An understatement, Mr. President."

"The Chinese like him, I suppose."

"The Chinese like anybody who doesn't like the Soviets."

"And do the Soviets know Castro is missing?"

"Oh, yes, they know he's missing, Mr. President. They have all those Red Army colonels down there dreaming up ways for Castro to do their dirty work for them. Troops in Africa and so on. They know he's missing, all right. But we don't think they know where he is."

"So what are the consequences if we prang him and get rid of the body?" Devol asked.

Chambliss smiled. "The Cubans would probably announce that he died of New York's water, hold private services, and make a big thing out of dumping his ashes over the Sierra Maestra, where the revolution began. There'll be poetry by José Martí, stuff like that."

"We'd be blamed, I suppose. There'd be rumors that we poisoned him."

Chambliss shrugged. "Maybe Paz would blame his death on the Soviets in order to open things up with us. It wouldn't make any difference: we'd have Paz in and the Russians out. The next day they'd want to import Coca-Cola and rock music."

Devol shook his head. "Paz in, the Russians out. How long do you think that would last?"

"We hope not long, Mr. President."

"Not long?" Devol didn't know what to say. Not long? We hope? What was this?

Chambliss leaned forward slightly. "Do you recall the line on Jaime Ramírez, next after Paz?"

"He was educated in the Soviet Union, as I recall, a pro-Russian hard-liner."

"No, no, Mr. President, you've got that wrong."

"Wrong?" Devol was certain. How could he forget about the number three Cuban?

"Jaime Ramírez, Mr. President, is an American mole."

"What?"

Chambliss allowed himself a short pause to let his statement lie there. It was more dramatic that way. "I'm his control, Mr. President."

"You?"

"Me. Tony set it up in 1959. Fidel doesn't know it, but the daughter of one of the men he had executed, a surgeon whose only sin was to have once performed a gallbladder operation on Fulgencio Batista, was to have married Ramírez."

Devol's demon anus, which had been calm like a dormant volcano, suddenly began to itch. He crumpled his doodles and threw them in the wastebasket. " 'Was to have married,' Mr. Chambliss?"

"The girl bungled an attempt to help her father escape to Miami. When she learned he had been tortured and castrated before he was executed, she killed herself."

"And you're his control?"

"I am, Mr. President."

"You were hoping not to have to tell me this, weren't you, Mr. Chambliss."

Chambliss looked embarrassed. Presidents come and go. A mole like Jaime Ramírez had to be kept secret, really secret.

Devol wondered if he had cornered Chambliss or if he was still being had somehow. "Tell me, Mr. Chambliss, is that why Bobby and Jack tried to kill Castro—to help your mole along?"

"Ramírez was a brilliant but minor Party functionary in those days. The Russians spot-

ted him and have been his chief sponsors
ever since. Mostly we just watch."

Devol laughed. "How do we know he's not
a double?"

Chambliss was calm. "Well, I guess we
don't. We never do in situations like this, do
we? Not really. Have you ever wondered how
the Soviets can be so sure about Kim Philby?"

Devol stood up.

"Well, Mr. President?"

"I'll let you know, Mr. Chambliss."

Chambliss didn't move, didn't speak.

"I said I'll let you know, Mr. Chambliss."

There was an awkward silence after which
Chambliss rose and left without shaking hands
with the President.

Devol had to go to the toilet.

CHAPTER

26

THE PREMIER'S SECRETARY USHERED IN VOL-
chak. Georgi Kagnanovich bade him to sit with
a wave of his hand. Volchak blinked once and
his tongue sought the pit on his front tooth.

Premier Kagnanovich winced when the
tongue moved but Volchak seemed not to
notice. Kagnanovich was grateful that Volchak's position required him to stay in the
background. The Premier was sensitive about
the image of the Russians with the rest of
the world. Nikita Khrushchev, for example, had
been especially embarrassing. Khrushchev had
a round face with jowls. He had porcine eyes
and a nose that looked like it had been stuck
on his face as a practical joke. The nose was a
shapeless blob covered with veins from Khrushchev's having consumed too much vodka.
Kagnanovich had been a rising young man in
the Party when Khrushchev whacked the podium with his shoe during a speech at the
United Nations. It had been an embarrassing
tirade. Kagnanovich was especially irritated
at what he thought was an international
stereotype of Russian women: solid, broad-

hipped with breasts hanging to their navels—pallid from staying inside all winter eating boiled potatoes and beet soup.

Kagnanovich did one hundred push-ups every morning then a hundred sit-ups and a six-mile run. He had been ambassador to the United Nations at one point in his career and had acquired a liking for Brut after-shave lotion, which was advertised on television in those days. He remembered that the American grid footballer Joe Namath appeared in the ads with beautiful women clinging to him. Tass correspondents bought his shirts in France, his shoes in Italy, his suits in London. Georgi Kagnanovich looked like a vice-president of Chase Manhattan.

Kagnanovich was vain but not dumb. Although Volchak was the man who looked like a breathing fish, Kagnanovich knew he had one of the quickest minds in Moscow. It was likely that Volchak was even brighter than Karpov but he would never succeed Karpov as head of the KGB, not with that tongue. Kagnanovich considered it fortunate that Volchak could be hidden from public view.

"Comrade Volchak." The Premier extended his hand.

"Comrade Kagnanovich." Volchak shook the Premier's hand and bowed his head slightly.

"I'm told we have a report from Colonel Strega in Havana."

Volchak's tongue paused. "Castro's missing," he said simply.

"Missing? How can that be?"

"Colonel Strega's of the opinion that he never returned from New York."

" 'Of the opinion'? Don't we know?" Kagnanovich was impatient with those who didn't do their job. It was Strega's duty to report Castro's every move to the Politburo. The KGB had a similar man in every Soviet client state in Eastern Europe, Asia, and Africa.

"Colonel Strega says he was told Castro has an intestinal virus from drinking the water in New York."

"Drinking the water in New York! That's good." Kagnanovich laughed. "What about his household staff, don't we have someone there?"

"Yes, Comrade, we have a young man named Paco Ortiz employed as the Premier's valet. Strega says Ortiz is missing also."

"Is it possible that the Cubans know this Ortiz is our man?"

Volchak pursed his lips. "Strega doesn't think so, but I disagree."

"Tell me about it," Kagnanovich said.

"I think Castro has known about Ortiz for at least two years now. I think he's been using Ortiz to tell us what we want to hear."

Kagnanovich looked at the French cuffs of his powder-blue shirt. He wondered if the sleeves might be a trifle long, the cuffs too showy. "Do you have any evidence of that, Comrade Volchak, or are you guessing?"

Volchak's tongue caressed his pitted tooth. "One rarely has proof of something like that, Comrade Kagnanovich. One watches and weighs. One understands deception. In the end, one learns to distrust anything that

works too well. This Ortiz, Comrade Kagnanovich, could be a double."

"Could be, Comrade Volchak?"

"Could be."

"But we don't know."

"One can never know in these matters."

Kagnanovich leaned back in his chair.
"But we do have to make decisions, don't
we, Comrade? We have a country to run,
responsibilities."

Volchak's tongue paused. He was, after all,
talking to Comrade Georgi Kagnanovich,
chairman of the Council of Ministers. "We do
have to make decisions. Would you say,
Comrade, that it is reasonable and in the best
interests of the motherland that we reasonably, dispassionately weigh the evidence and
proceed from there?"

Comrade Kagnanovich was not used to
people asking *him* questions; he, Georgi
Kagnanovich, asked others questions. Should
this man be silenced? No, thought Kagnanovich. He would hear what Volchak had
to say. "Of course that is how we should
proceed, Comrade Volchak. Say what you
have to say."

Volchak could feel his heart thumping. He
liked being second in command of the KGB.
He had spent his life struggling upward
through the hierarchy. Did he really want to
say what he thought? "I've been running
some programs through our computers the
last couple of months, Comrade Kagnanovich.
It's my opinion, based on what I think is a
valid analysis of our covert foreign operations, that in cases where we may be dealing

with a double—and that includes virtually all cases where we are working with an indigenous informant—we're fooling ourselves if we think we have any evidence to weigh.''

Kagnanovich muffled a cough with his hand. He had been in control of both the State and Party apparatus for two years and had never had a subordinate make a statement like that. Volchak was risking Siberia. Kagnanovich wondered why and concluded it was Volchak's accursed tongue. No one would defend a man with a mouth like a breathing fish. Volchak must have despaired and decided the hell with it all. "I said say what you have to say, Comrade Volchak. I meant it."

Volchak smiled. He leaned forward eagerly. His tongue sprang into action, punctuating everything he said. "Thank you for hearing me out, Comrade. I appreciate it. Take the case of Ortiz, sir. He's a political, recruited by Strega as a student in Havana. As you know there are those who believe politicals are the most reliable."

"And you, what do you think?"

"Infidelity is nothing anymore, and there are known homosexuals in the British Parliament and the American Congress. It's getting hard to blackmail anyone." Volchak laughed. "There's little risk in the approach though, I'll admit that. Entrepreneurs have always been the riskiest. You never know what they're liable to do. Never. As I said, take Ortiz, a political, ambitious, resentful that he's going nowhere. We put him next to Castro, the Premier. Ortiz is just a kid. What does a kid know? How can we be so sure of him? Castro's a bore in public but he has his charm in private. There's status in going everywhere with the Premier. It's easy enough to shift your loyalty in a situation like that."

"Easy to double, you're saying, Comrade Volchak."

Volchak nodded. "I'd say almost certain to double. Every foreign national has a situation that is uniquely his. It's virtually impossible for us to know all the details, Comrade Kagnanovich. A man may act as he does because of his environment, because of some tragedy in his past. We can never know for sure. Strega says Ortiz is missing. He could be ours and be burned. He could be held somewhere. He could be dead. He could be ours and not be burned, I'll grant you that. Maybe he just can't communicate with his case officer. He could be theirs also, Comrade, theirs, and wanting us to think he's ours and unable to communicate. The problem is the possibilities split off and divide almost geometrically until we're lost in a maze of what could have happened."

Kagnanovich considered that. "So in your opinion what do we do, Comrade Volchak?"

"We check and recheck everything we get from an indigenous. We look for something that isn't right somehow. It may not be much. It may be subtle, a hint, a suggestion, no more. We allow only our most experienced people to handle a source in Ortiz's position. Colonel Strega is an example. But we suspect the worst, always."

"How far back did you take your inquiry, Comrade Volchak?"

For Aleksandr Cherenenkovich Volchak there was no turning back. "To Beria, Comrade."

"So, Fidel Castro is missing and so is our young man Ortiz. Comrade Karpov and Comrade Rubashov are in the United States on the Goldman matter. What do we make of it?"

"We learned about the manna enzyme from Fidel at a place he thought was safe. We relied on an electronic listening device. For our own protection we are forced to conclude Castro believes in the potential of the enzyme. He believes it is real. We don't even think about Ortiz anymore. Whether he's ours or theirs makes no difference. We write him off. We assume, again for our protection, that Castro is somewhere outside Havana directing an operation to kidnap Goldman and deliver manna to the Third World. We assume he doesn't trust us and doesn't want us involved."

"Are you saying, Comrade Volchak, that we were foolish to send Comrade Karpov and Comrade Rubashov to join the Americans and the Brit?"

Volchak shook his head no. His tongue kept moving. "The risks are great but so are the stakes. No, what I'm asking is how we know manna is real and if it is real, how do we know Laurence isn't ahead of us, using us rather than the other way around?"

Kagnanovich was momentarily distracted by his cuff. He'd have to have another tailor brought in. "We cannot make mistakes, Comrade Volchak. We can't afford it. We represent the Soviet workers." It was a stupid statement. He knew it and knew Volchak knew it.

"We have backup contacts and alternate communications. Comrade Karpov is the best in the world. We have Strega." The tongue paused. "We also have Rubashov, Comrade." It was Volchak's turn to feel like a fool.

Kagnanovich rose from behind his desk. "Keep me informed."

Volchak bowed his head slightly, rose, and prepared to leave.

Kagnanovich stopped him with a gesture of his hand. Kagnanovich cleared his throat. "Comrade Volchak, I have a personal question for you."

"Certainly, Comrade," said Volchak.

"I don't mean to be prying, but do you have any kind of personal life? I mean is there a woman or someone?" He knew from having read Volchak's dossier that there was none.

Volchak blinked once and wet his lips. He wondered why he was being quizzed about his personal life. Was he about to be sent to Siberia?

"Comrade Volchak, I want you to have your teeth capped. My secretary will call the appropriate surgeons and make an appointment. I want it done immediately. The next time I see you, I want that accursed tongue of yours stopped. I want it to remain inside your mouth, where it belongs. And I want you to get yourself laid. Is that clear?"

Volchak grinned, forgetting his tongue. "Yes, Comrade."

Kagnanovich winced. "Go now, Comrade Volchak. If Karpov communicates with you, I want to know immediately. Do you understand?"

"I understand."

Kagnanovich waved him out and Volchak was gone. The Premier sat alone in his office. It was either have Volchak's teeth fixed or shoot him. There seemed no other way.

CHAPTER

27

THEY COULDN'T SEE THE DAM AT SODA SPRINGS or the reservoir above it. The highway cut to the far right of the valley, hugging the rising mountains. The reservoir at Soda Springs, low and to the left, was obscured by manzanita and stands of Douglas fir. The reservoir was not accessible by automobile, so the water was underfished except by those willing to float down from above and paddle back. Outboards were forbidden. Fishermen told stories of enormous lunkers there, lurking fat-bodied in the shadows of the steep banks that lead up from the water—German Browns and rainbows.

There was a ranger station at the upper end of the reservoir and behind that a small powerhouse at the end of an enclosed aqueduct that delivered water from high in the mountains. The water roiled up from the mouth of the generator. Trout gathered there for reasons known only to God and forest rangers, for they were the only fishermen willing to endure the noise of the generator to drift wet flies in the wake. They caught their limit.

Perini drove with his elbow hanging out of the window. Laurence and Rubashov sat in the rear. If they minded the wind, they said nothing. Perini slowed so Laurence could see pumice in the slopes where the engineers had sliced the mountains with earthmovers to make way for the highway. A mile past the power station, Perini was forced to stop for a blacktail doe who waited on the bad end of a blind corner. She stood looking at them like a large dog with one ear slightly askew.

"I wish I had a camera," Rue said.

"She's beautiful," Laurence said.

"They have deer like that in the Urals," Rubashov said. "My father has a dacha on the Volga, near Kalinin. There is a game preserve there. The deer are lovely." He started to say something more but shut up.

"These are blacktails," Perini said. "The mulies on the eastern side are larger."

"I started to say I wish Karpov were here," Rubashov said.

The doe blinked at last, as though acknowledging, reluctantly, that she must leave. She turned in one twisting, graceful leap, and scrambled up a slope kicking loose yellow hunks of pumice and a fine cloud of dust that floated in the thin mountain air. When she was gone there was an odd silence, broken only by the popping of timber expanding from the heat.

"And what does your father do at Kalinin, Comrade Rubashov?" Laurence asked.

"My father? Nothing," Rubashov said. He paused. "He works for the government."

"Doesn't everybody in the Soviet Union?" Laurence asked.

"Ahh." Rubashov smiled. "Yes, they do."

Diamond Lake, the headwaters of the Umpqua, is just north of the national park at Crater Lake. It remains frozen through the early summer. The lake is flanked on three sides by steep, jagged slopes. Like its more famous neighbor, Diamond Lake appears to sit in the mouth of one of the many extinct volcanoes that form the Cascade Chain, part of a geologic flaw that runs from the Aleutians to the tip of Chile.

In the winter, rainbow trout planted by the Oregon State Game Commission feed unmolested in the lake, isolated by snowdrifts that pile to the eaves of the lodge. In July, the fishermen come, trailed closely by mosquitoes and tourists with cameras and overheated automobile engines. It is possible in the summer for a fisherman with a good trolling motor to limit out on three- to five-pound trout. For that reason schoolteachers, vacationers, and tourists in Winnebagos, Ford pickups with aluminum canopies, and sedans pulling U-Haul trailers compete for parking spaces on the road leading into the lodge.

The sky above Diamond Lake was a pale, cool blue that became paler still as it approached the horizon. There it washed to nothing on the crest of jagged mountains. The lodge itself was heavy, built in the 1930s, with the musty smell of old worms and half-rotted wood of fishing resorts everywhere.

Inside, a girl in a white blouse totaled bills on an old-fashioned cash register decorated with elaborate floral designs. A name tag on her blouse identified her as Bobbi. Pictures of grinning fishermen holding trout by the gills were taped on the underside of a glass case. There was a wooden toothpick dispenser on top of the glass along with a box of chocolate-covered mints and a wire rack of postcards. The rack squeaked when it was turned. One of the postcards showed a man riding a giant jackrabbit. The guests, older people enjoying the view of the lake, an assortment of fishermen, and younger people trying not to stare too hard at the menu prices, ate in a large hall. The sound of scraping chairs and fishermen laughing off the frustrations of a long day on the water echoed off the hardwood floor and high ceiling. It was a place where sunburned anglers enjoyed a cold beer and a cheeseburger with a thick slice of onion.

It was there that Eddie Perini, flanked by Rue Kadera and Comrade Rubashov, opened a bag of onion-flavored potato chips and looked out on the lake beyond the windows. They could see a stretch of grass near the lodge where wives waited and girl friends sunned, listening warily for the faint buzz of bloated mosquitoes. On the lake itself floated so many aluminum and Fiberglas boats as to make Perini shake his head in dismay. Out there somewhere was Bernard Goldman hoping for a fishing story to tell back in Edinburgh.

Laurence could see the three of them from the phone booth. "Well, what did my cousin say?"

"He wouldn't say anything, Tony," Chambliss replied.

"We take him then," Laurence said.

"If you get the chance. Use your judgment."

"If something goes wrong they'll blame it on him, anyway."

"That's the way I see it."

Laurence laughed. He thought of telling Chambliss about Karpov but thought better of it. He didn't have time to explain. "Later, James." He hung up.

They rented two aluminum boats: one for Laurence and Rubashov, the other for Perini and Kadera. Laurence was reading the starting instructions on his ten-horsepower Evinrude when Rue Kadera tapped him on the shoulder.

"Fishing must not be too good here, Tony."

Laurence looked up. "Huh?"

"There goes our professor friend." She pointed to a maroon Volkswagen bus that was pulling out of a nearby parking lot.

"You get the license?"

"It's the same."

Rubashov looked impressed. "You British have a way, Miss Kadera."

Rue Kadera didn't answer. Rubashov didn't expect her to. Both were running after Perini, who was unlocking their car. Laurence took the passenger side on the front seat. Perini drove. "Stay back, Eddie, but don't take a chance of losing him. So far as we know, he doesn't have any reason to believe anybody is following him."

They followed Goldman to Soda Springs Reservoir, which lay two hundred yards downstream from the ranger station and powerhouse they had passed earlier. Laurence motioned for Perini to park their car well short of where Goldman parked his bus. "I think we need to consider this."

Perini felt his heart thumping. "Consider what, Tony?"

"We could take him from here," Rubashov said.

Laurence shook his head no. "Not with the ranger station there. I think one of us should talk to him first and verify what he told the student, Vivanco, and what his son told Perini."

"Americans." Rubashov shook his head in disgust.

"Oh, we have the stomach," Laurence said mildly. "We just want to be certain. We've got him to ourselves. We always have a responsibility to make sure in a case like this, if at all possible. We should do it right." Laurence watched as Goldman removed a rubber life raft from the rear of the bus and began filling it with a hand pump. Goldman worked in the shadow of a high bluff that flanked the highway side of the reservoir— which was several miles long and no more than twenty to thirty yards across at its widest—sloped gently up into sugar pine and Douglas fir.

"I agree with Tony," Rue Kadera said. She

wondered who would have to shoot Goldman. She didn't want to be the one.

Laurence shifted on the front seat and looked back at Kadera and Rubashov. "The way I see it the three of us should hike upstream there, cross the bridge, and work our way down on the far side of the reservoir. We'll take the heavy stuff. Eddie, Goldman knows you. I want you to take a handgun and work your way along the top of the bluff until you can find a way to get down to the water. When you do, I want you to tell Goldman he's in danger. Tell him we're on the far side waiting to help." Laurence would have preferred to let the mercenaries do it but they were nowhere in sight. He couldn't take a chance on the Cubans finding him first.

Perini closed his eyes. "Just like that! Say 'Hello there, Doc. There're some good people across the way who wanna ask you a few questions then blow your head off.'"

"Unless you prefer we just hike down the other side and take him out, no questions asked. We can do that. I never said this was going to be any fun."

Perini watched as the figure at the water's edge wrestled the raft into the river. "I'll take the Walther PPK."

Rubashov looked disgusted. "You Americans have the minds of grocers. You weigh everything."

Laurence glared at him. "Maybe you're right there, friend. Maybe we should have followed George Patton's advice."

"What's that?" Rubashov looked puzzled.

"Maybe we should have kept those tanks rolling right on through to Moscow."

Rubashov laughed. "Hitler tried."

Eddie Perini stopped them with his hand. "What do you say let's get this awful business over with and get on out of here?"

"Done," Laurence said. He was still irked.

"I think so," Rubashov said. He was wondering who the hell George Patton was. Rubashov's brush with history had been brief.

A half hour later Laurence, Kadera, and Rubashov eased through the bushes and settled in some twenty yards from the shoreline where a solitary man fished for trout in the shadows of the bluff on the far side of the reservoir. There was a break in the bluff. The break led to a narrow strip of beach by the water and would put Eddie Perini not ten yards from Goldman.

"Little bit of luck for Eddie," Laurence whispered.

Rue Kadera nodded but didn't reply. Rubashov settled down for the wait.

Laurence's right index finger caressed the trigger of the M21. He was a reflective man. When he was alone he watched and listened, weighed and judged. He adjusted the 2-by-10.5 Leopold and Vary, bringing the figure on the raft into sharp clarity. Laurence could see the individual hairs on Goldman's neck. He could see the stitching on the seams of Goldman's short-sleeved shirt. He could watch Goldman's fingernails when he scratched his jaw.

A slight breeze stirred, making a lowing

sound in the Douglas firs on the mountain above him and ruffling the water on the reservoir. Laurence remembered practicing on the M21 in the forests of Virginia. The forests were different in Virginia. The trees were deciduous. In the winter the trees, stripped of color, were barren and hard as the cold wind swept down from northwestern Maryland. In the spring the trees turned, the sap rose, leaves appeared, promising warmth and life. In the summer the forests were impenetrable. No breeze stirred in the wet heat. There was no soft lowing as here in the Cascades.

Laurence traced the cut of Goldman's sideburns with the cross hairs of the telescopic sight.

In the fall, when the leaves were dying, Virginians, Marylanders, and residents of the District took to the highways to watch the color on the Skyline Drive in the Appalachians. The third week of October was when the leaves turned. The third week, almost always. It was in a secluded place, where the Appalachians rose from the fields and farms of the Virginia flatlands, that Anthony Laurence learned how to shoot an M21.

There were no farms or fields at the firing range, however. There was the sound of insects, he remembered, then the sound of his instructor's quiet voice telling him how to put the cross hairs of the telescopic sight on the cardboard head in the distance, telling him how to pull the trigger. The instructor had spoken of nerves, of breathing, of anticipation. Now, watching Goldman shift positions on the rubber raft, he remembered the colors of that distant day, remembered the blue of his instructor's eyes, the soft greens of summer.

He remembered that the cardboard men appeared without warning in the distance. Laurence moved the scope. Nothing. "I'll never understand where they get guys like you," said the instructor, who wore plastic earmuffs clipped over his head with a metal band. "There, there, and there," the instructor pointed again. He picked up his own M21 and fired three shots, crack, crack, crack, snapping a cardboard man with each shot. When he was finished he removed his earmuffs and looked at Laurence, saying nothing.

Laurence remembered the cardboard faces. They had straight noses, straight lines for mouths. The mouths did not turn down, suggesting hate. They did not turn up, suggesting warmth. They were not Europeans, Asians, or black men. They were targets. They were morally neutral. You shot them because you had to. Laurence put the cross hairs on Goldman's ear then moved to the bridge of his nose. He watched as Goldman changed flies, sitting spraddle-kneed, working on a knot with his front teeth and both hands. He finished his knot, trimmed the ends with fingernail clippers, and lofted the line gracefully into the shadows of the bluff.

There were no muffled drums. There was no soaring music by Elmer Bernstein, Maurice Jarre, or Dmitri Tiomkin to warn of an approaching climax. There was the sound of insects. Laurence could not tell by a dimly lit fluorescent clock on the far wall of the theater that his time was near. There was no commercial break to let him relieve his bladder and warn him the finale was at hand. There were no tricks of artists, wizards, and storytellers with their editors and directors to ease his tension and soften his anxiety, to let him know that justice would somehow triumph. Laurence had no way of knowing how many pages were left. There could be a hundred. There could be a paragraph. Could be.

Laurence knew only what was. He knew his forearm itched. He knew the acrid smell of pine and fir. He knew the musty odor of the crumbling log against which he rested his M21 and the future of those fortunate to have been born in the developed, temperate world. He knew the sun that moved left to right above the highest reaches of the valley of the Umpqua, named for a tribe of American aborigines that were no more. He knew insects rustling nervously in the heat of the afternoon. He knew the reservoir. He knew the steep bluff on the far side.

He knew there was a man in a rubber life raft on the water whose name was Bernard Goldman, who held a secret that could either feed the poor people of the world or destroy the economies of the industrial nations.

Anthony Laurence knew something, only something, of history and history's ills. He knew about the tight, self-righteous Swedes and their taxes, Volvos, and collaboration with the Nazis. He knew about the brutally efficient Germans. He knew about the Italians and their sharp wine and good food. For a while the Italians changed their governments more often than some men change their underwear. He knew about the Spaniards and the debilitating heat of the Mediterranean sun. Was that classic North-South? he wondered. Was that sun, which leached and baked and sapped, also responsible for North Vietnam–South Vietnam, Japan–Southeast Asia, North America–South America, even North–South in the Civil War?

Laurence wondered where Perini was. Had he crossed the bridge behind the forest camp? He had, Laurence concluded. He must be on the other side, picking his way through the underbrush. In the underbrush it would be easy for Perini to lose his sense of time and distance. In order to reach the break in the cliff, he would have to ease his way to the edge periodically to gauge his progress by Laurence's side of the river. If Goldman should move either upstream or downstream from Perini's access to the water, Laurence's plan was ruined.

Goldman, however, seemed content to stay where he was.

Laurence adjusted the Leopold and Vary and scanned the brush at the top of the embankment, hoping to catch a glimpse of Perini. He listened also, not for Perini, on the other side of the reservoir, but for movement on his own side. The Cubans might be coming soon.

Kadera stirred beside him. Rubashov muffled a cough. "What do you think, Mr. Laurence?" he whispered.

"I think it's hard to wait, Comrade." Although Laurence was director of the CIA, he was in fact a soldier. He understood that and accepted it. Institutions exist for reasons that are outwardly logical, if sometimes unacceptable. Being a member of the Company was much like being married. It had its moments of excitement but it also made its demands. Laurence understood that also. There was no use being frightened or having second thoughts—it was too late. Following the logic of the institution and its reason for being, one did what one had to do.

There were less than sixty yards between the curve of the reservoir and the shadow of the bluff where Goldman worked the still waters with his fly rod.

They were ten yards around the curve before Anthony Laurence realized they were there: canoes. Aluminum canoes. Rented from the lodge at Diamond Lake.

There were two of them.

Laurence heard a fish slap the water as he scanned the occupants of the canoes.

From front to back, the first canoe contained three figures Laurence recognized as Jan deJonette, R. Cardinal, and Mikki Scanlan. Scanlan was wearing a pastel-blue hat with a wide brim and flowered blouse. Shit!

Laurence did not recognize the first two men in the far canoe. He recognized the third man: Fidel Castro.

He understood the wacko circumstance that the men in each canoe were oblivious of the identity of the other. They were both pretending to be out for trout this lovely sunny day.

He also knew they recognized Bernard Goldman straight ahead in the water. It was his time. Their time.

Anthony Laurence was aware that he was an agent acting on behalf of the government of the United States and ultimately on behalf of the economies of the NATO and Warsaw Pact countries.

Eddie Perini had not been able to talk to Bernard Goldman.

Stroke, stroke, stroke. The canoes shot through the water, drawing closer to Goldman with each dip of the paddle.

Laurence pulled to the right and held the cross hair on the ear of Bernard Goldman.

Laurence pulled the scope to the left.

Mikki Scanlan, looking dead ahead at Goldman, adjusted the brim of his hat.

Fidel Castro dug the blades of his paddle into the water with great, deep, hard strokes.

There is no aspect of the cybernetic revolution, not one, equal to the human brain. No memory chip, no machine capable ultimately of distinguishing only between one and zero, between plus and minus, can equal the human brain in comprehending instantly the consequences of the decision now facing Anthony Laurence.

It was now. All at once.

Consider:

If Laurence pulled down on Castro and scored, thus assuring an American mole in charge of Cuba, Goldman might live.

If he pulled down on Castro and missed, Goldman still might live.

If he pulled down on Goldman and hit, Castro might live. Manna might be real; it might be fake. But the market would continue.

If Laurence pulled down on Goldman and missed, both manna and the mole in Havana might be lost.

Laurence moved the cross hairs onto the side of Bernard Goldman's head and pulled the trigger. Goldman's head exploded like an egg under a hammer. Shards of his skull ripped across Soda Springs Reservoir.

Dann, sitting at the point of Castro's canoe, turned with an automatic weapon and raked Scanlan's canoe. R. Cardinal's magnificent chin disappeared. So too his shoulder and most of his chest.

Scanlan was caught in the throat, a pumper squirting great crimson streaks of blood, one catching deJonette in the eye as deJonette turned his weapon on the Castro canoe and the general direction of Laurence and Rubashov.

He took Dann and Rivera cleanly, halving their torsos.

Two survived.

Castro, who was underwater stroking deep and hard.

And deJonette, who did likewise. A ribbon of blood from a chest wound trailed him in the water.

As Eddie Perini plunged thirty feet down the cut in the embankment, he lost his Walther PPK automatic pistol. Laurence was on his feet, scanning the reservoir with the

Leopold and Vary. If Castro surfaced, he had missed him.

"Castro! Goddammit, Castro!" he screamed at Perini, who was on his hands and knees on the narrow shelf at the base of the bluff, his left hand covering most of his face.

"What?" Perini called back.

"Castro! Get him, you son-of-a-bitch, get him!"

Perini looked stupidly at his hand, which was covered with blood. It was coming from his nose. He wiped a handful of blood on his thigh. The blood kept flowing. "Lost my grip up there," he said. He looked back up the bluff.

"Castro!" Laurence yelled at the back of his head.

Perini seemed not to understand. He knelt to slosh some cold water on his face when he saw, for the first time, the corpses on the water. Soda Springs Reservoir had virtually no current; the corpses, minus a head here, a shoulder or a torso there, floated like rag dolls in soft, billowing folds of pink. It was surreal, as though it had been painted in acrylics of startling clarity by Salvador Dali. The slight breeze had pushed the yellow life raft to the shore. He looked across the narrow reservoir again. Had Laurence spoken to him? What was Laurence doing? "What happened?" he asked vaguely. He did not look at Laurence. He looked at the bodies on the water in front of him. He had drunk beer with one of them at the Horse Brass Pub.

The man who discovered manna had part of a neck, but no head.

"I said, get Castro!" Laurence yelled.

"Get him? I don't understand." Perini slumped back against the bluff. Rue Kadera now stood behind Laurence.

Laurence looked upstream and downstream. He had completely lost Castro in the confusion. If he was alive, Castro would come out on Perini's side of the reservoir, not his own. Laurence was enraged at being on the wrong side. "Waste him, Eddie."

Perini shook his head. "I don't think I understand."

"Kill him."

Perini turned his empty palms up. "With what? I lost my Walther. And who says so?" A few days ago he was shooting a game of English darts in a tournament, now this. He felt like Walter Mitty.

"My cousin says so."

"Your cousin?"

"The President of the United States, Eddie. If Castro's alive, he's gonna come out of the water on your side. When he does, I want you to run him down and choke him with a pine cone or scratch his eyes out with your fingernails. I don't care how you do it but I want him dead."

Perini could hear a grasshopper. "Me?"

"You."

Perini looked down his side of the reservoir. They were no more than thirty yards apart and their discussion had an odd, conversational quality about it that was eerie. "You tell me what I do now, Tony. You tell me." He rubbed his hand on his nose and looked at the fingers. The blood had stopped coming.

"Listen, I can't circle up to the bridge to help you out. The minute I tried he would swim to this side and be gone in the woods. That's if he's still alive. I'll stay here with my M21. We'll assume for starters that he went downstream on your side."

"You want me to go downstream?"

"Downstream looking for footprints in the sand. I'll send Rue Kadera downstream on this side. When you find him, yell. I'll circle upstream and cross the bridge to join you."

"Where's Rubashov?"

"Rubashov's bleeding to death."

Perini remembered Aldo Ray dying a sweaty, dramatic death on an atoll in the Pacific. But that was in the movies—against the Japanese. Afterward, Perini had gone with a girl named Leanne Graebner, she of the great butt, to drink beer in a parked car. "Who shot him? One of these?" Perini gestured at the corpses which had floated six or eight feet downstream in the slow-moving water.

"None of those. DeJonette," Laurence said.

"Who the hell's deJonette?"

"It doesn't make any difference now, Eddie. We have to think about Castro. We've got our orders."

Without saying another word and wondering why he was doing it, Perini began trotting downstream on the narrow shelf of beach at the base of the bluff overlooking Soda Springs Reservoir. He was thinking how lucky Valery Karpov was to have died

n his sleep. He remembered studying exis-
entialism in a philosophy course as an undergraduate. There were certain questions,
he recalled, that were held to be unanswer-
able and therefore absurd to ask. He couldn't
remember what they were and laughed to
himself as he watched for a sign of Castro's
having emerged from the reservoir. He wondered what would happen if Castro had
drowned or one of the privates had cut him
in half in the confusion. They couldn't leave
him there in the water. What if some fisherman found him and a small-town cop sent
his fingerprints in to the FBI for identifica-
tion? Perini wondered if Castro's prints were
recorded in whatever computer bank held
the records for national agency checks.

No, it wouldn't do for a stranger to find
Fidel Castro's corpse in Soda Springs Reservoir.

CHAPTER

28

EDDIE PERINI DIDN'T FIND FIDEL CASTRO'S
corpse. He did find the place where Castro
had crawled out of the reservoir. He'd hunted
big buck mule deer in the Blue Mountains of
eastern Oregon as a youngster and knew how
to follow a spoor. Mulies are tough. They can
leap fifteen feet sideways as casually as a
five-year-old picks his nose. Castro was easier.
He was overweight, lead-footed, predictable, and running for his life. Castro's footprints led out of the reservoir basin into an
almost impenetrable thicket of lodgepole pine.

"Hey, here!" Perini yelled. He had covered
nearly a half mile since he left Laurence but
knew Laurence would be able to hear him in
the silence of the mountain afternoon.

A hundred and fifty miles to the west, on
the Oregon coast, lodgepole pines are swept
by salt air and beaten by gales. They're
short, stocky trees with widespread foliage
and twisted crowns. In the interior and at
higher elevations in the Cascades, lodgepoles
grow in dense stands of slender trees six
inches or less in diameter, rising fifty feet or

more in height. The thicket at Soda Springs was so dense as to be nearly impassable. The trees rose from tangles of sharp-pointed Pinemat manzanita struggling under a burden of generations of lodgepoles felled by lightning, disease, and old age—resembling nothing so much as scrambled pickup-sticks of a child's game. The tops of the lodgepoles bore thin foliage. The bottom three-fourths were bare except for the stubs of dead branches. The thicket was mountain gothic: dark, silent, forbidding, brooding; the ground beneath the manzanita was barren save for lichen, fungus, and moss.

Perini followed Castro's trail into the thicket.

He heard Castro before he saw him. He followed a dull pop into the brooding thicket, realizing a man had to look almost straight up to see the sky. He heard another popping sound, parted manzanita with his hands and began scrambling over fallen lodgepoles in the direction of his quarry. Twenty feet into the thicket a dead tree gave way under Perini, and sent him crashing onto the forest floor which was brick-hard from summer heat and lack of rain.

Castro, up ahead, must have heard the pine give way.

Perini picked up the pace, maneuvering over, under, and around lodgepole pines in the direction of the retreating Fidel Castro. He had gotten no more than forty yards into the thicket when the wind began to blow in earnest. Earlier in the day there had been a fitful wind, stopping and starting, moving this way and that according to changes in temperature of the land mass. It blew hard now.

"Laurence!" Perini shouted as loud as he could. "Laurence!" He wondered if Castro would recognize the name of the head of the Central Intelligence Agency.

Perini heard the sound of a rifle somewhere behind him. Laurence had heard the shot too and was on his way. The sounds of Castro's retreat were becoming louder. Perini was gaining on his quarry.

The rifle fired again.

"Here!" Perini yelled. "Laurence!"

Laurence's weapon sounded twice. One was a question: Where are you? Two was the affirmative: I hear you. Laurence hadn't heard the first time. He had the second.

Perini worked his way through the tangles of manzanita. He didn't see the manzanita, however. The pointed leaves raked his forearms but he didn't feel them. Nor the sweat that slid down from his eyebrows and ran into his eyes. He wiped his eyes with the back of his hand, which was itself caked with dust. The wind, which swayed the tops of the creaking lodgepoles, didn't penetrate the interior of the thicket. It was hot and quiet on the floor. Perini took a spiderweb across his open mouth. He batted at it with his hand, nearly gagging when he inadvertently inhaled. He stopped to scratch his ankle and realized he was being pursued by a swarm of mosquitoes. The lodgepoles creaked and groaned. There was a shrill whistling high above where the tops of the pines twisted and lashed against one another. The pines sounded like people weeping.

Perini wished he had worn a long-sleeved shirt. He slapped a mosquito on the side of his face and continued through the manzanita. He ignored the heat, ignored the mosquitoes. He saw only the headless corpse of Bernard Goldman floating in a pink aura in the cold water of Soda Springs Reservoir. There had been whitish strings of flesh floating from the stump of his neck. Perini remembered it clearly; an artery that led nowhere, the color of the water.

He heard something in the thicket up ahead: Fidel Castro.

He heard the sound of a rifle behind him: Anthony Laurence.

"Here!" he heard himself shout. "Here, Tony!"

The rifle sounded twice behind him. Eddie Perini felt history closing in.

Then, as abruptly as it had begun, the thicket of lodgepoles ended. Perini stepped onto a large, sunny meadow covered with yellow flowers and meadowgrass that was bent nearly double by the wind. The meadow broke gently downhill to a lazy, stagnant creek. The creek was marked by cattails and broad-leafed swamp grass. Perini saw a magpie in the distance and the figure of a man, Fidel Castro, dragging himself out of the muck.

"Tony!" Perini yelled again. He began running downhill toward Castro.

Castro slapped a mosquito. "¡Mierda!" He had welts all over his neck and streaks of blood on his forehead, where he had swatted bloated mosquitoes before they could move. Castro was exhausted. He couldn't move any longer. He had heard the shots back there in the pine forest. He knew they were after him. That little twit, Ortiz, had probably gotten word to the Soviets before Rodríguez had a chance to take him out. Or else it was the Americans who were chasing them. They probably had a man on his staff, too.

Well, it didn't make any difference now. Castro had had it. He was trembling from fatigue. He felt like vomiting. He wondered what in heaven had persuaded him he could return to the mountains at his age. It was stupid. He saw the distant figure of a man running down the meadow in his direction. Castro's mouth was dry. He was thirsty. He looked up the meadow in front of him. It was another three hundred yards to the next thicket of lodgepoles. He sighed and got up. He'd have to try.

Perini's knees buckled from fatigue at each stride. He was so tired he couldn't lift his arms up. He ran openmouthed, his eyes stung from sweat. He saw Castro get to his feet on the far side of the swampy stream. He wondered why Castro didn't run. He just stood there.

It was a hundred and seventy-five, maybe two hundred yards. Anthony Laurence adjusted the Leopold and Vary on the M21 and moved the cross hairs along the dark ribbon of swamp grass until he found Castro. He trained it on Fidel's face to assure himself it was Castro. It was. He moved the cross hairs lower and eased off the safety. He would take Castro first, then Perini. Laurence was exhausted and couldn't hold the mark. He moved the stock higher on the fallen lodgepole. The cross hairs moved slowly left and right but wouldn't hold. Laurence, remembering the advice of an instructor one far-off day in Virginia, took a deep breath and let it out slowly, smoothly, watching the slow sway of the cross hairs for the right moment.

It was time.

Anthony Laurence's head exploded as Bernard Goldman's had an hour earlier.

Perini turned when he heard the shot and saw a man emerge from the thicket of lodgepoles. That would be Laurence. He looked down the meadow at the stream and saw that Fidel Castro had sat down again. He had apparently given up.

Castro looked up the sloping meadow at the man with a rifle. It was no use running. They would take him in the open. His only chance was to wait. Maybe something would happen. Maybe he could take them by surprise. What a fool he was. What a jackass. All this and no manna. No speeches. No parades. No telling the Americans and Russians where they could shove it. All this and no beard even. He felt like an asshole without his beard. All this and he would be killed and buried in a mountain meadow, fertilizer for swamp grass and yellow flowers.

Valery Karpov unscrewed the curved metal stock from the Russian machine pistol that Rubashov had hidden for him outside the cabin. He strolled casually down the meadow.

It was a nice walk. The Cascades were lovely mountains. He had to admit that. There had been a mountain meadow like this in the Urals where he had gone fishing with some army officers from the Kremlin. There had been yellow flowers too. A swampy stream. And mosquitoes. He wondered how Perini would react when he saw him.

Perini acknowledged the shot with a wave of his arm, then sat, then flopped on his back, arms outstretched, looking at the sky. He felt the breeze and waited for whatever was to happen next. He unbuttoned his shirt and let the cooling air race across his sweaty chest. Laurence was here. It was Laurence's show now. Murdering Castro was Laurence's doing, not his. Perini was a sportswriter. He waited in the cooling wind when a shadow crossed his face. There was a man standing above him, looking down.

Valery Karpov.

"What?" Perini stared up, openmouthed.

Karpov grinned. "You're surprised, I take it."

Perini blinked. "That's hardly the word for it. How?"

Karpov squatted beside Perini, who made no move to get up. Karpov plucked a blade of meadow grass and began chewing on it, keeping an eye on Castro at the bottom of the swale. "Scientists call it biofeedback. With proper training, Eddie, one has the ability to train and manipulate what we are taught are automatic responses of the central nervous system; pulse, heartbeat, and so on. I studied for two years under Swami Tarmananda at the Yoga Center at Chandigarh almost fifteen years ago. I've practiced it ever since as a form of relaxation and meditation. Given a couple of hours of concentration, I can reduce my pulse to twelve beats a minute."

Perini was too exhausted to look either surprised or bewildered. "Twelve beats a minute. No wonder Laurence thought you were dead."

"Tarmananda could get by on six. I'm surprised Laurence didn't get a clue from my dossier. He always struck me as a careful man. He should have studied my dossier." Karpov got to his feet. "Well, Señor Castro is waiting. Won't you join me, Eddie?"

Perini didn't think he had much choice in the matter. He got to his feet and walked by Karpov's side for the remaining one hundred yards to Castro, who watched them from the far side of the swampy creek. "And Tony, Comrade Karpov?"

"Dead," said Karpov. "The last shot you heard. He was about to murder Premier Castro." Karpov gestured back up the meadow toward Laurence's corpse.

Perini looked back at the lodgepoles. He was too tired to be shocked or alarmed. He was ready to believe anything. Laurence was a bit of a jerk, in his opinion, but he was sorry to see him dead. Laurence had been acting according to the inexorable logic of an institution Perini regarded as barbaric but necessary. Perini didn't like the Soviets because they had long lines at grocery stores, because they would rather buy tanks than refrigerators and blue jeans, and because the Soviets threw poets into labor camps. "How do you know he was about to murder Castro?"

Karpov stopped to pick up an orange-colored agate with delicate swirls of red in it. "I know because he had Castro in the sights of his M-twenty-one."

"How could you know that for sure—I mean really sure?"

Karpov flipped the agate down the meadow. "I suppose I can't for sure. The CIA has been eager to take a pop at Fidel for twenty years now. Besides, I'm like Laurence. I'm his flip side. That's what I would have done."

"I thought Langley was finished with that business of trying to kill Castro. I thought we had been through all that. Why?"

"Rolando Paz, Mr. Perini."

"I don't know him."

"I'll bet there would be good deer hunting here. Castro's brother, Raúl, has cancer, Mr. Perini. Rolando Paz is next in the line of succession after Raúl. Señor Paz hates Russians."

Perini suddenly remembered Rubashov. "Your comrade was bleeding to death when I left the reservoir to chase Castro."

Karpov sighed. "Just as well, I suppose." He slowed to find a place where they could cross the muck without sinking up to their knees in mud.

Castro had recognized Karpov from thirty yards away. He was relieved. "Ahh, Señor Karpov," he called.

"Comrade Castro," Karpov called back. He turned to Perini and shook his head. "Poor

Rubashov is dead by now, Mr. Perini. He was the Premier's nephew."

"What?"

"Comrade Kagnanovich has a sister, Irina. She always had great hopes for Rubashov, but he never seemed able to do much of anything right. All he seemed to be able to do is repeat those mindless slogans. Irina had apparently been nagging her brother to give Vasily something really important, something that would make his career. We all knew he would never amount to much but we couldn't say anything. Rubashov was the Premier's nephew, after all."

"So Kagnanovich sent him along with you."

Karpov sighed. "Yes, he sent him with me. 'Need,' he said. We had to keep it tight. What better way than to send a member of the family? That way he could get Irina off his back."

Karpov stopped at the edge of the cattails and gave a tentative test of the mud with his toe. "No sense in us wading across the mud, Comrade Castro. You may as well join us."

Castro looked foolish. "We tried to get word to you, Comrade, but there wasn't time. We knew the Americans would be coming. We had to move quickly." He wasn't a convincing liar.

"You arrived late," Karpov said.

"Sí, we were late." Castro stood up and slapped a mosquito on his forehead. He looked heavy and awkward. He didn't want to have to wade back through the mud but there was no other way.

Perini thought Castro looked embarrassed, as though he'd been caught masturbating by his father.

Castro began wading across the mud and suddenly sank waist-deep in the goo. "We would have fed the poor people of the earth," he said. He ran his hand across his beardless face. It still felt odd not having a beard. "Mosquitoes. *¡Mierda!*" He extended a hand in Karpov's direction, expecting help.

Karpov looked at Perini. "Would you care to give him a hand, Eddie?"

Perini grinned. "Not me, Comrade. I'm a running dog lackey of the capitalist imperialists. He's Soviet bloc."

"Ahhh!" said Karpov. "Mr. Perini says no, Comrade. I don't like wading in mud either."

Castro's face reddened. He began cursing them in Spanish that was too fast for either of them to understand. By now he was up to his chest in smelly mud.

Perini and Karpov sat on the meadow discussing the differences between Douglas firs, sugar pines, and ponderosa pines while Castro struggled to extricate himself from the mud. The harder he worked the deeper he sank until he managed to screw himself down to his armpits. He finally got a handhold on some cattail roots and managed to drag himself out of the slime. The problem was that when he came unstuck his shoes remained behind. It was a long walk up the rocky meadow with no shoes.

Karpov and Perini walked slowly back up the meadow, each holding one foot of Laurence's corpse. They talked about trout fish-

ing as they dragged the body behind them.
Castro followed, swearing loudly in Spanish
as he picked his way carefully among the
sharp volcanic rocks that littered the ground.
The corpse made it slow going through the
thicket of lodgepoles. Laurence's body had to
be alternately pushed and pulled through the
underbrush. The mosquitoes, sensing easy
marks, rose in malevolent swarms to press
their advantage. Castro swore even louder,
and slapped angrily at his ankles and neck.

When they got back, they found Rue Kadera
sitting in a narrow strip of sun on the far
side of the reservoir. She was soaking wet.
The corpses of Rubashov, Dann, Rivera,
Scanlan, and Cardinal lay in a neat row in
the shade of a Douglas fir.

Perini dropped Laurence's foot and flopped
on the ground. He was exhausted.

"Is it Tony?" Kadera asked. She could see
that it was.

Perini looked at the body. "He tried to kill
Señor Castro."

"I shot him," Karpov said.

"And where did you come from?" Kadera
stared at Karpov in bewilderment.

Perini said, "Remember those yoga exercises he did back there in Portland last
night? He stopped his pulse for our benefit
this morning."

Kadera shivered. "That water is bloody
cold," she said. She looked at the corpses.
"Poor sods."

"And this is Premier Castro," Perini said.

"*Buenos días*, Señor Castro. Eddie, I think
I heard someone in the woods back there."

"I suppose we'll want to bury the bodies and get out of here," Perini said.

"I heard someone. I know I did."

Karpov said, "I think we should do what we have to do."

"If I swim Laurence's body to the other side, do you suppose you and the Premier can break into Goldman's van to see if he had anything in there we can dig with? You can cross over on the bridge again." Perini scratched at a mosquito bite.

It turned out Goldman did have something to dig with, a folding metal shovel. An hour later, Perini and Kadera began dragging the corpses into the forest.

It was there that they found Jan deJonette's body pitched forward in a pool of blood.

Perini kneeled and turned the body over. "The third mercenary. He's the one you heard back here in the brush."

"Whoever I heard was here just fifteen or twenty minutes before you returned."

"You think this one's been dead longer than that?"

"I don't know," Kadera said. "It's hard to say."

"It was probably this one," Perini said.

They buried the eight corpses in a shallow grave, along with the rubber life raft, while Castro took a bath and rinsed out his clothes in the reservoir. Karpov laughed as the Premier cupped his genitals in his hands and lowered himself slowly into the icy water.

"¡*Mierda!*" he yelled.

Perini had lifted the wallets from the corpses before he slipped the bodies into their com-

non grave. He swam the reservoir again and
buried the wallets on the other side.

"Say, do you think it would be possible for
me to buy some blue jeans on the way
back?" Castro asked when they were in the
car at last. "For a friend," he added quickly.

Three hours later, Perini stopped at a
shopping center in Eugene where the Premier bought twelve pairs of blue jeans—size
38 waist to accommodate the revolutionary
paunch.

AFTERWORD

BERNARD GOLDMAN'S
IRISH COFFEE

1½ ounces Irish whiskey   1 teaspoon sugar
5 ounces very hot strong   1 spoonful whipped
   black coffee   cream

   1. Rinse an 8-ounce stemmed goblet with ver
hot water.
   2. Place the sugar in the glass, pour in the Iris
whiskey and coffee; stir to dissolve sugar and to
with whipped cream.

CHAPTER

29

PRESIDENT DEVOL REREAD THE PRESS RELEASE announcing the appointment, subject to ratification by the Senate, of James Chambliss to be director of the Central Intelligence Agency. It was a popular appointment with the Senate hawks—those senators from the South, the Southwest, and states with large defense contracts. Chambliss was a professional with the proper credentials, not some jackass professor pumped full of grand theories and lacking common sense. Common sense, to Senator Beauchamp of South Carolina, was that the fucking Soviets were bent on running the world. They had so stated in 1917, according to Beauchamp, and had not changed their mind since—their desire for American grain and computers notwithstanding. The announced appointment was being made under something of a cloud in view of the disappearance of Anthony Laurence. Devol made Chambliss interim director and Chambliss had sense enough to kiss the proper asses on the Hill. For that, at least, Devol was grateful. Chambliss brought Eddie Perini

to the Oval Office and the President ques
tioned him at length as to Laurence's fate
Perini said they had watched as professiona
killers murdered Bernard Goldman. He sai
the killers had pursued himself and Laurenc
into a thicket of lodgepole pines where the
had become separated. Perini returned bu
couldn't find Laurence.

There were gunshots, Perini said, and tha
was the last he saw of Tony Laurence.

Chambliss had his appointment. He wa
satisfied. President Devol had $20 million fc
his election campaign. He was satisfied. H
announced the formation of a special con
mission to investigate Laurence's disappea
ance. The commission was headed by th
Chief Justice of the Supreme Court. Its men
bers included the head of The Rockefelle
Foundation, the director of Paramount Pic
tures, the director of the FBI, the presiden
of the NAACP, the President's niece—a senic
at Stanford—and those senators and cor
gressmen who liked to appear on televisio
and be quoted in the newspapers and fro
whom the President expected favors in r
turn for the appointment.

President Devol corrected a comma splic
and changed a "finalized" to "completed" i
a press release and put his initials on to
His press secretary, a former televisio
newsman, was illiterate but the polls showe
the public trusted him.

That done, Devol turned his attention to
memo from Donald Proctor, his campaig
adviser, on how the $20 million should b
spent. Proctor advised, as Devol knew l

would, that the President should ignore his challenger—an attractive and intelligent if unknown liberal from Pennsylvania. In the immediate weeks before the election, Proctor said, the President should do something generous to some civilized countries in Western Europe—give them money or airplanes. He should then visit the countries (Japan would be okay, too, he noted parenthetically), participating in the usual state receptions, and parades. The television networks wouldn't dare ignore an American President riding in a black limousine to cheering multitudes. He would be on television every night. The public liked to see their President cheered by people who eat fish and garlic.

Devol made a mental note to leave France out of this scenario. He didn't like the French. People who made cars as ugly as the Peugeot were hardly to be trusted. Also the French had a hangup about their Godalmighty Precious Damned Language. Devol had made a point of making a bullshit little speech in French for the French President at a State dinner and afterward, while sipping Devol's bourbon whiskey, the Frenchman had the nerve to correct Devol's pronunciation.

During the last week of the campaign, Proctor advised, the President should flood the networks with a series of television commercials. The commercials would show him at work, looking concerned, looking serious, answering questions from the press, holding a child, and so on. He wouldn't have to say anything. The commercials, said Proctor, would show it all. Proctor had once been

associated with a national campaign that
had dramatically increased the use of Copenhagen chewing tobacco. That was good. Proctor was a bit simple and predictable but
then again the United States was a simple
and predictable country. There was no sense
getting fancy when you didn't have to. Devol
trusted him.

Eddie Perini returned to Portland to cover
the Trail Blazers. The Los Angeles Summer
League was starting up, and Perini was sent
south to report back to the city of rain that,
as usual, Portland had failed to draft anybody who knew how to rebound the basketball or play defense. On the day he got on
the plane there was an interesting story in
the *Oregonian* written by the newspaper's
correspondent in Roseburg. The story wasn't
important enough to be carried out of state
by the wire services:

There are still no clues to the where-
abouts of Roseburg fisherman, Dale
Springer, 33, who failed to return from
an outing on Soda Springs Reservoir
Sunday afternoon. Douglas County Sheriff Raymond Daniels said a thorough
dragging of the reservoir has failed to
produce any evidence of a body.

Springer was visiting his uncle, Clar-
ence Springer, 58, a ranger who lives in
one of the Forest Service cabins near the
upper end of the narrow reservoir. Clar-
ence Springer said his nephew had set
out alone in an inflatable raft.

Sheriff Daniels said Springer's disappearance was complicated by a van found parked near the top of the reservoir. The van belongs to a visiting professor at Lewis and Clark College in Portland—who is also missing. Daniels said Dr. Bernard Goldman, on leave from the University of Edinburgh, was apparently fishing the reservoir too.

Daniels said searchers would comb the area until they had exhausted all possibilities.

He said he had no evidence to link the missing fisherman with the abandoned vehicle or with Goldman, who could not be found either.

In reading the story, Perini remembered that he had only seen the fisherman from the top of the bluff. At that distance it was impossible to know it was Goldman for certain. And the corpse that was Goldman had no face. What if Goldman had been fishing farther downstream when the shooting started?

Perini thought of sending a copy of the clipping to Rue Kadera but thought better of it. There were some dart tournaments coming up. He preferred on-darts and out-darts to Langley's games.

Besides that, he had liked Goldman.

Rue Kadera, having well-served the honor of Her Majesty's Government, returned to London, still wondering about the noise in the woods. It wasn't deJonette, the third mercenary. She was sure of that. No matter. As far as Archie Smethurst was concerned, the problem was resolved.

Valery Karpov returned to Moscow and was startled to find Comrade Volchak sporting slick new front teeth. There was no pit. Volchak actually smiled. Karpov was disconcerted to find the new teeth were there as a result of an order from Premier Kagnanovich. It didn't make any difference, however. Volchak's tongue returned to the tooth as before, going round and round on the smooth surface.

Fidel Castro hid his new blue jeans in an antique sea trunk that had been a gift from Communist guerrillas in Timor. The trunk was his special place. Housekeepers were forbidden to open it. It took several months for the Premier's beard to grow back. Castro didn't care. He was able to relax in his blue jeans and T-shirt late at night, and drink rum and coke and watch *Solid Gold* on the tube.

THE BEST IN SUSPENSE

BESTSELLING BOOKS FROM TOR

☐ 58725-1 *Gardens of Stone* by Nicholas Proffitt $3.95
  58726-X   Canada $4.50

☐ 51650-8 *Incarnate* by Ramsey Campbell $3.95
  51651-6   Canada $4.50

☐ 51050-X *Kahawa* by Donald E. Westlake $3.95
  51051-8   Canada $4.50

☐ 52750-X *A Manhattan Ghost Story* by T.M. Wright
                                              $3.95
  52751-8   Canada $4.50

☐ 52191-9 *Ikon* by Graham Masterton $3.95
  52192-7   Canada $4.50

☐ 54550-8 *Prince Ombra* by Roderick MacLeish $3.50
  54551-6   Canada $3.95

☐ 50284-1 *The Vietnam Legacy* by Brian Freemantle
                                              $3.50
  50285-X   Canada $3.95

☐ 50487-9 *Siskiyou* by Richard Hoyt $3.50
  50488-7   Canada $3.95

Buy them at your local bookstore or use this handy coupon:
Clip and mail this page with your order

TOR BOOKS—Reader Service Dept.
49 W. 24 Street, 9th Floor, New York, NY 10010

Please send me the book(s) I have checked above. I am enclosing
_____ (please add $1.00 to cover postage and handling).
Send check or money order only—no cash or C.O.D.'s.

Mr./Mrs./Miss _____

Address _____.

City _____ State/Zip _____

Please allow six weeks for delivery. Prices subject to change without
notice.

MORE BESTSELLERS FROM TOR